THE FIX

volume 3
Deal of Fortune,

Robert Kirkman
Chief Operating Officer

Erik Larsen
Chief Financial Officer

Todd McFarlane
President

Marc Silvestri
Chief Executive Officer

Jim Valentino
Vice President

Eric Stephenson
Publisher /
Chief Creative Officer

Corey Hart
Director of Sales

Jeff Boison
Director of Publishing
Planning & Book Trade Sales

Chris Ross
Director of Digital Sales

Jeff Stang
Director of Specialty Sales

Kat Salazar
Director of PR & Marketing

Nicole Lapalme
Controller

Heather Doornink
Production Director

Drew Gill
Art Director

THE FIX, VOL. 3.
DEAL OF FORTUNE.
First printing. September 2018.
ISBN: 978-1-5343-0374-4.
Published by Image Comics, Inc. Office
of publication: 2701 NW Vaughn
St., Suite 780, Portland, OR 97210.

image

IMAGECOMICS.COM

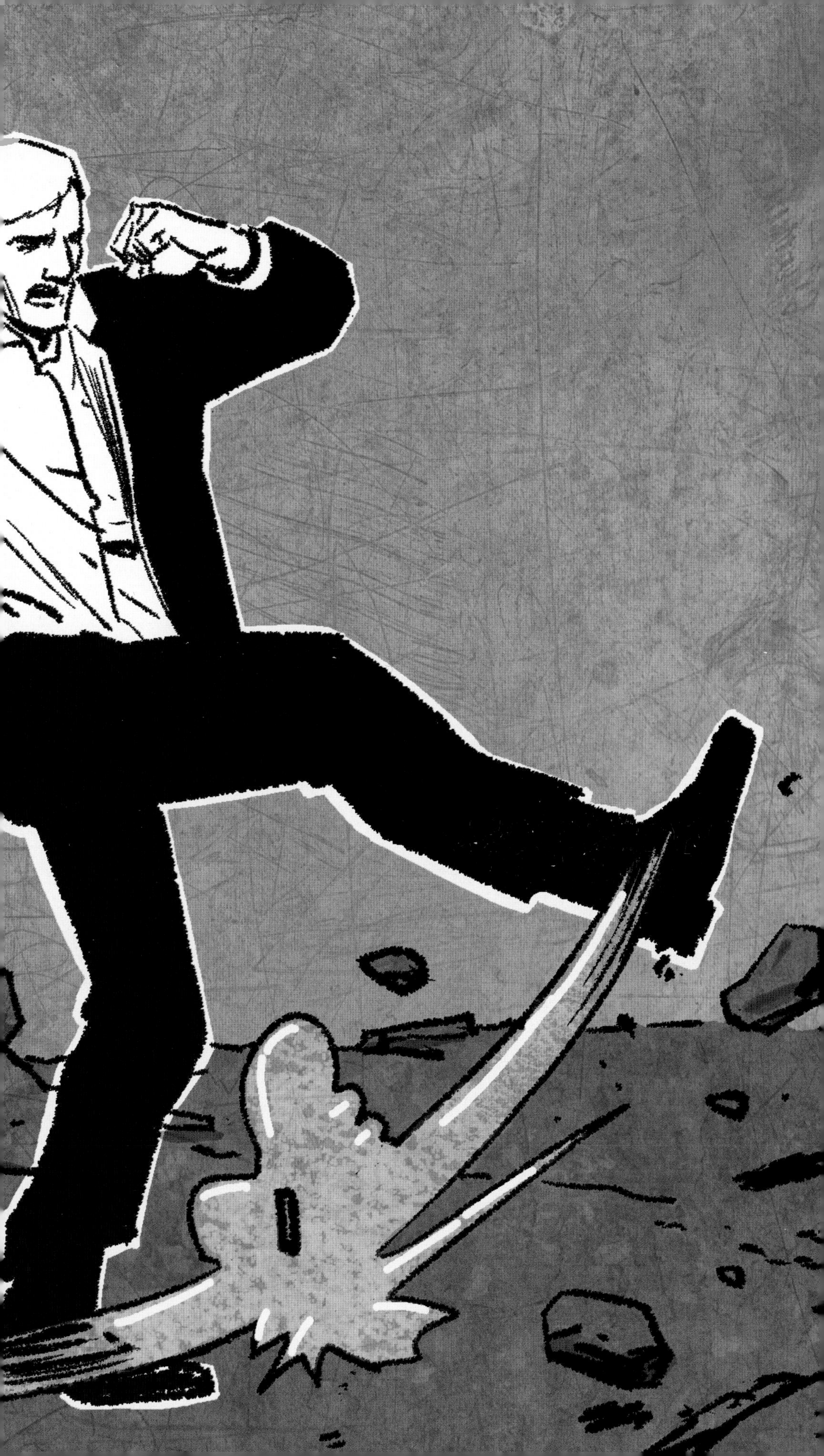

THE
FIX

volume 3
Deal of
Fortune

writer
NICK SPENCER

artist
STEVE LIEBER

colors
RYAN HILL

letters/design
MARSHALL DILLON
& IRONBARK

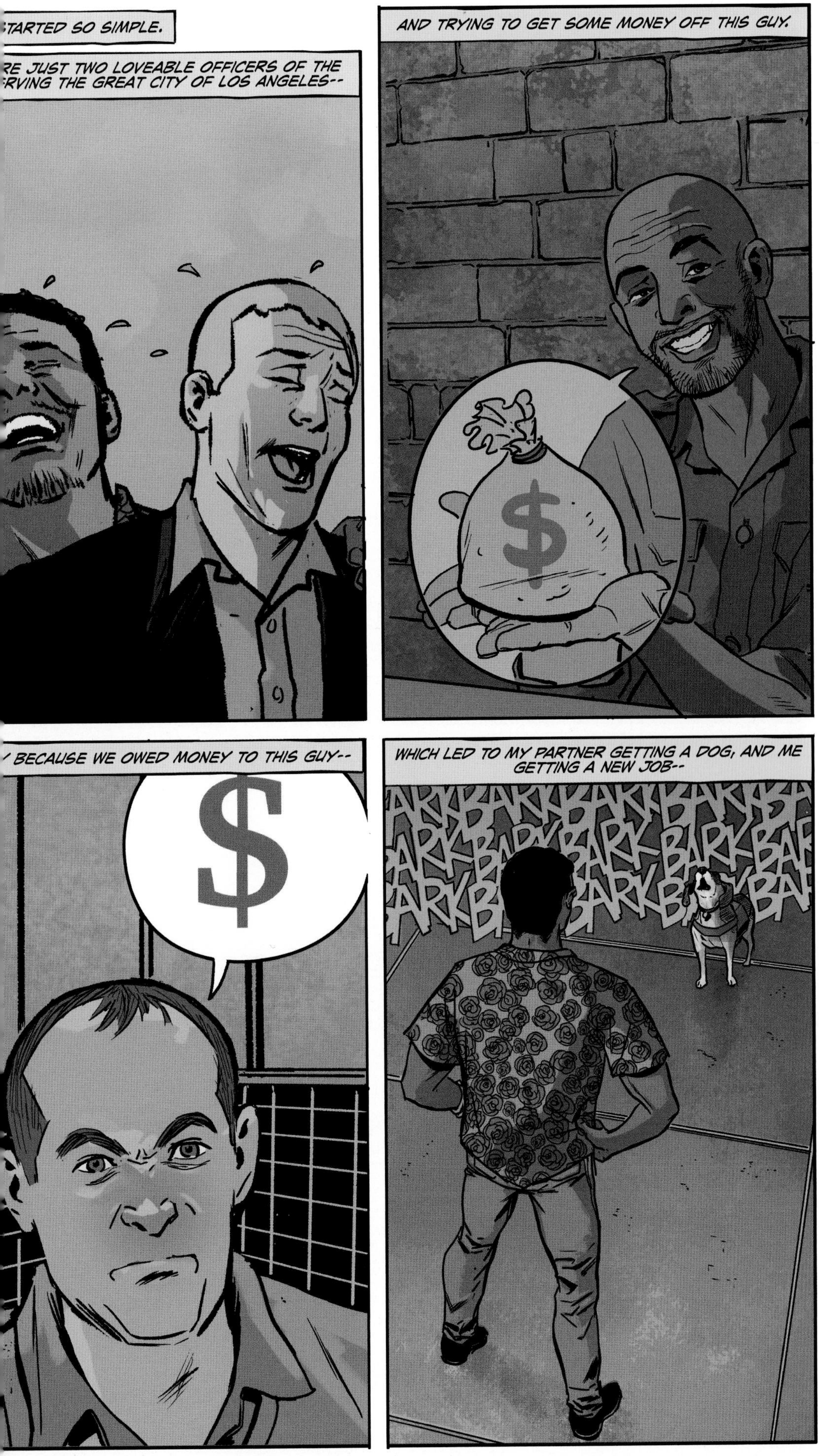
STARTED SO SIMPLE.
RE JUST TWO LOVEABLE OFFICERS OF THE
RVING THE GREAT CITY OF LOS ANGELES--
AND TRYING TO GET SOME MONEY OFF THIS GUY.
$
BECAUSE WE OWED MONEY TO THIS GUY--
$
WHICH LED TO MY PARTNER GETTING A DOG, AND ME GETTING A NEW JOB--
BARK BARK BARK BARK BARK BARK BARK BARK

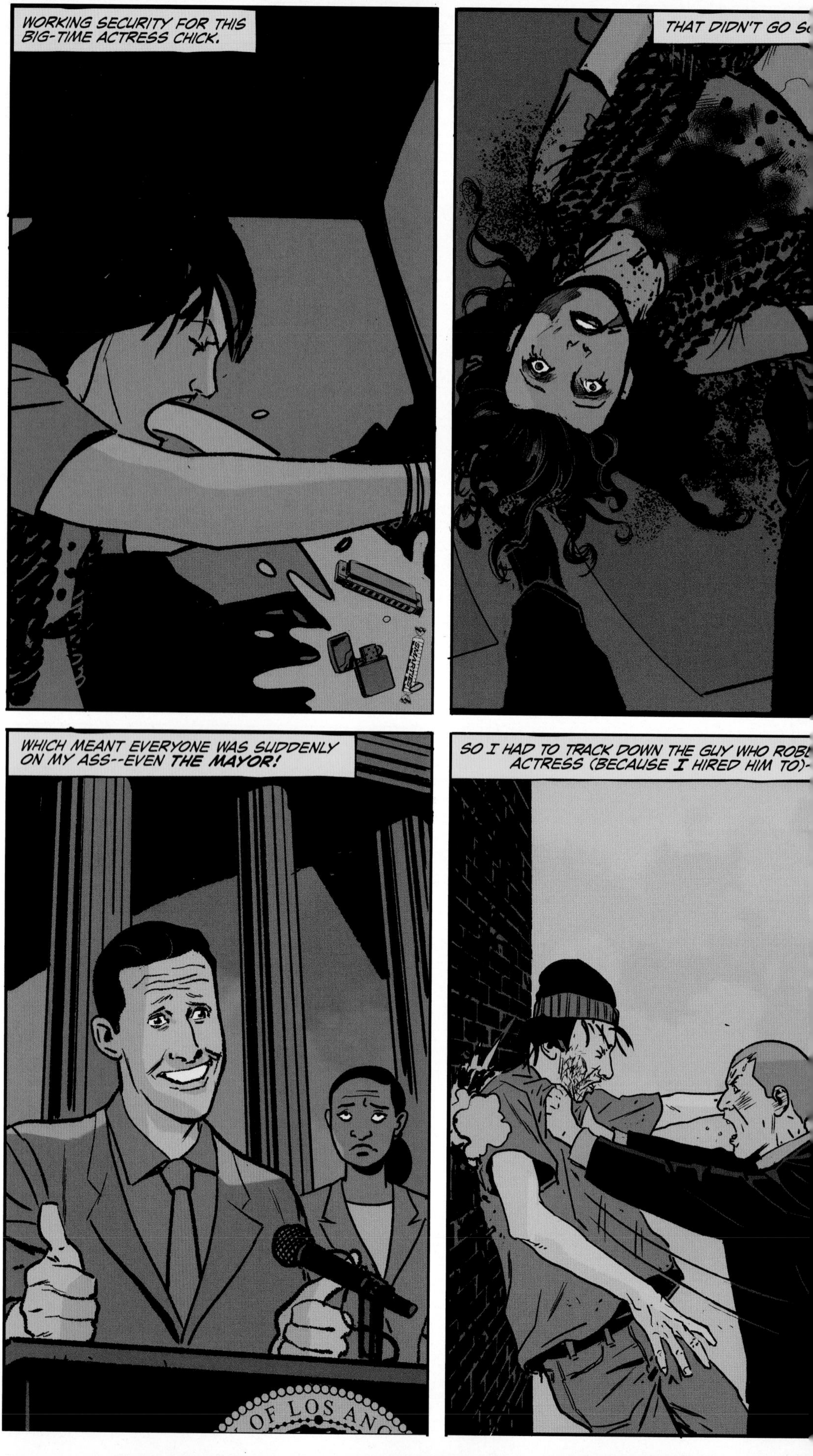
WORKING SECURITY FOR THIS BIG-TIME ACTRESS CHICK.
SMARTIES
THAT DIDN'T GO
WHICH MEANT EVERYONE WAS SUDDENLY ON MY ASS--EVEN THE MAYOR!
OF LOS
SO I HAD TO TRACK DOWN THE GUY WHO
ACTRESS (BECAUSE I HIRED HIM TO)-

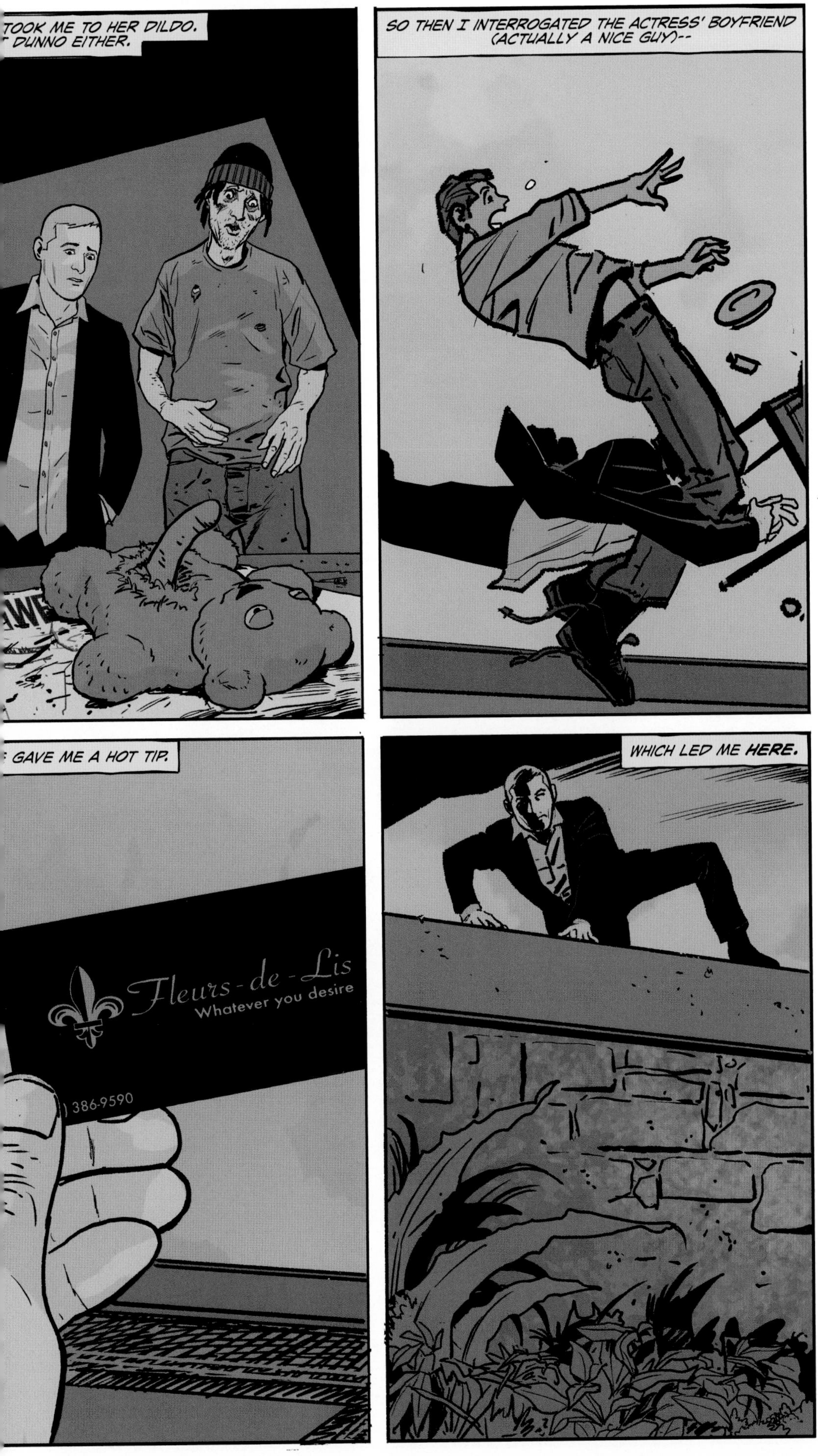

TOOK ME TO HER DILDO.
T DUNNO EITHER.
SO THEN I INTERROGATED THE ACTRESS' BOYFRIEND (ACTUALLY A NICE GUY)--
E GAVE ME A HOT TIP.
Fleurs-de-Lis
Whatever you desire
) 386-9590
WHICH LED ME HERE.

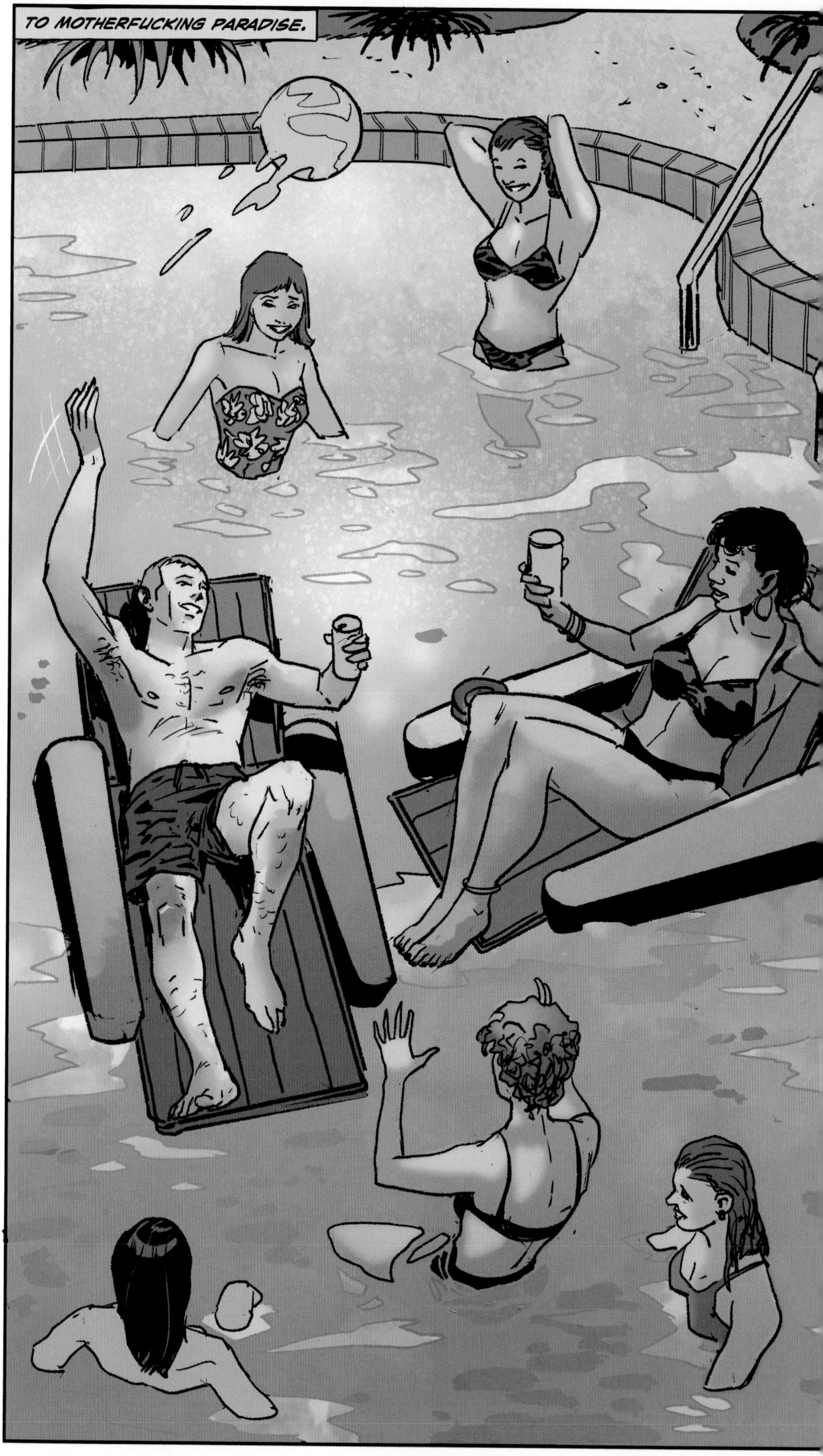
TO MOTHERFUCKING PARADISE.

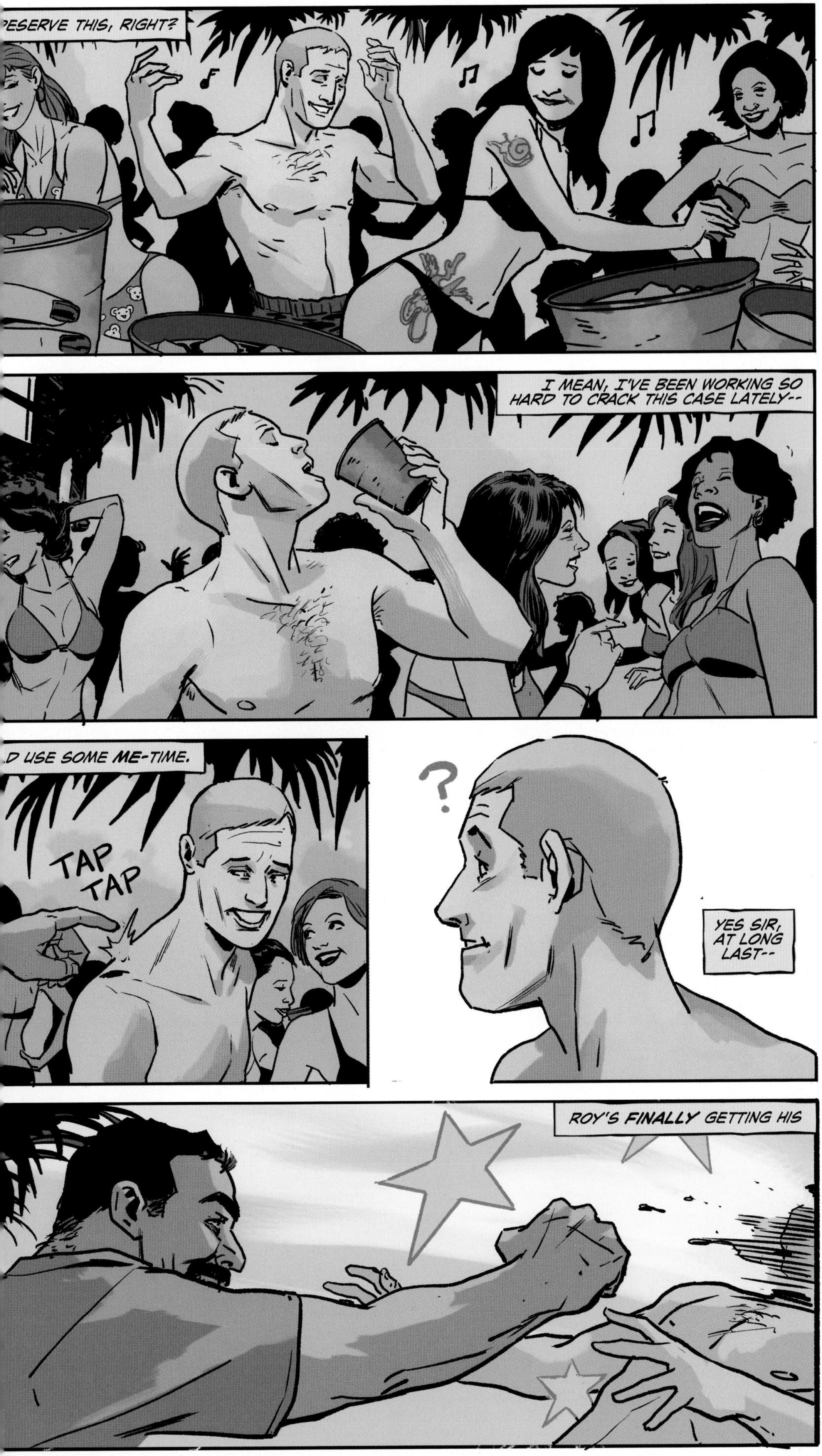

DESERVE THIS, RIGHT?
I MEAN, I'VE BEEN WORKING SO HARD TO CRACK THIS CASE LATELY--
D USE SOME ME-TIME.
TAP TAP
?
YES SIR, AT LONG LAST--
ROY'S FINALLY GETTING HIS

THE

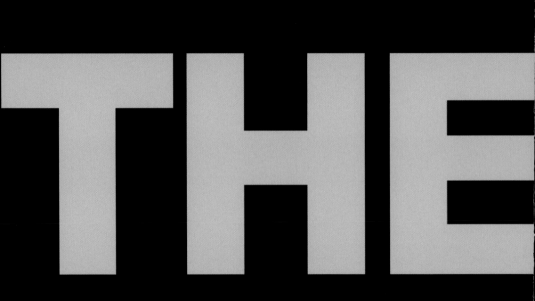

FIX

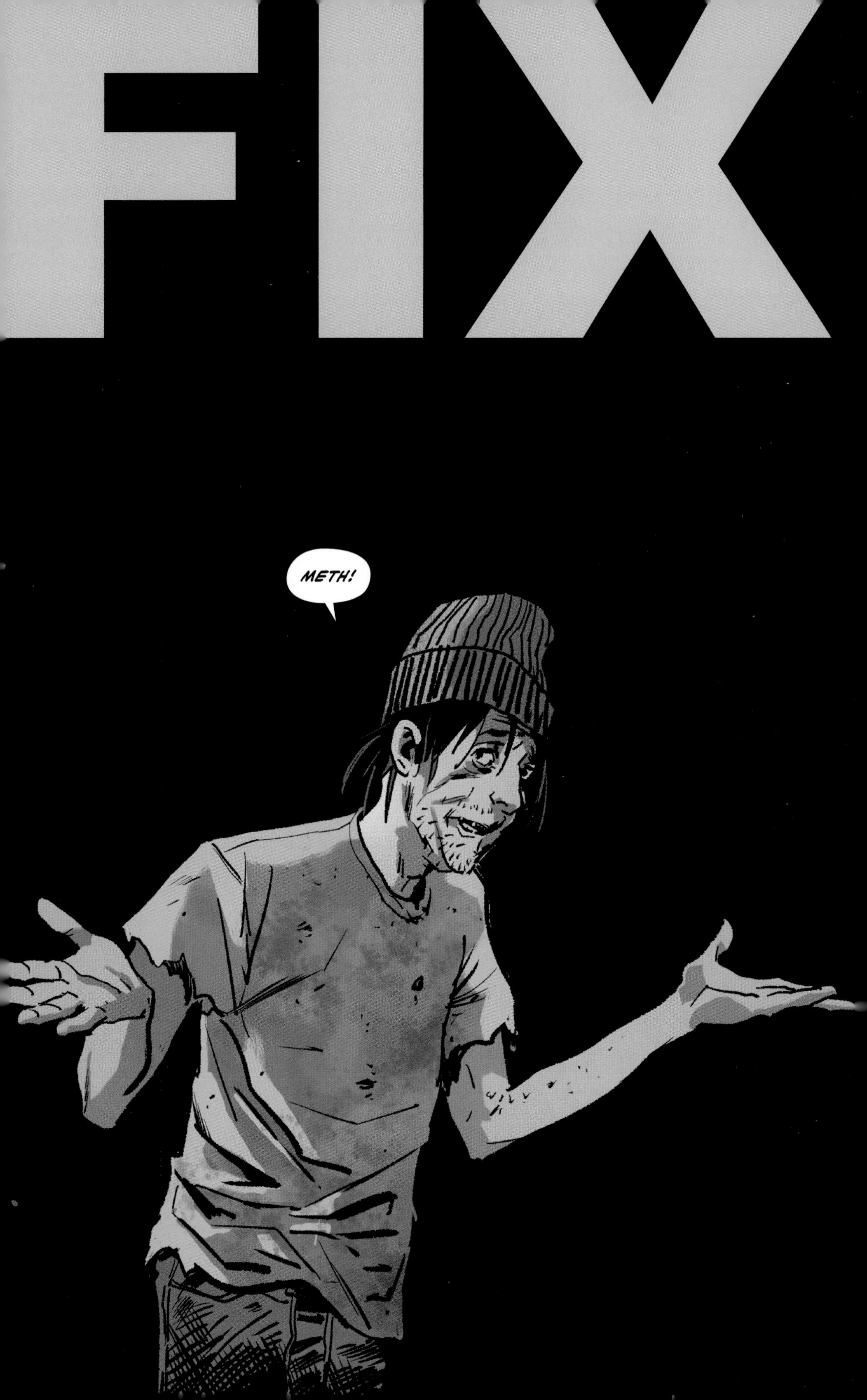
METH!

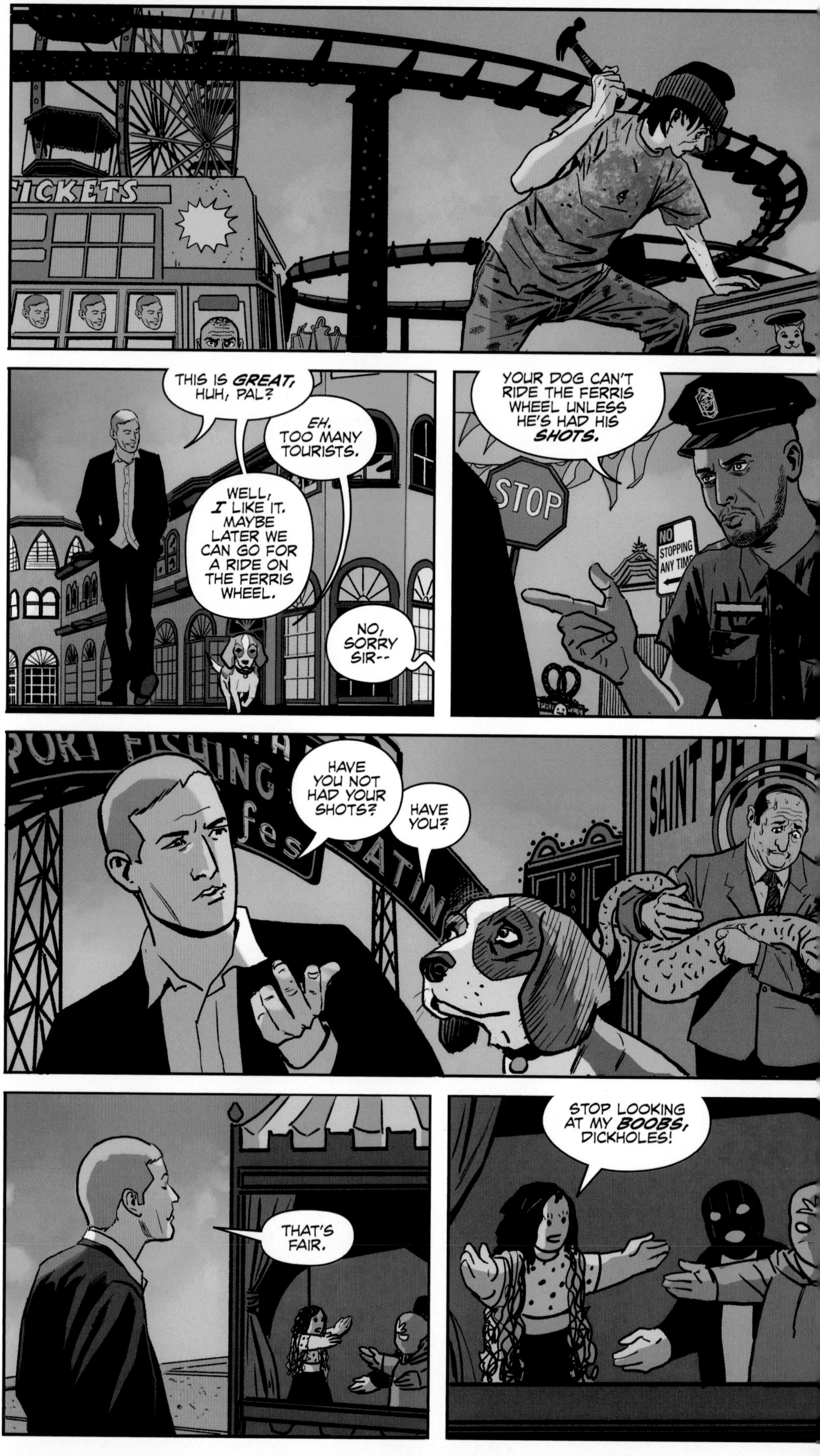
TICKETS
THIS IS GREAT, HUH, PAL?
EH. TOO MANY TOURISTS.
WELL, I LIKE IT. MAYBE LATER WE CAN GO FOR A RIDE ON THE FERRIS WHEEL.
NO, SORRY SIR--
YOUR DOG CAN'T RIDE THE FERRIS WHEEL UNLESS HE'S HAD HIS SHOTS.
STOP
NO STOPPING ANY TIME
HAVE YOU NOT HAD YOUR SHOTS?
HAVE YOU?
THAT'S FAIR.
STOP LOOKING AT MY BOOBS, DICKHOLES!

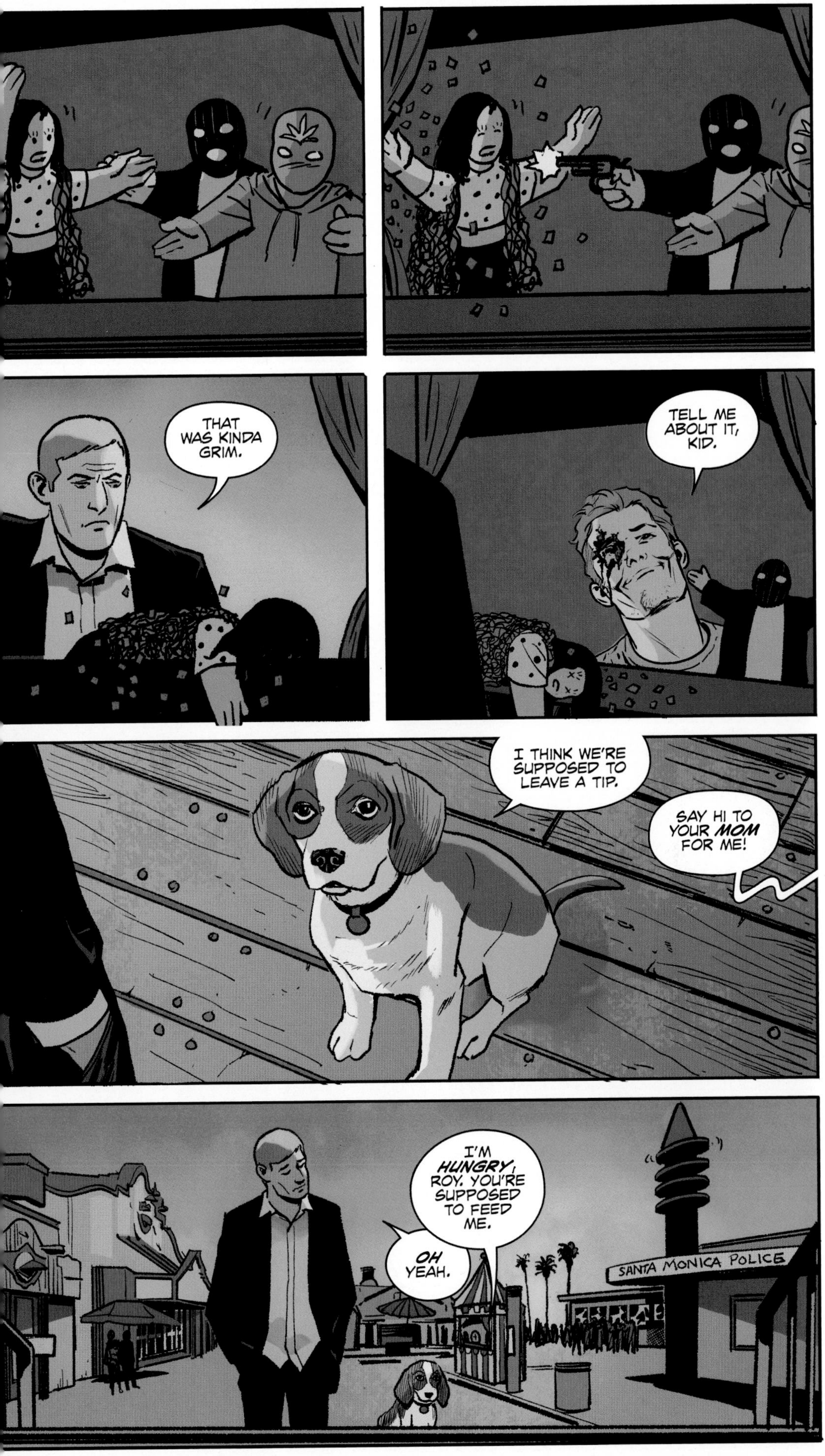
THAT WAS KINDA GRIM.
TELL ME ABOUT IT, KID.
I THINK WE'RE SUPPOSED TO LEAVE A TIP.
SAY HI TO YOUR MOM FOR ME!
I'M HUNGRY, ROY. YOU'RE SUPPOSED TO FEED ME.
OH YEAH.
SANTA MONICA POLICE

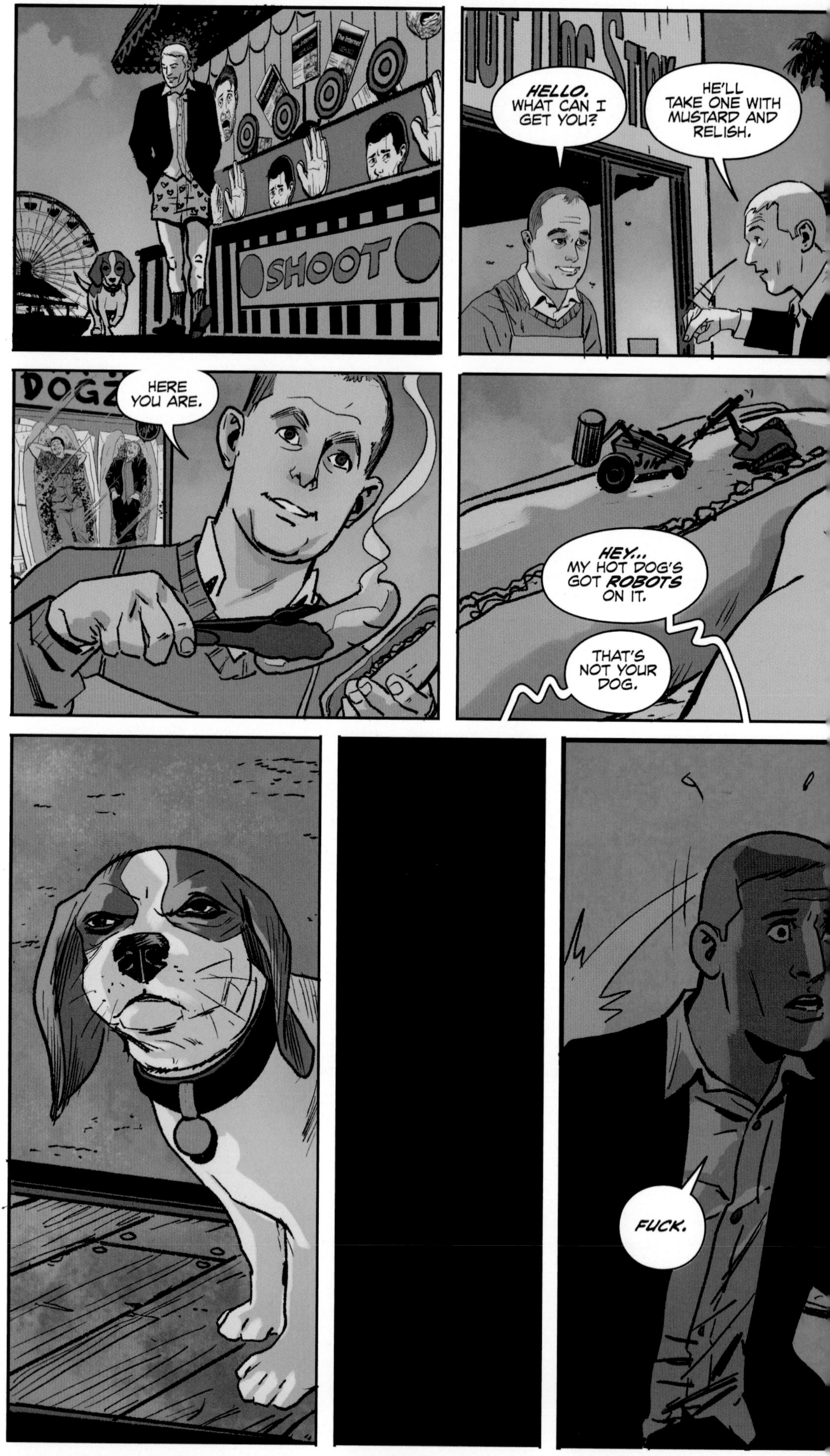
SHOOT
HELLO. WHAT CAN I GET YOU?
HE'LL TAKE ONE WITH MUSTARD AND RELISH.
DOGZ
HERE YOU ARE.
HEY... MY HOT DOG'S GOT ROBOTS ON IT.
THAT'S NOT YOUR DOG.
FUCK.

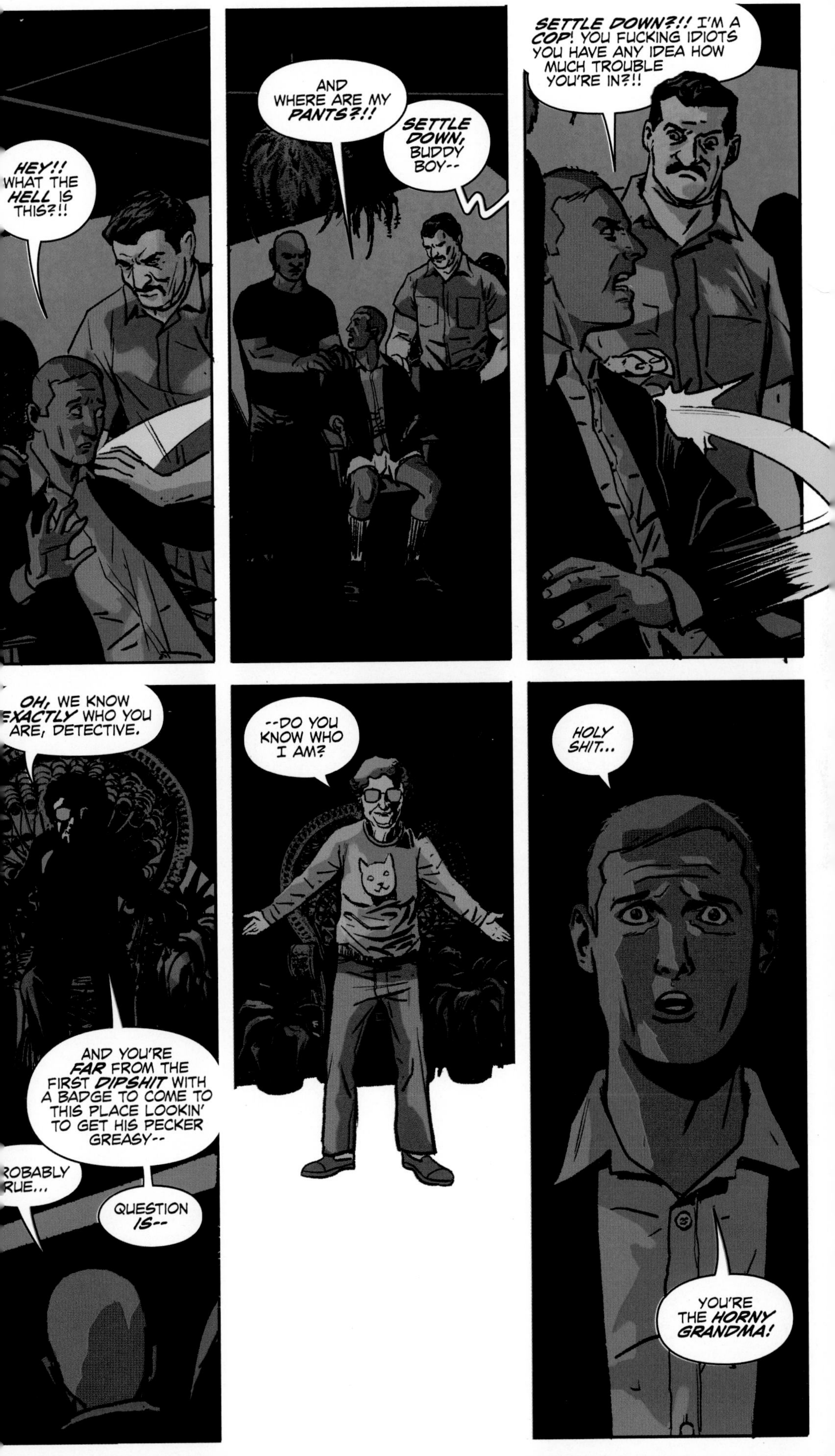
HEY!! WHAT THE HELL IS THIS?!!
AND WHERE ARE MY PANTS?!!
SETTLE DOWN, BUDDY BOY--
SETTLE DOWN?!! I'M A COP! YOU FUCKING IDIOTS YOU HAVE ANY IDEA HOW MUCH TROUBLE YOU'RE IN?!!
OH, WE KNOW EXACTLY WHO YOU ARE, DETECTIVE.
AND YOU'RE FAR FROM THE FIRST DIPSHIT WITH A BADGE TO COME TO THIS PLACE LOOKIN' TO GET HIS PECKER GREASY--
ROBABLY RUE...
QUESTION IS--
--DO YOU KNOW WHO I AM?
HOLY SHIT...
YOU'RE THE HORNY GRANDMA!

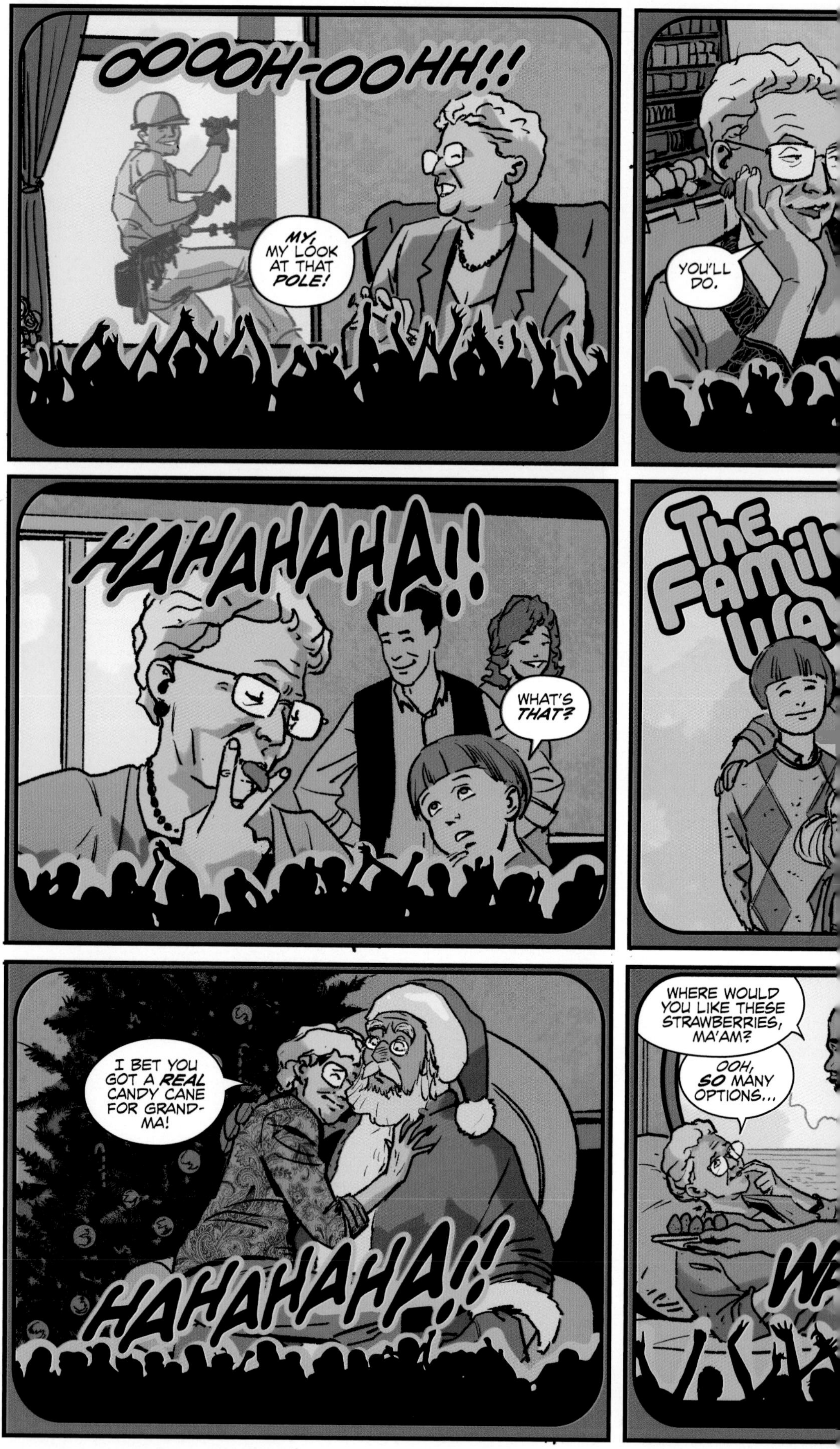
OOOOH-OOHH!!
MY, MY LOOK AT THAT POLE!
YOU'LL DO.
HAHAHAHA!!
WHAT'S THAT?
I BET YOU GOT A REAL CANDY CANE FOR GRAND-MA!
HAHAHAHA!!
WHERE WOULD YOU LIKE THESE STRAWBERRIES, MA'AM?
OOH, SO MANY OPTIONS...

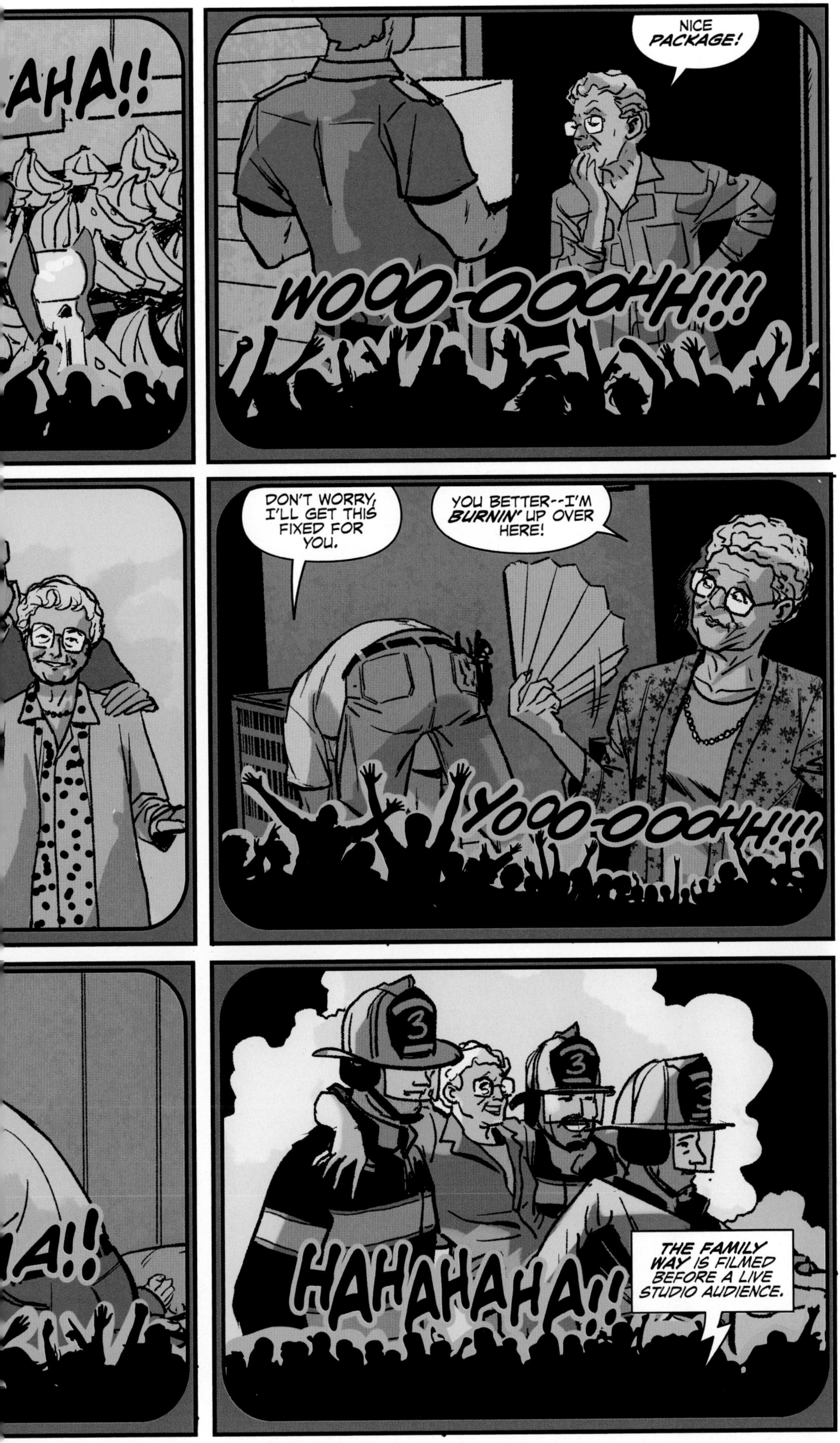
AHA!!
NICE PACKAGE!
WOOO-OOOHH!!!
DON'T WORRY, I'LL GET THIS FIXED FOR YOU.
YOU BETTER--I'M BURNIN' UP OVER HERE!
YOOO-OOOHH!!!
A!!
HAHAHAHA!!
THE FAMILY WAY IS FILMED BEFORE A LIVE STUDIO AUDIENCE.

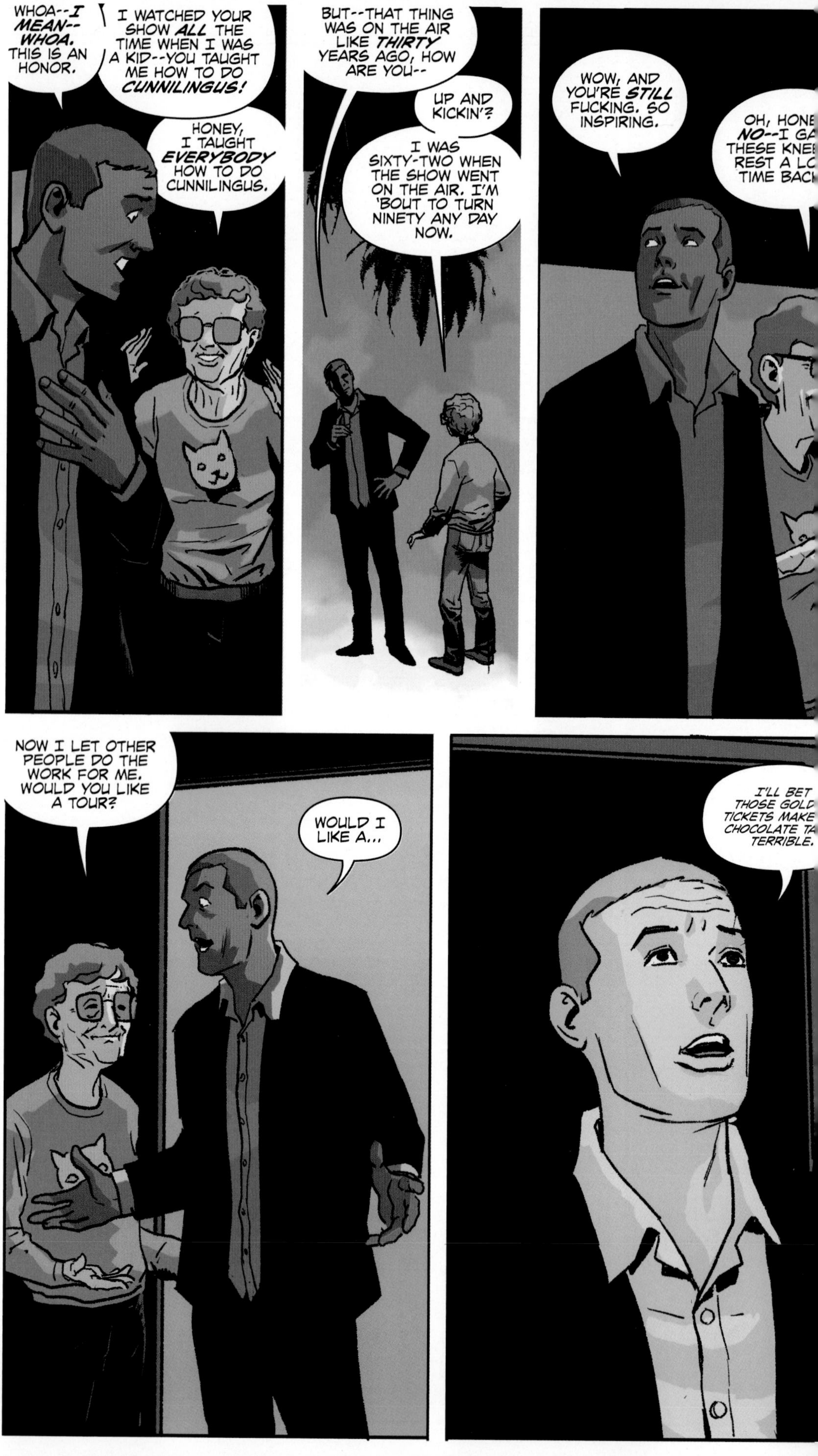
WHOA--*I MEAN--* *WHOA.* THIS IS AN HONOR.
I WATCHED YOUR SHOW *ALL* THE TIME WHEN I WAS A KID--YOU TAUGHT ME HOW TO DO *CUNNILINGUS!*
HONEY, I TAUGHT *EVERYBODY* HOW TO DO CUNNILINGUS.
BUT--THAT THING WAS ON THE AIR LIKE *THIRTY* YEARS AGO, HOW ARE YOU--
UP AND KICKIN'?
I WAS SIXTY-TWO WHEN THE SHOW WENT ON THE AIR. I'M 'BOUT TO TURN NINETY ANY DAY NOW.
WOW, AND YOU'RE *STILL* FUCKING. SO INSPIRING.
OH, HONE *NO--*I GA THESE KNEE REST A LO TIME BACK
NOW I LET OTHER PEOPLE DO THE WORK FOR ME. WOULD YOU LIKE A TOUR?
WOULD I LIKE A...
I'LL BET THOSE GOLD TICKETS MAKE CHOCOLATE TA TERRIBLE.

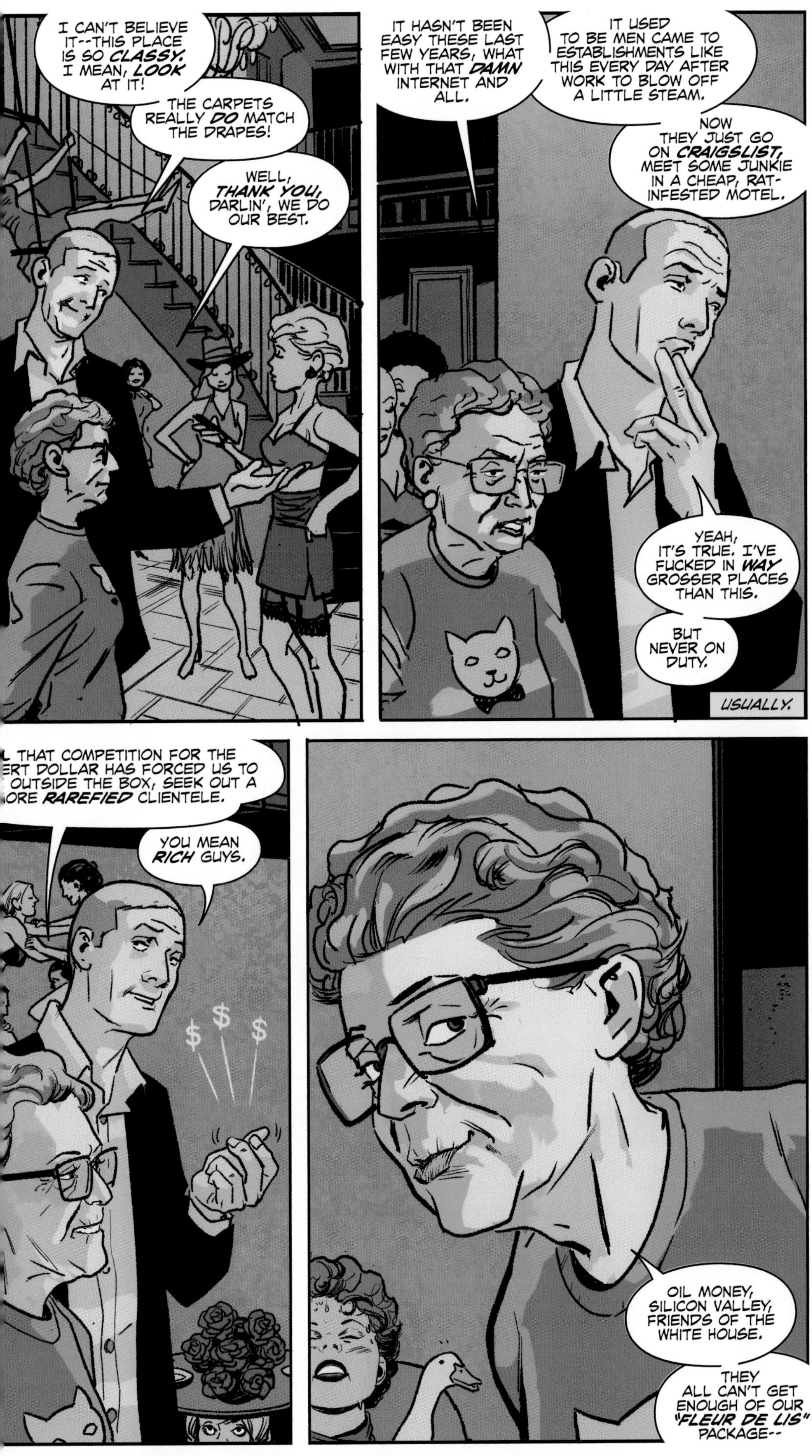

I CAN'T BELIEVE IT--THIS PLACE IS SO CLASSY. I MEAN, LOOK AT IT!
THE CARPETS REALLY DO MATCH THE DRAPES!
WELL, THANK YOU, DARLIN', WE DO OUR BEST.
IT HASN'T BEEN EASY THESE LAST FEW YEARS, WHAT WITH THAT DAMN INTERNET AND ALL.
IT USED TO BE MEN CAME TO ESTABLISHMENTS LIKE THIS EVERY DAY AFTER WORK TO BLOW OFF A LITTLE STEAM.
NOW THEY JUST GO ON CRAIGSLIST, MEET SOME JUNKIE IN A CHEAP, RAT-INFESTED MOTEL.
YEAH, IT'S TRUE. I'VE FUCKED IN WAY GROSSER PLACES THAN THIS.
BUT NEVER ON DUTY.
USUALLY.
L THAT COMPETITION FOR THE ERT DOLLAR HAS FORCED US TO OUTSIDE THE BOX, SEEK OUT A ORE RAREFIED CLIENTELE.
YOU MEAN RICH GUYS.
$ $ $
OIL MONEY, SILICON VALLEY, FRIENDS OF THE WHITE HOUSE.
THEY ALL CAN'T GET ENOUGH OF OUR "FLEUR DE LIS" PACKAGE--

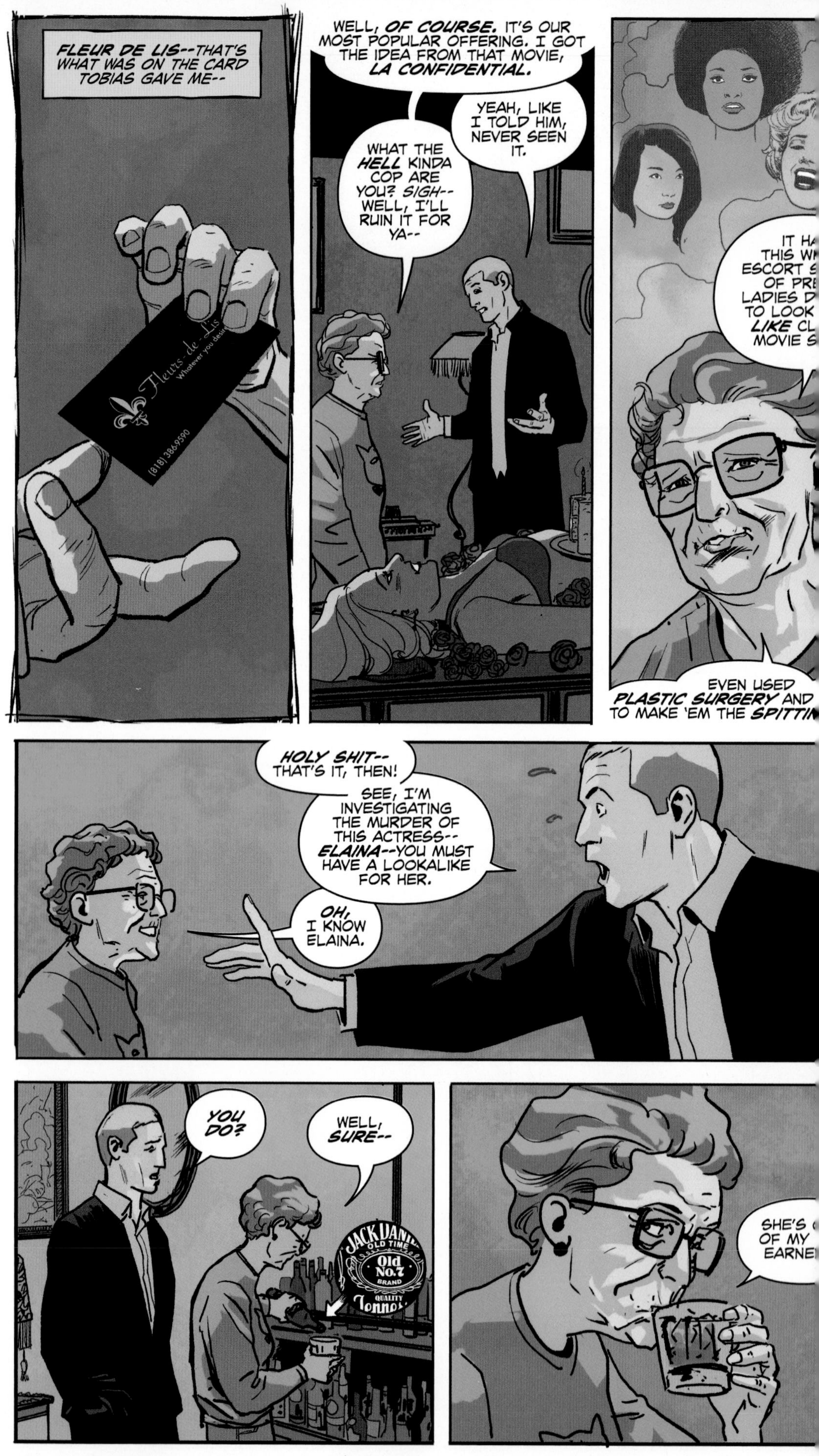
FLEUR DE LIS--THAT'S WHAT WAS ON THE CARD TOBIAS GAVE ME--
Fleurs-de-Lis
Whatever you desire
(818) 386-9590
WELL, OF COURSE. IT'S OUR MOST POPULAR OFFERING. I GOT THE IDEA FROM THAT MOVIE, LA CONFIDENTIAL.
YEAH, LIKE I TOLD HIM, NEVER SEEN IT.
WHAT THE HELL KINDA COP ARE YOU? SIGH-- WELL, I'LL RUIN IT FOR YA--
IT HA THIS WH ESCORT S OF PRE LADIES D TO LOOK LIKE CL MOVIE S
EVEN USED PLASTIC SURGERY AND TO MAKE 'EM THE SPITTIN
HOLY SHIT-- THAT'S IT, THEN!
SEE, I'M INVESTIGATING THE MURDER OF THIS ACTRESS-- ELAINA--YOU MUST HAVE A LOOKALIKE FOR HER.
OH, I KNOW ELAINA.
YOU DO?
WELL, SURE--
SHE'S OF MY EARNE

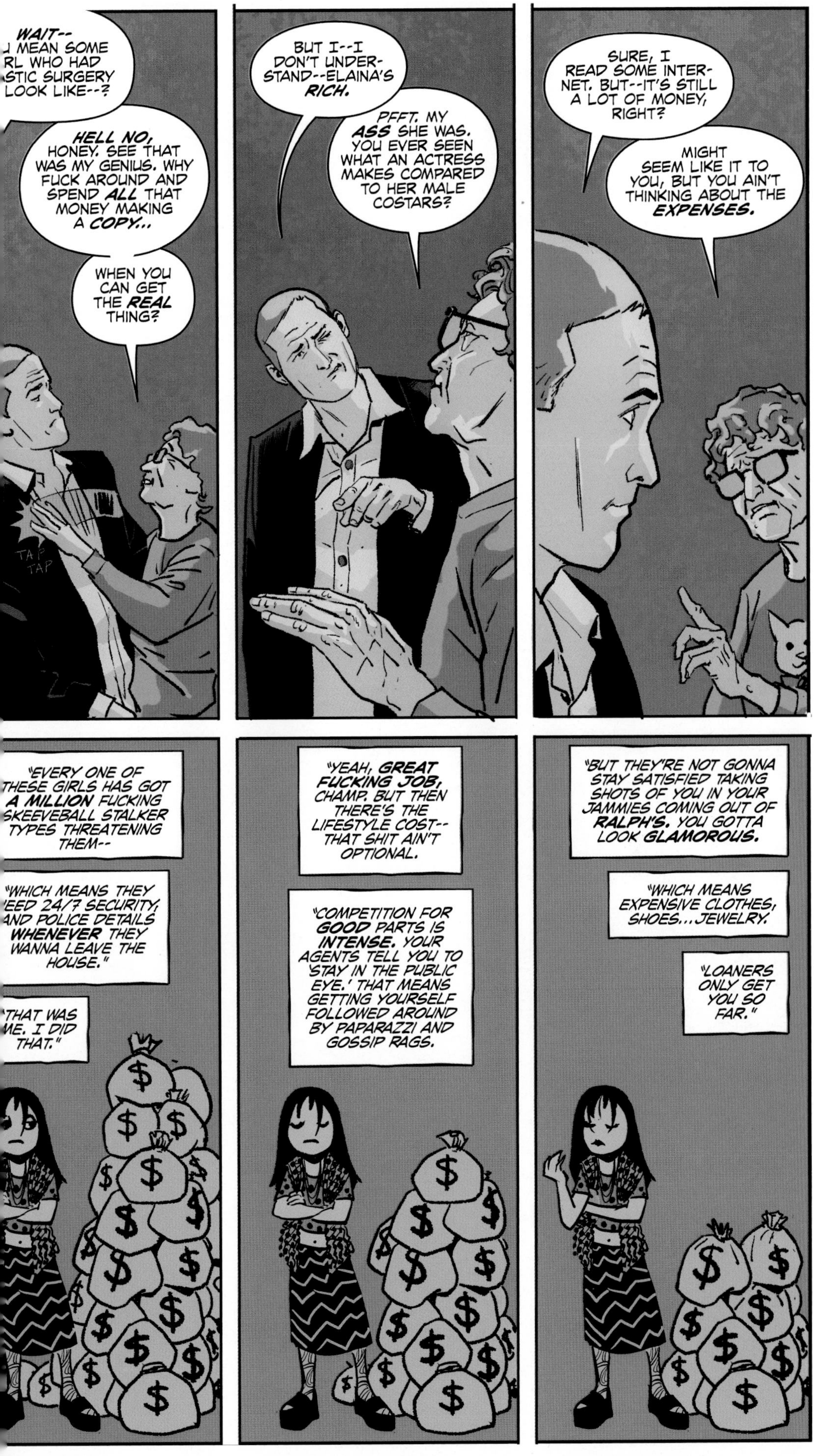
WAIT-- ...U MEAN SOME ...RL WHO HAD ...STIC SURGERY ...LOOK LIKE--?
HELL NO, HONEY. SEE THAT WAS MY GENIUS. WHY FUCK AROUND AND SPEND ALL THAT MONEY MAKING A COPY...
WHEN YOU CAN GET THE REAL THING?
TAP TAP
BUT I--I DON'T UNDER-STAND--ELAINA'S RICH.
PFFT. MY ASS SHE WAS. YOU EVER SEEN WHAT AN ACTRESS MAKES COMPARED TO HER MALE COSTARS?
SURE, I READ SOME INTER-NET. BUT--IT'S STILL A LOT OF MONEY, RIGHT?
MIGHT SEEM LIKE IT TO YOU, BUT YOU AIN'T THINKING ABOUT THE EXPENSES.
"EVERY ONE OF THESE GIRLS HAS GOT A MILLION FUCKING SKEEVEBALL STALKER TYPES THREATENING THEM--
"WHICH MEANS THEY ...EED 24/7 SECURITY, AND POLICE DETAILS WHENEVER THEY WANNA LEAVE THE HOUSE."
"THAT WAS ...ME. I DID THAT."
"YEAH, GREAT FUCKING JOB, CHAMP. BUT THEN THERE'S THE LIFESTYLE COST--THAT SHIT AIN'T OPTIONAL.
"COMPETITION FOR GOOD PARTS IS INTENSE. YOUR AGENTS TELL YOU TO 'STAY IN THE PUBLIC EYE.' THAT MEANS GETTING YOURSELF FOLLOWED AROUND BY PAPARAZZI AND GOSSIP RAGS.
"BUT THEY'RE NOT GONNA STAY SATISFIED TAKING SHOTS OF YOU IN YOUR JAMMIES COMING OUT OF RALPH'S. YOU GOTTA LOOK GLAMOROUS.
"WHICH MEANS EXPENSIVE CLOTHES, SHOES...JEWELRY.
"LOANERS ONLY GET YOU SO FAR."

"THEN THERE'S ALL THE WILD NIGHTS OUT ON THE TOWN-- WHERE EVERYBODY EXPECTS THE FAMOUS ACTRESS TO PICK UP THEIR TAB. BUT THAT'S CHUMP CHANGE--

"--GETTING ON THE GOOD SIDE OF DIRECTORS MEANS PRIVATE JETS AND WEEKENDS IN EUROPE.

"NOT TO MENTION ALL THE SCAMMERS. HANGER-ON ASSHOLES WHO GET YOU TO SINK YOUR MONEY INTO THEIR RESTAURANTS AND THEIR REAL ESTATE SCHEMES, TELLIN' YOU YOUR 'BRAND' WILL DO ALL THE WORK--

"THEN LEAVE YOU HOLDING THE BALL IN COURT.

"SO YEAH, THAT MONEY GOES QUIC[K] AND THAT'S IF YOU[RE] LUCKY ENOUGH NO[T] TO PICK UP ANY BA[D] HABITS--

"MY SHOW GOT TH[E] BIGGEST SYNDICATI[ON] DEAL IN HISTORY AT THE TIME, AND [I] GOT SOME ROYALT[IES] OFF THAT, SURE--B[UT] BY THE TIME MY CO[KE] BUDGET WAS FACTO[RED] IN, I DIDN'T HAVE A [POT] TO PISS IN."

WELL, IT WAS THE EIGHTIES. LOOK, ALL THAT MAKES SENSE, BUT STILL--I MEAN, PROSTITUTION?

TRUST ME HONEY, WHORIN'S ABOUT THE LEAST DEGRADING THING AN ACTRESS HAS TO DO IN THIS TOWN.

WOW... BUT THINK ABOUT WHAT THIS MEANS FOR THE CASE.

I MEAN, IF SHE WAS YOUR TOP EARNER, SHE MUST'VE HAD SOME BIG DEAL CLIENTS.

WHO ARE ALL NOW SUSPECTS.

YOU BET, DARLING. AND WE'RE GONNA GET TO THE BOTTOM OF ALL THA[T] BUT FIRST--

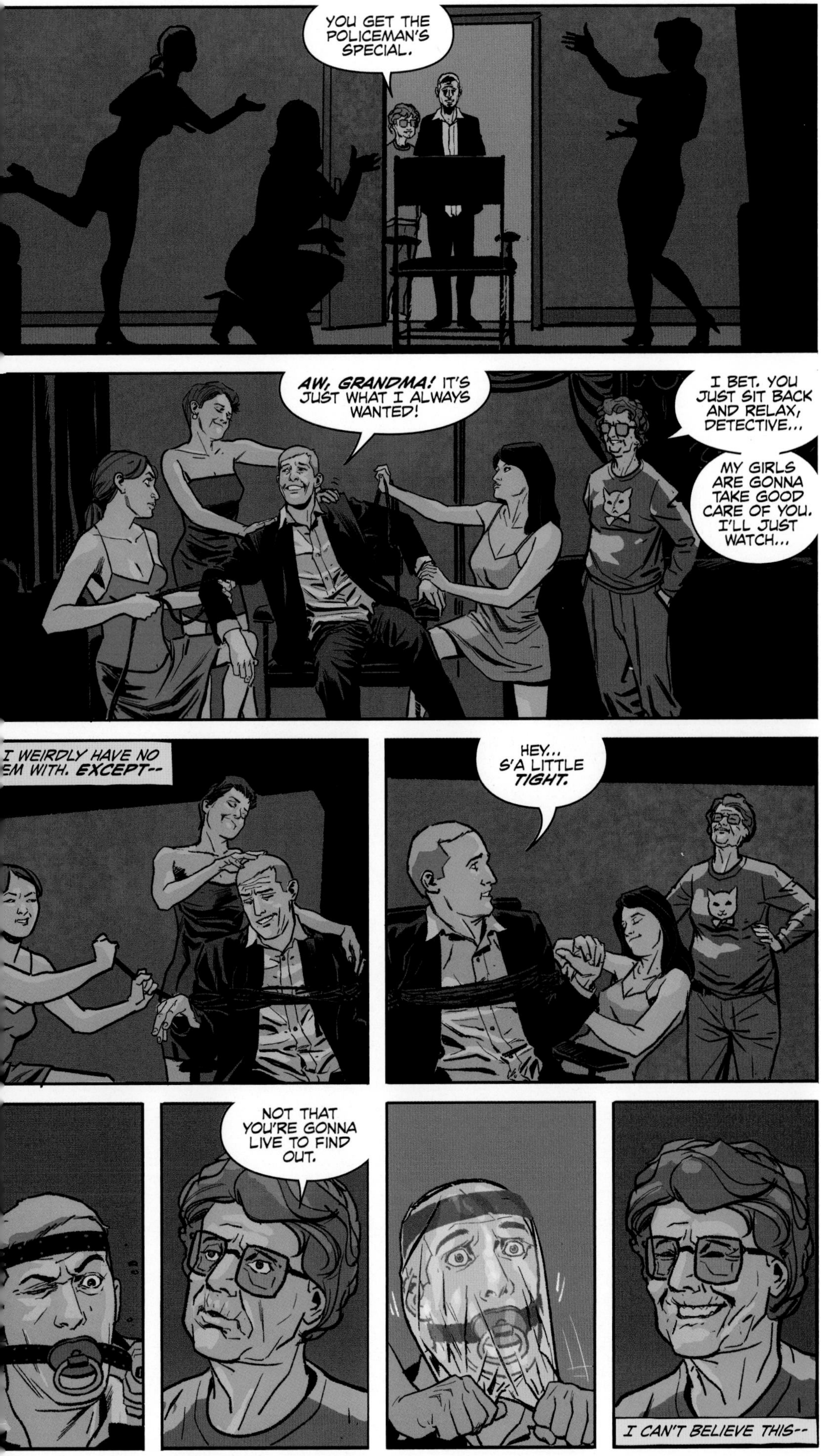
YOU GET THE POLICEMAN'S SPECIAL.
AW, GRANDMA! IT'S JUST WHAT I ALWAYS WANTED!
I BET. YOU JUST SIT BACK AND RELAX, DETECTIVE...
MY GIRLS ARE GONNA TAKE GOOD CARE OF YOU. I'LL JUST WATCH...
I WEIRDLY HAVE NO
EM WITH. EXCEPT--
HEY... S'A LITTLE TIGHT.
NOT THAT YOU'RE GONNA LIVE TO FIND OUT.
I CAN'T BELIEVE THIS--

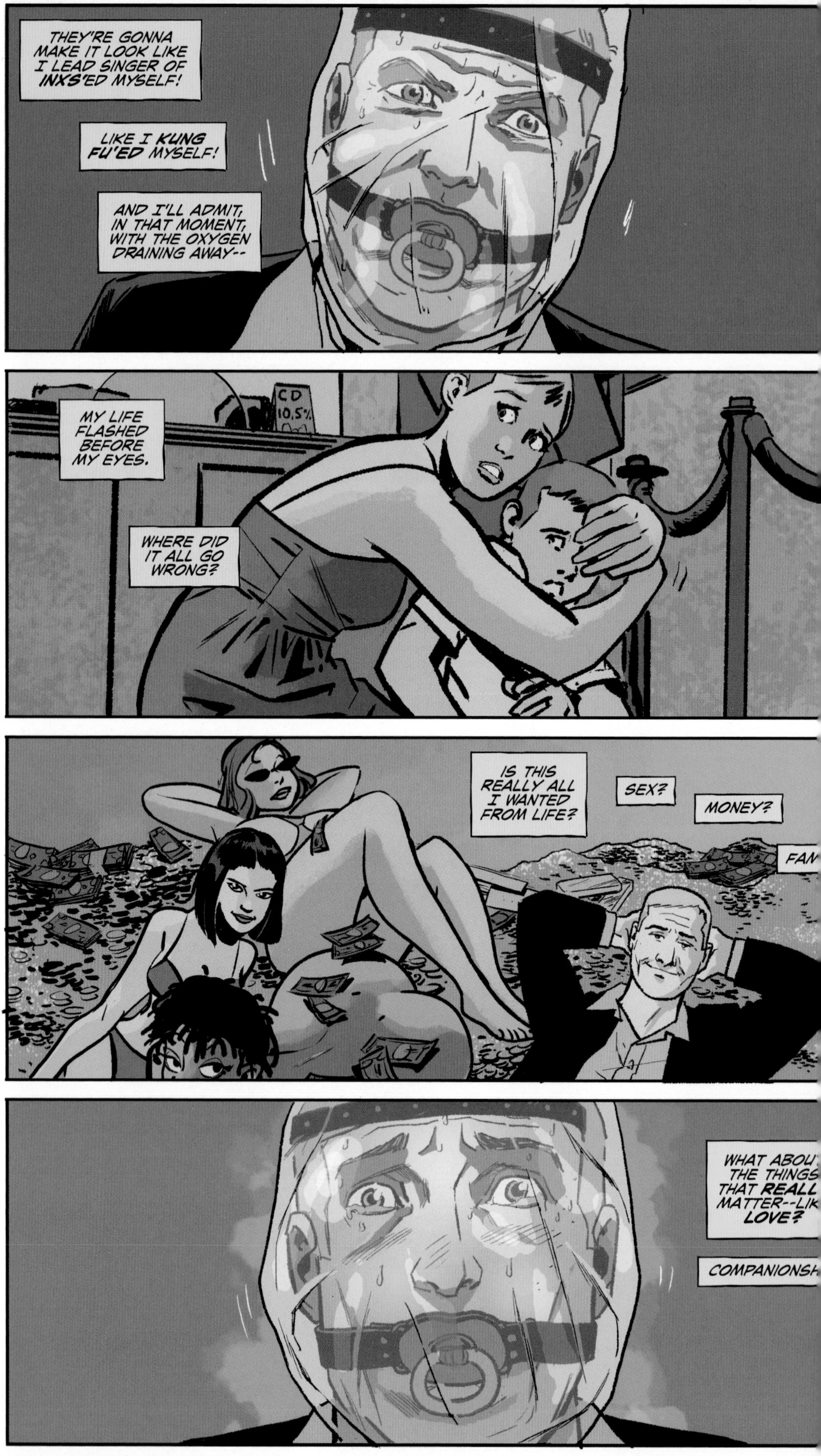
THEY'RE GONNA MAKE IT LOOK LIKE I LEAD SINGER OF INXS'ED MYSELF!
LIKE I KUNG FU'ED MYSELF!
AND I'LL ADMIT, IN THAT MOMENT, WITH THE OXYGEN DRAINING AWAY--
CD 10.5%
MY LIFE FLASHED BEFORE MY EYES.
WHERE DID IT ALL GO WRONG?
IS THIS REALLY ALL I WANTED FROM LIFE?
SEX?
MONEY?
WHAT ABOU THE THINGS THAT REALL MATTER--LIK LOVE?

NDSHIP.

C FOUND
HAT WITH
RETZELS,
T ME...

WAIT,
THAT'S IT--

AC! AT LEAST
ALWAYS HAD
HAT GUY. MY
ST FRIEND--
SOMETHING,
RIGHT?

JUST A SHAME
I'LL NEVER GET
TO TELL HIM WHAT
HE MEANS TO ME.

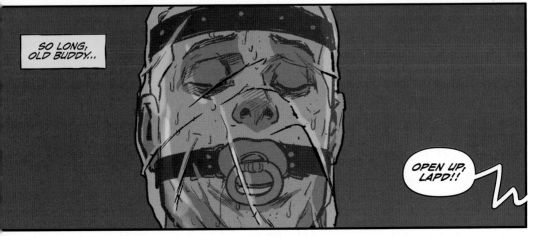

SO LONG,
OLD BUDDY...

OPEN UP,
LAPD!!

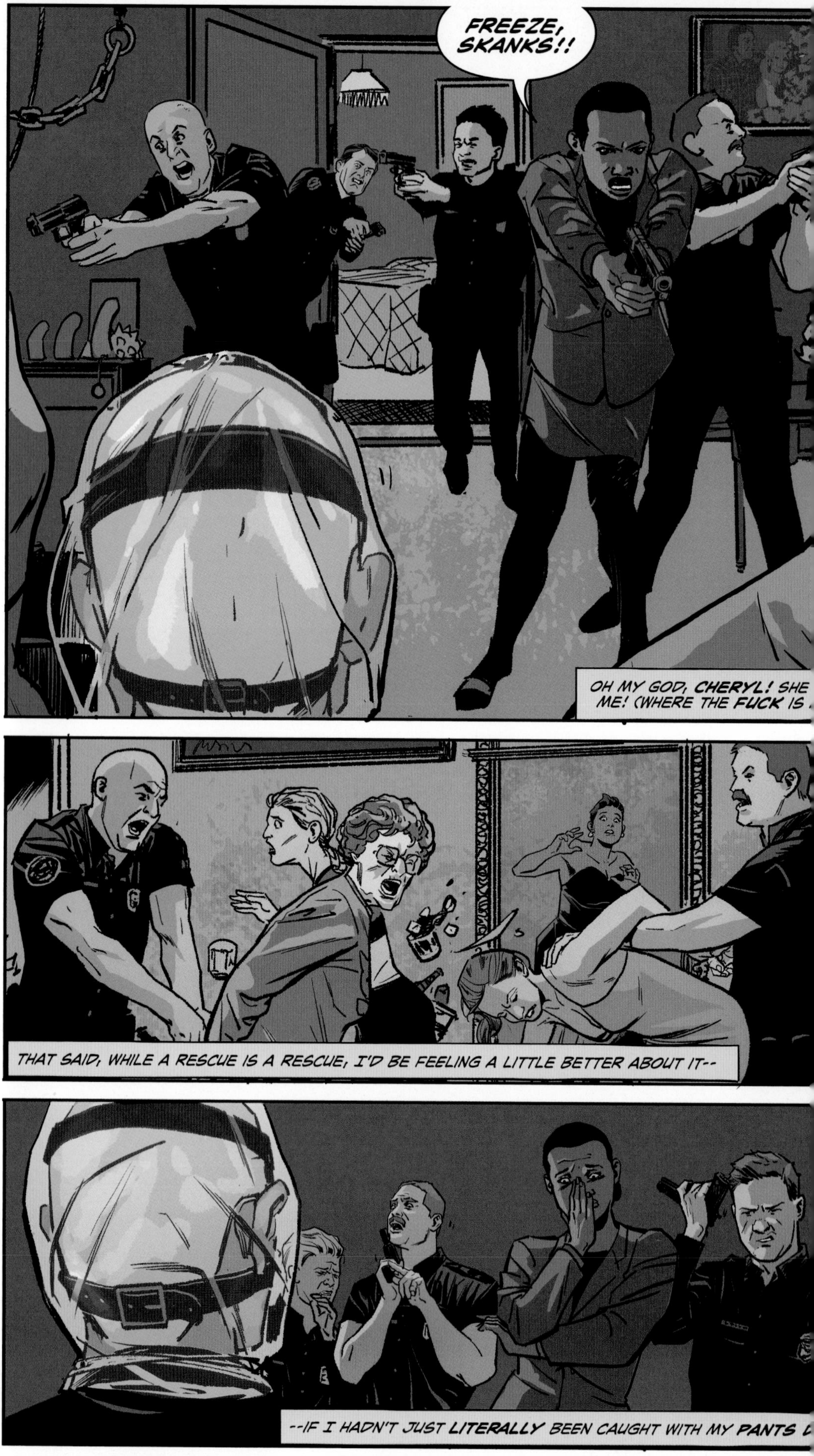
FREEZE, SKANKS!!
OH MY GOD, CHERYL! SHE
ME! (WHERE THE FUCK IS
THAT SAID, WHILE A RESCUE IS A RESCUE, I'D BE FEELING A LITTLE BETTER ABOUT IT--
--IF I HADN'T JUST LITERALLY BEEN CAUGHT WITH MY PANTS

ROY, WHAT THE *FUCK* ARE YOU DOING?!!

AT YOU N?!!

—*THEY* DID THIS—THEY WERE GONNA *KILL ME* AND MAKE IT LOOK LIKE *AUTOEROTIC ASPHYXIATION!*

I GET *THAT*—

—BUT WHY ARE YOU *ACTUALLY JERKING OFF?!!*

WELL, I FIGURED IF I WAS GONNA DIE *THAT* WAY, MIGHT AS WELL GET THE FULL EXPERIENCE...

OKAY—

—BUT WHY ARE YOU *STILL* DOING IT?!!

I DUNNO, *STRESS?!!*

CHERYL—THIS *WAY* BIGGER E THOUGHT.

NA—THE ESS. SHE KED HERE. E WAS...

OW. ER

WHAT ARE YOU TALKING ABOUT?

CAN YOU BELIEVE THAT?

ONE OF *THE MOST* FAMOUS GIRLS IN THE WORLD, NOW KILLED MYSTERIOUSLY—DID WORK HERE.

ALRIGHT...

TUG!

DON'T YOU REALIZE WHAT THIS MEANS?!!

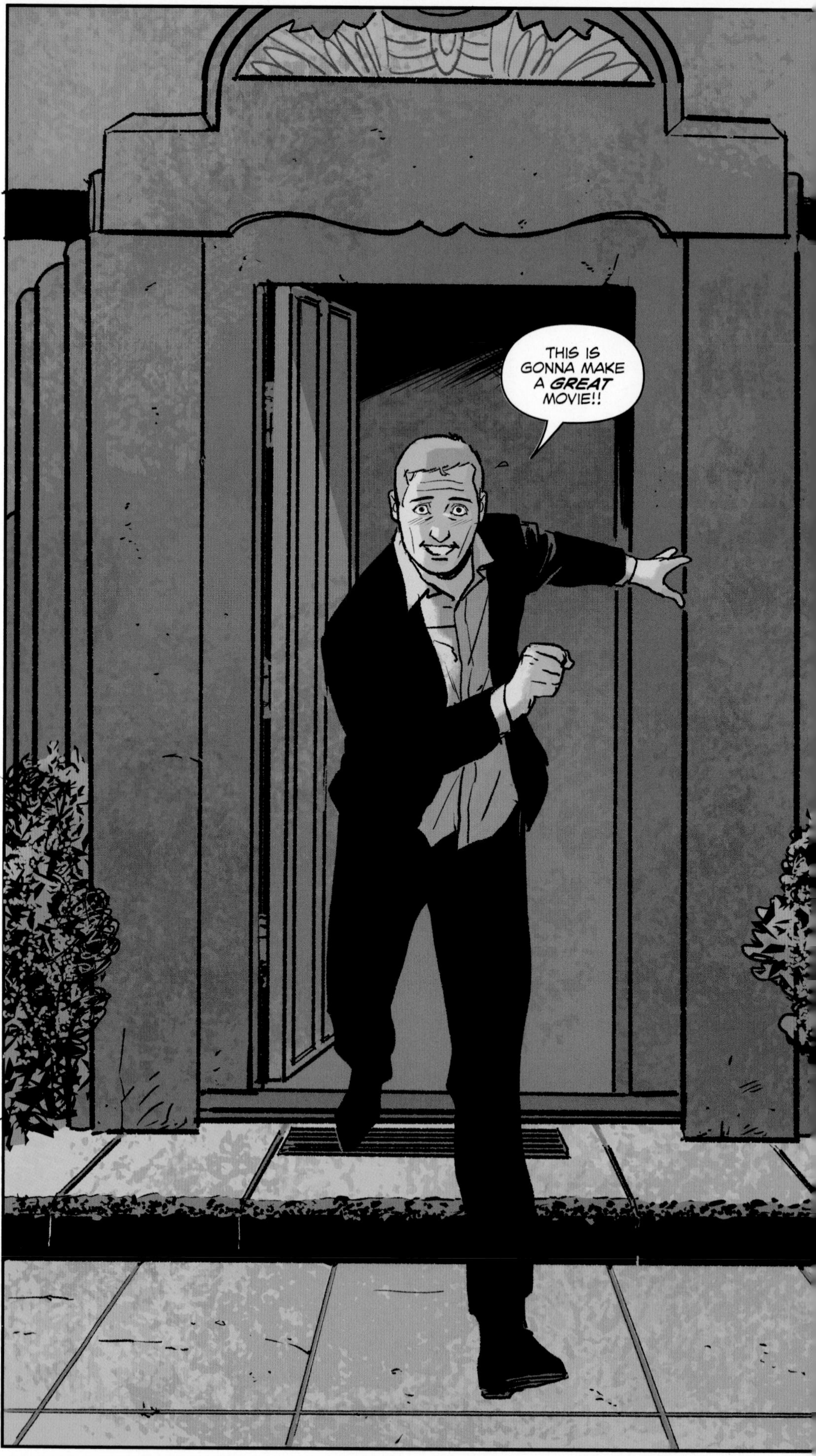
THIS IS GONNA MAKE A GREAT MOVIE!!

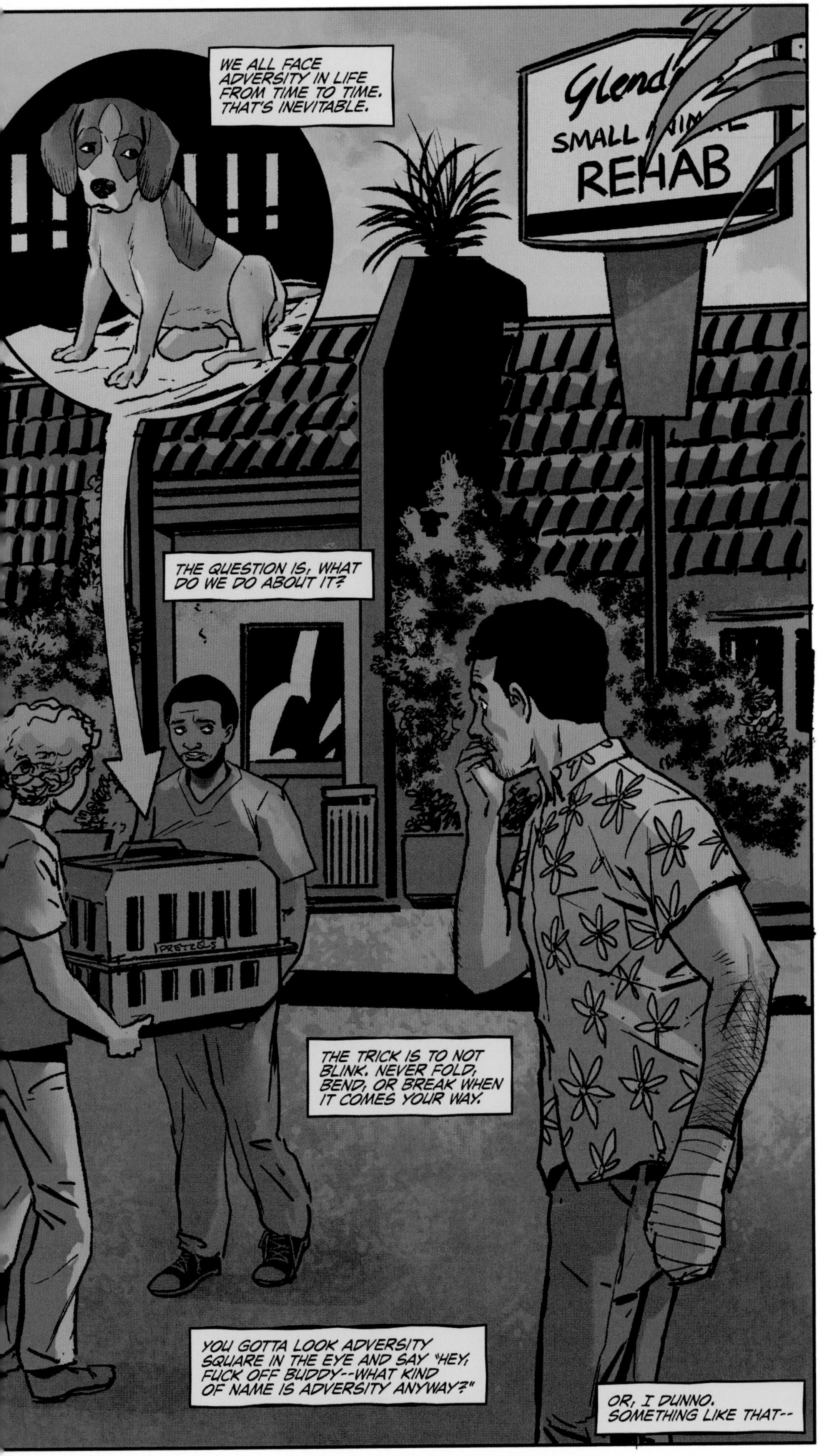
WE ALL FACE ADVERSITY IN LIFE FROM TIME TO TIME. THAT'S INEVITABLE.
REHAB
THE QUESTION IS, WHAT DO WE DO ABOUT IT?
PRETZELS
THE TRICK IS TO NOT BLINK. NEVER FOLD, BEND, OR BREAK WHEN IT COMES YOUR WAY.
YOU GOTTA LOOK ADVERSITY SQUARE IN THE EYE AND SAY "HEY, FUCK OFF BUDDY--WHAT KIND OF NAME IS ADVERSITY ANYWAY?"
OR, I DUNNO. SOMETHING LIKE THAT--

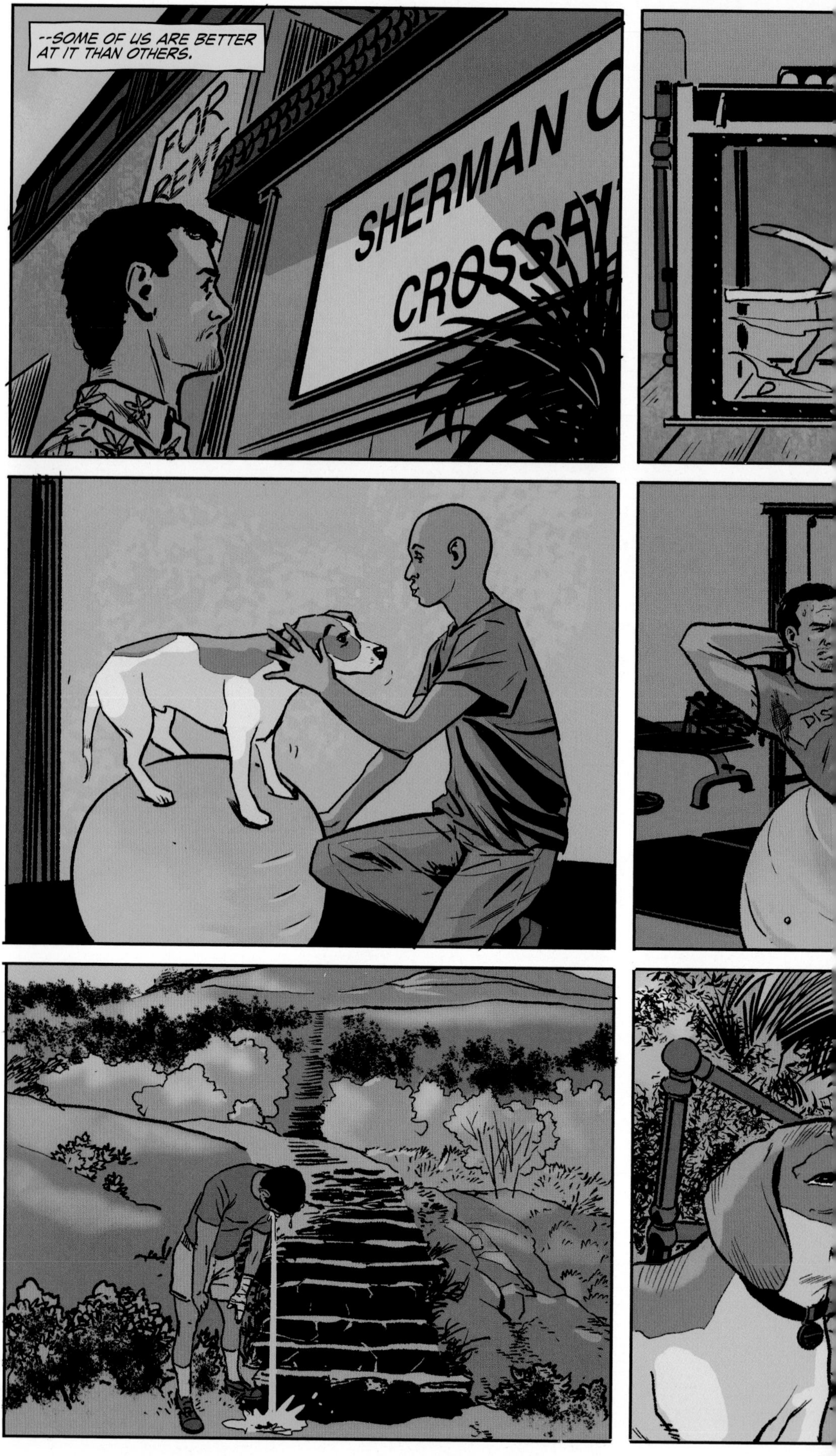
--SOME OF US ARE BETTER AT IT THAN OTHERS.
FOR RENT
SHERMAN C
CROSSF

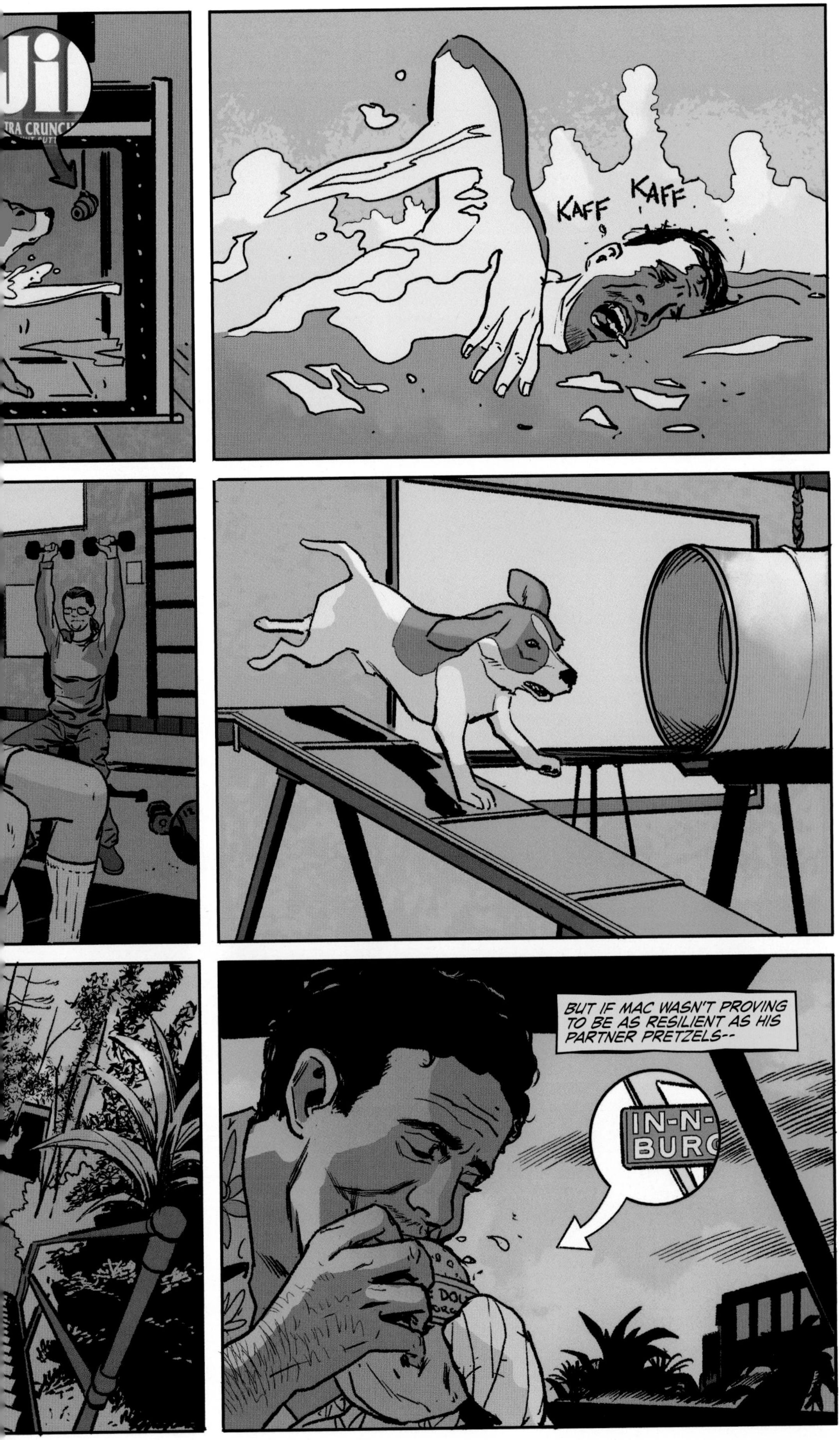

Jif
TRA CRUNCH
KAFF
KAFF
BUT IF MAC WASN'T PROVING TO BE AS RESILIENT AS HIS PARTNER PRETZELS--
IN-N-
BURG

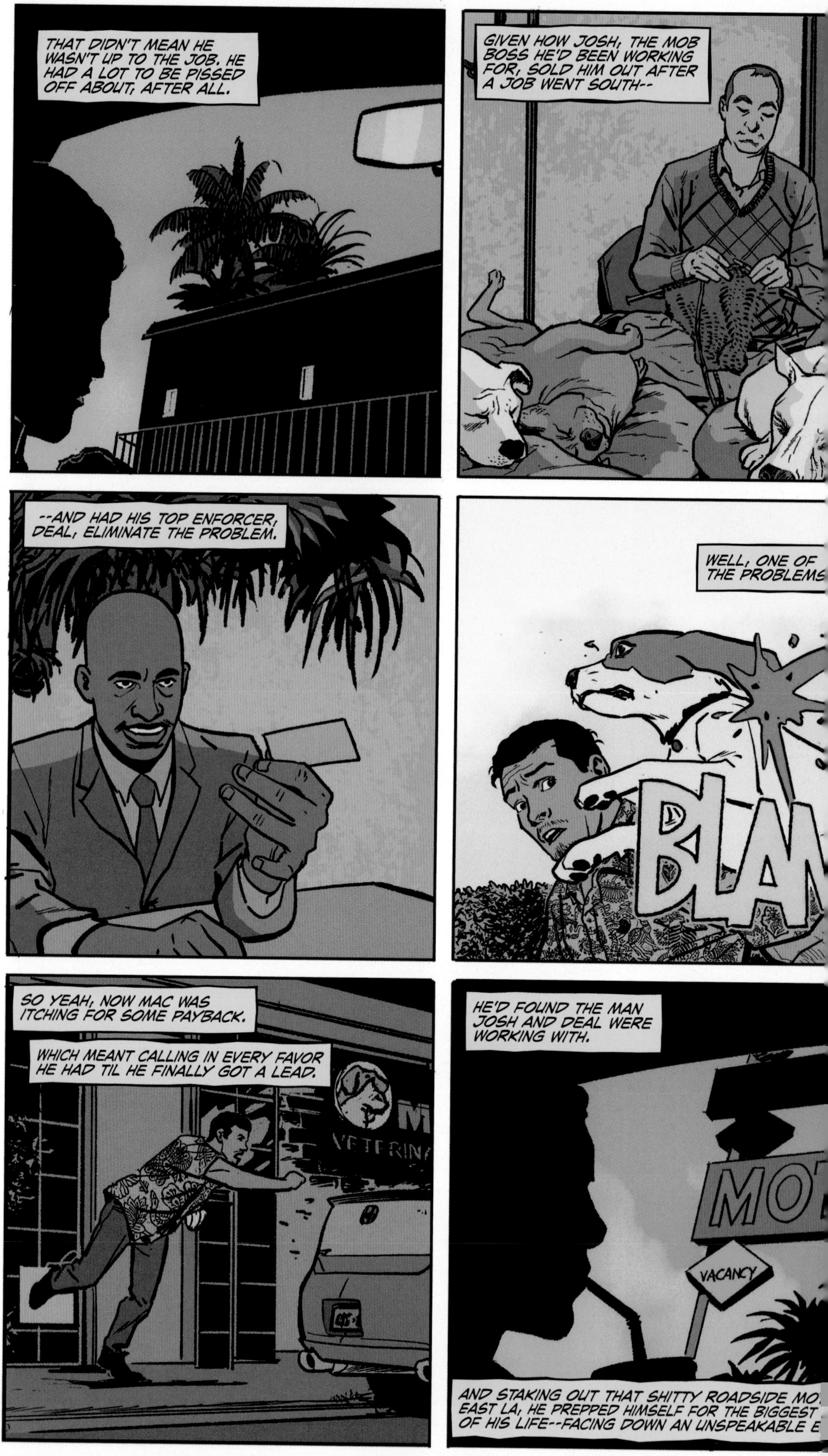
THAT DIDN'T MEAN HE WASN'T UP TO THE JOB. HE HAD A LOT TO BE PISSED OFF ABOUT, AFTER ALL.
GIVEN HOW JOSH, THE MOB BOSS HE'D BEEN WORKING FOR, SOLD HIM OUT AFTER A JOB WENT SOUTH--
--AND HAD HIS TOP ENFORCER, DEAL, ELIMINATE THE PROBLEM.
WELL, ONE OF THE PROBLEMS
BLA
SO YEAH, NOW MAC WAS ITCHING FOR SOME PAYBACK.
WHICH MEANT CALLING IN EVERY FAVOR HE HAD TIL HE FINALLY GOT A LEAD.
VETERINA
HE'D FOUND THE MAN JOSH AND DEAL WERE WORKING WITH.
MOT
VACANCY
AND STAKING OUT THAT SHITTY ROADSIDE MO
EAST LA, HE PREPPED HIMSELF FOR THE BIGGEST
OF HIS LIFE--FACING DOWN AN UNSPEAKABLE E

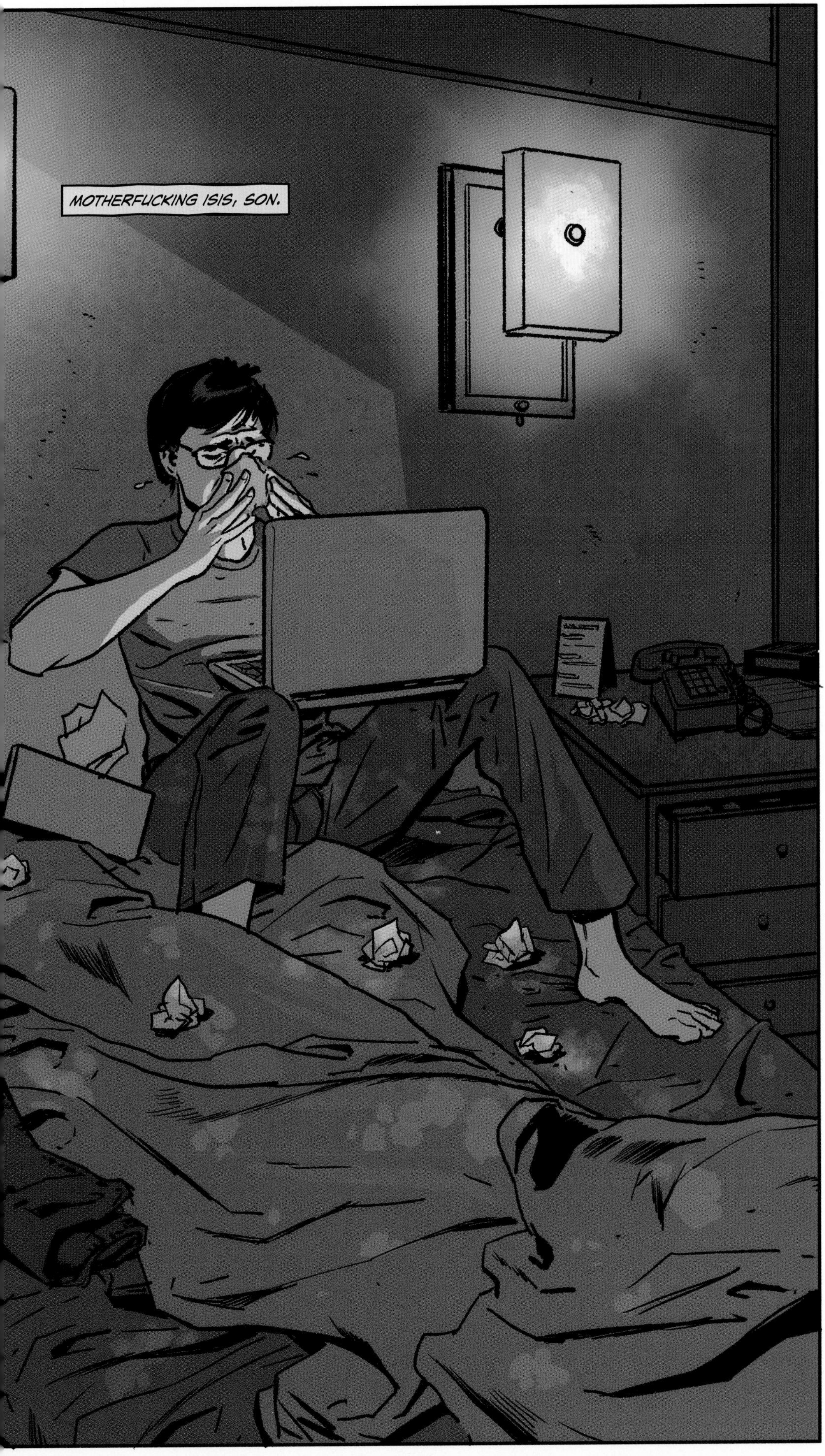
MOTHERFUCKING ISIS, SON.

THE

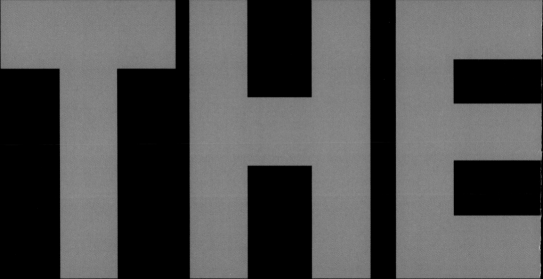

FIX

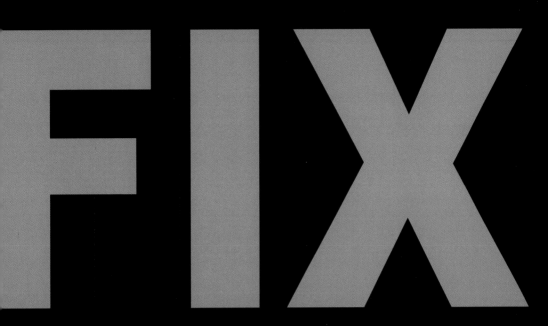

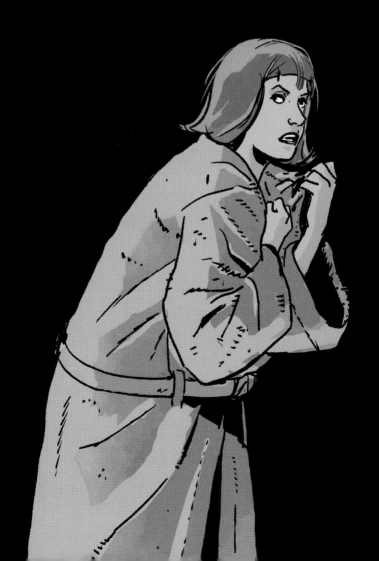

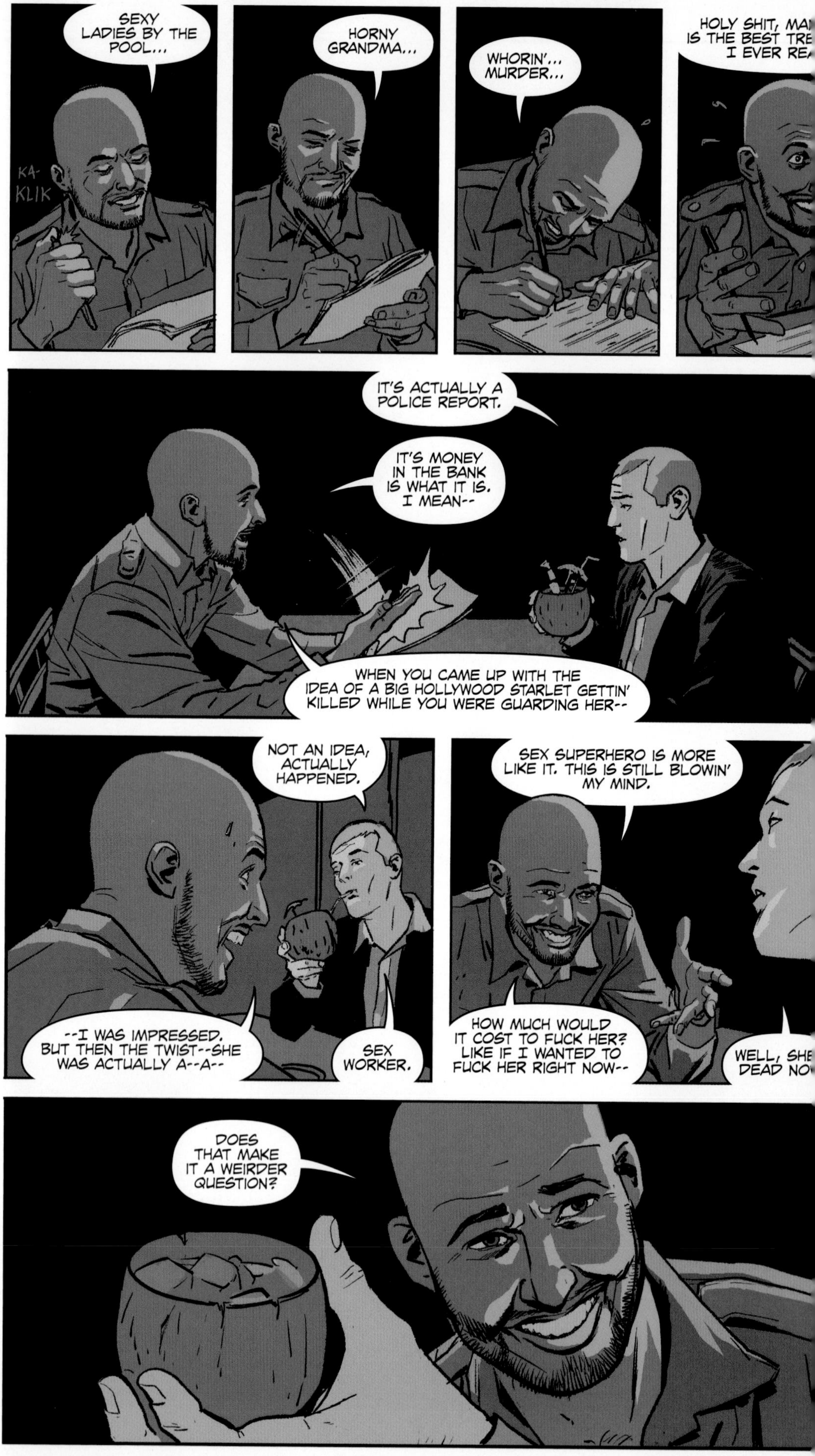
SEXY LADIES BY THE POOL...
KA-KLIK
HORNY GRANDMA...
WHORIN'... MURDER...
HOLY SHIT, MA
IS THE BEST TRE
I EVER RE
IT'S ACTUALLY A POLICE REPORT.
IT'S MONEY IN THE BANK IS WHAT IT IS. I MEAN--
WHEN YOU CAME UP WITH THE IDEA OF A BIG HOLLYWOOD STARLET GETTIN' KILLED WHILE YOU WERE GUARDING HER--
NOT AN IDEA, ACTUALLY HAPPENED.
--I WAS IMPRESSED. BUT THEN THE TWIST--SHE WAS ACTUALLY A--A--
SEX WORKER.
SEX SUPERHERO IS MORE LIKE IT. THIS IS STILL BLOWIN' MY MIND.
HOW MUCH WOULD IT COST TO FUCK HER? LIKE IF I WANTED TO FUCK HER RIGHT NOW--
WELL, SHE
DEAD NO
DOES THAT MAKE IT A WEIRDER QUESTION?

I DUNNO--SHE'S PRETTY MUCH JUST ASHES AT THIS POINT, SO--

SO YOU'RE STILL NOT ANSWERING MY QUESTION.

I'LL TRY TO LOOK INTO IT--BUT DONOVAN--NOW THAT YOU GOT THIS--WHAT'S NEXT? I MEAN, IN TERMS OF PAYING FOR THE RIGHTS TO THE STORY AND ALL THAT--

WHOA, WHOA, WHOA-- COOL YOUR JETS. I LOVE THIS, OKAY? I LOVE IT LIKE I LOVE--COCAINE. AND THERE IS NOTHING I LOVE MORE THAN COCAINE. EXCEPT MAYBE THIS.

NO WAIT, COCAINE.

IT'S ONE HELL OF A FIRST ACT, FOR SURE--BUT YOU KNOW WHAT ELSE HAD GREAT FIRST ACTS? *HANCOCK. I AM LEGEND. BIG WILLIE STYLE.*

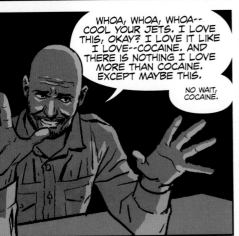

ARE--ARE YOU THINKING OF WILL SMITH FOR THIS?

WHO ELSE IS LIKEABLE ENOUGH TO PLAY ME? BUT LOOK, YOU'RE MISSING THE POINT--

WE NEED TO SEE WHERE THIS GOES. YOU GET ME? WE NEED TO SEE THE THIRD ACT. ROY-- YOU'RE ALL SET UP--

--I JUST NEED A BIG ENDING.

WHICH IS ALL WELL AND GOOD I GUESS--IF I SURVIVE THE SECOND ACT.

LUCKILY I DO HAVE SOMETHING STASHED AWAY TO HELP ENDS MEET IN THE MEANTIME--

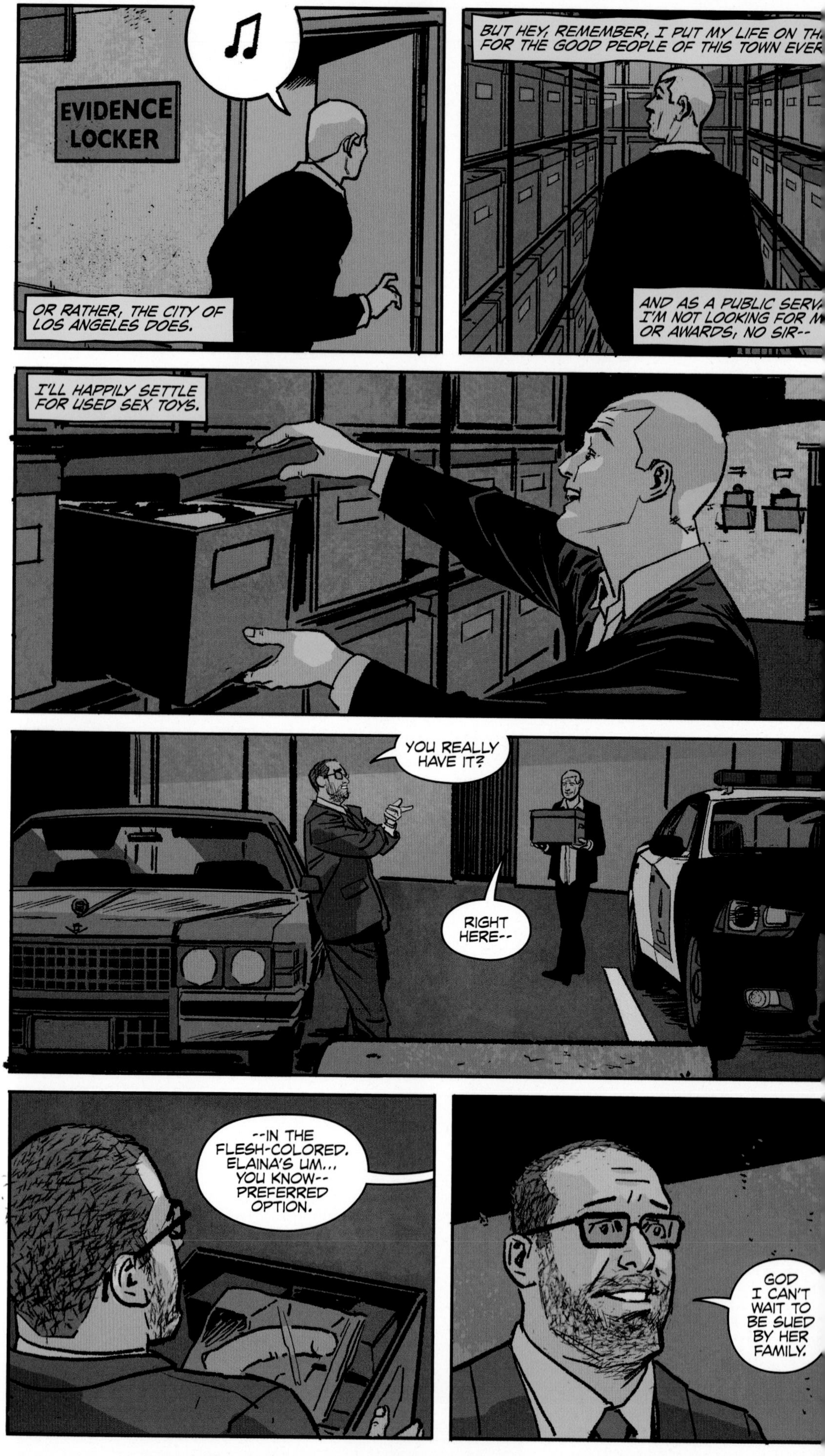
♫
EVIDENCE LOCKER
OR RATHER, THE CITY OF LOS ANGELES DOES.
BUT HEY, REMEMBER, I PUT MY LIFE ON TH FOR THE GOOD PEOPLE OF THIS TOWN EVER
AND AS A PUBLIC SERV I'M NOT LOOKING FOR M OR AWARDS, NO SIR--
I'LL HAPPILY SETTLE FOR USED SEX TOYS.
YOU REALLY HAVE IT?
RIGHT HERE--
--IN THE FLESH-COLORED. ELAINA'S UM... YOU KNOW-- PREFERRED OPTION.
GOD I CAN'T WAIT TO BE SUED BY HER FAMILY.

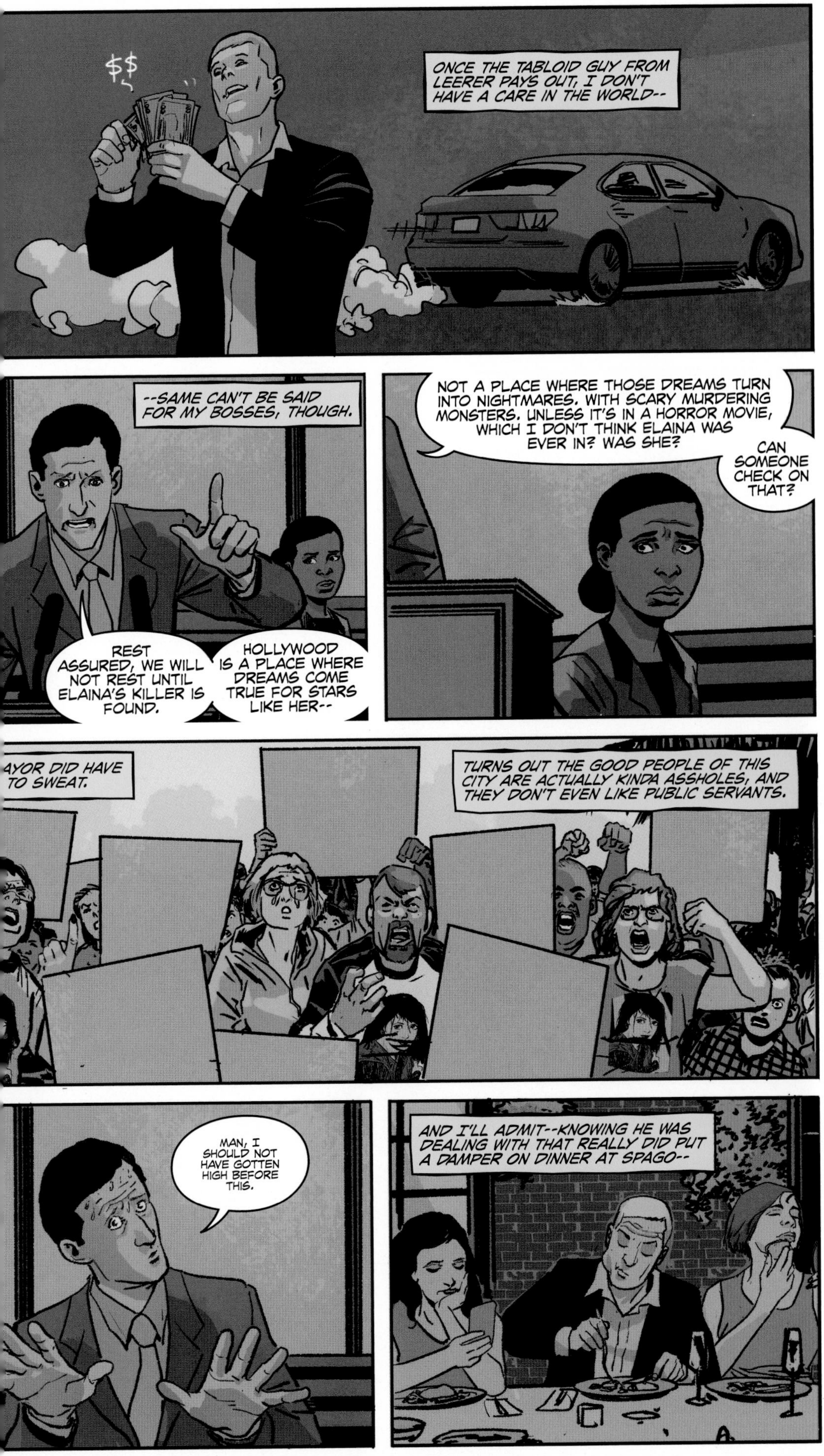
$$
ONCE THE TABLOID GUY FROM LEERER PAYS OUT, I DON'T HAVE A CARE IN THE WORLD--
--SAME CAN'T BE SAID FOR MY BOSSES, THOUGH.
REST ASSURED, WE WILL NOT REST UNTIL ELAINA'S KILLER IS FOUND.
HOLLYWOOD IS A PLACE WHERE DREAMS COME TRUE FOR STARS LIKE HER--
NOT A PLACE WHERE THOSE DREAMS TURN INTO NIGHTMARES. WITH SCARY MURDERING MONSTERS. UNLESS IT'S IN A HORROR MOVIE, WHICH I DON'T THINK ELAINA WAS EVER IN? WAS SHE?
CAN SOMEONE CHECK ON THAT?
AYOR DID HAVE TO SWEAT.
TURNS OUT THE GOOD PEOPLE OF THIS CITY ARE ACTUALLY KINDA ASSHOLES, AND THEY DON'T EVEN LIKE PUBLIC SERVANTS.
MAN, I SHOULD NOT HAVE GOTTEN HIGH BEFORE THIS.
AND I'LL ADMIT--KNOWING HE WAS DEALING WITH THAT REALLY DID PUT A DAMPER ON DINNER AT SPAGO--

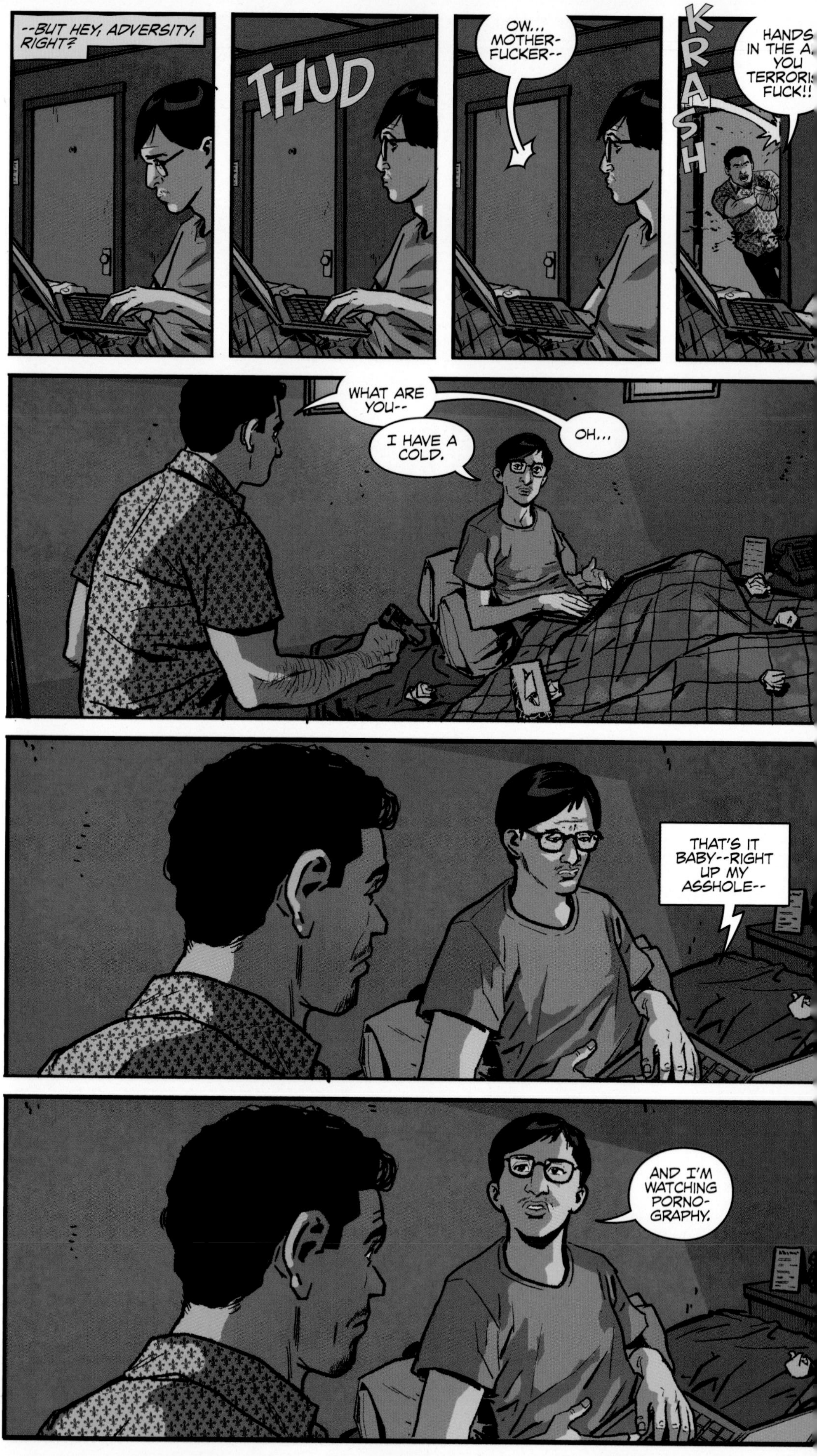
--BUT HEY, ADVERSITY, RIGHT?
THUD
OW... MOTHER-FUCKER--
KRASH
HANDS IN THE A. YOU TERRORI FUCK!!
WHAT ARE YOU--
I HAVE A COLD.
OH...
THAT'S IT BABY--RIGHT UP MY ASSHOLE--
AND I'M WATCHING PORNO-GRAPHY.

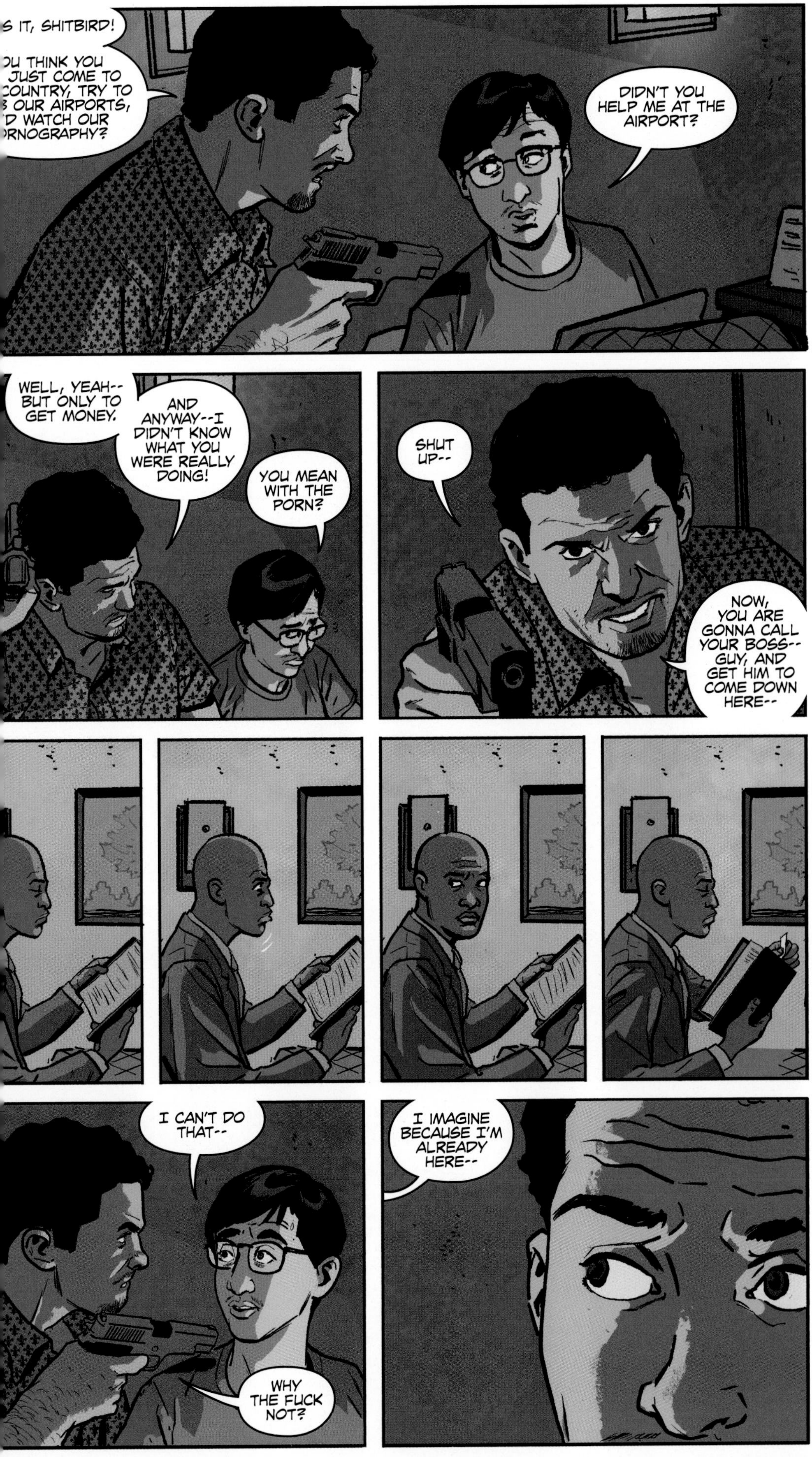
S IT, SHITBIRD!
OU THINK YOU JUST COME TO COUNTRY, TRY TO B OUR AIRPORTS, D WATCH OUR ORNOGRAPHY?
DIDN'T YOU HELP ME AT THE AIRPORT?
WELL, YEAH-- BUT ONLY TO GET MONEY.
AND ANYWAY--I DIDN'T KNOW WHAT YOU WERE REALLY DOING!
YOU MEAN WITH THE PORN?
SHUT UP--
NOW, YOU ARE GONNA CALL YOUR BOSS-- GUY, AND GET HIM TO COME DOWN HERE--
I CAN'T DO THAT--
WHY THE FUCK NOT?
I IMAGINE BECAUSE I'M ALREADY HERE--

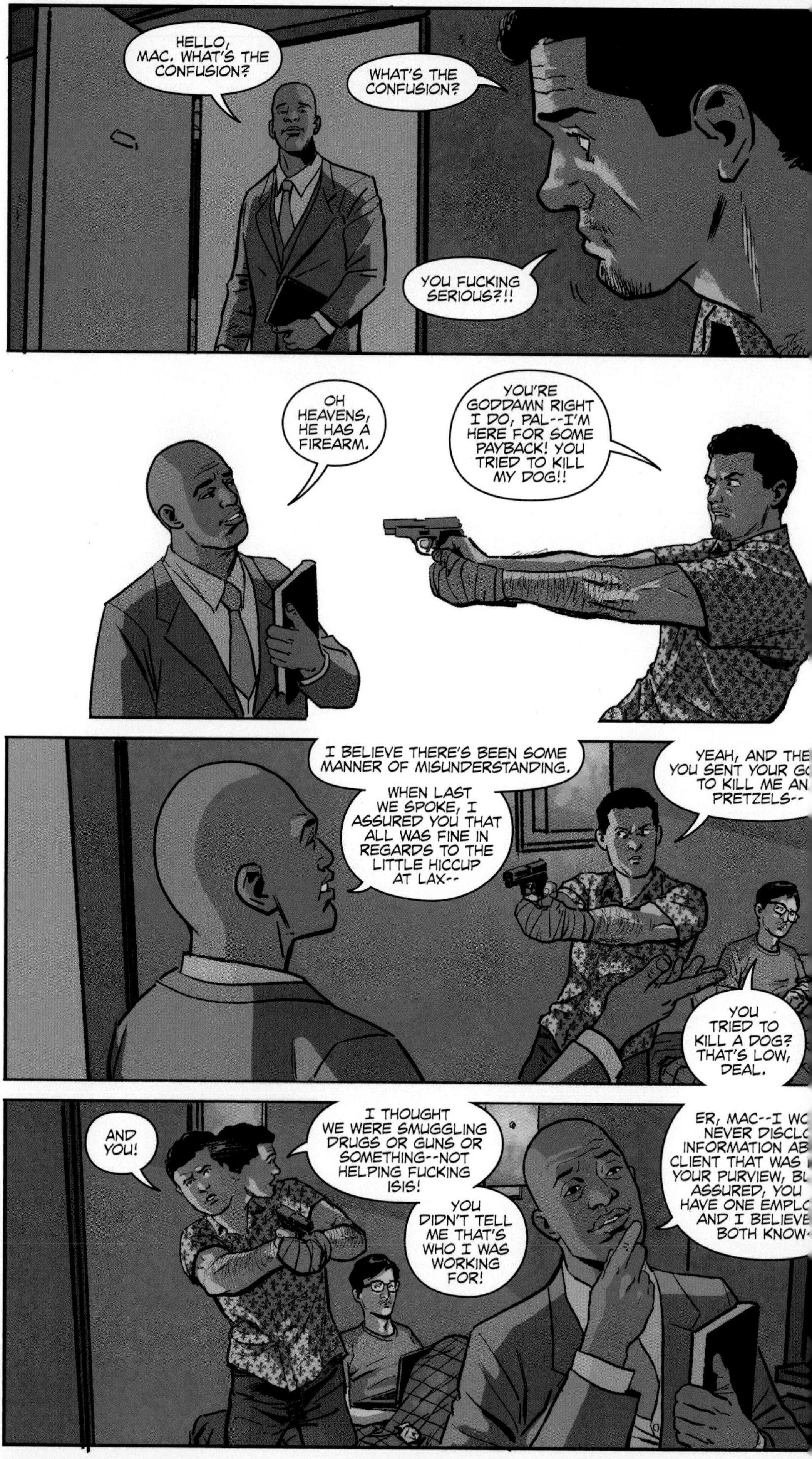
HELLO, MAC. WHAT'S THE CONFUSION?
WHAT'S THE CONFUSION?
YOU FUCKING SERIOUS?!!
OH HEAVENS, HE HAS A FIREARM.
YOU'RE GODDAMN RIGHT I DO, PAL--I'M HERE FOR SOME PAYBACK! YOU TRIED TO KILL MY DOG!!
I BELIEVE THERE'S BEEN SOME MANNER OF MISUNDERSTANDING.
WHEN LAST WE SPOKE, I ASSURED YOU THAT ALL WAS FINE IN REGARDS TO THE LITTLE HICCUP AT LAX--
YOU TRIED TO KILL A DOG? THAT'S LOW, DEAL.
AND YOU!
I THOUGHT WE WERE SMUGGLING DRUGS OR GUNS OR SOMETHING--NOT HELPING FUCKING ISIS!
YOU DIDN'T TELL ME THAT'S WHO I WAS WORKING FOR!

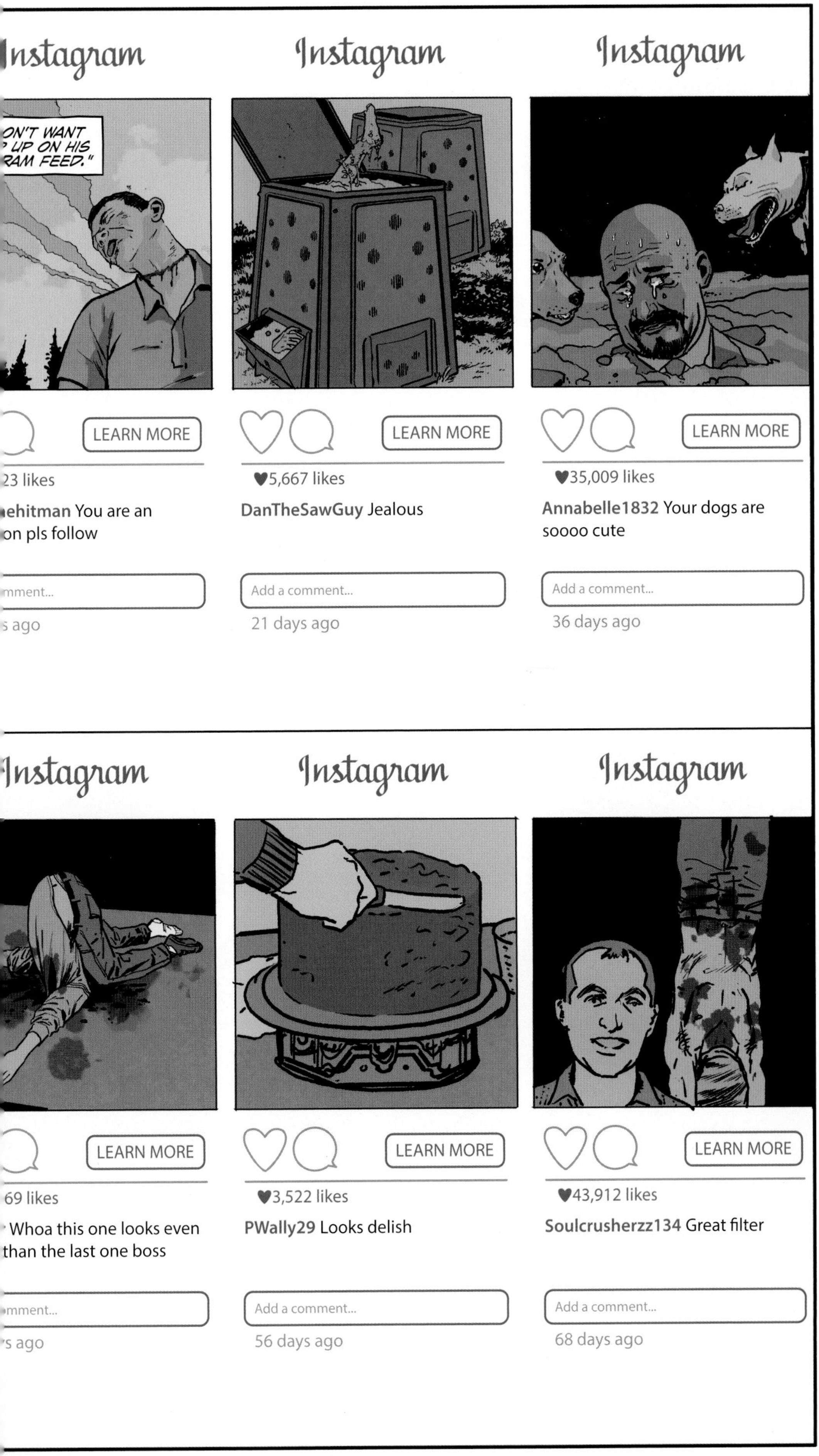

Instagram
ON'T WANT
UP ON HIS
RAM FEED."
LEARN MORE
23 likes
ehitman You are an
on pls follow
mment...
s ago
Instagram
LEARN MORE
♥5,667 likes
DanTheSawGuy Jealous
Add a comment...
21 days ago
Instagram
LEARN MORE
♥35,009 likes
Annabelle1832 Your dogs are soooo cute
Add a comment...
36 days ago
Instagram
LEARN MORE
69 likes
Whoa this one looks even
than the last one boss
mment...
s ago
Instagram
LEARN MORE
♥3,522 likes
PWally29 Looks delish
Add a comment...
56 days ago
Instagram
LEARN MORE
♥43,912 likes
Soulcrusherzz134 Great filter
Add a comment...
68 days ago

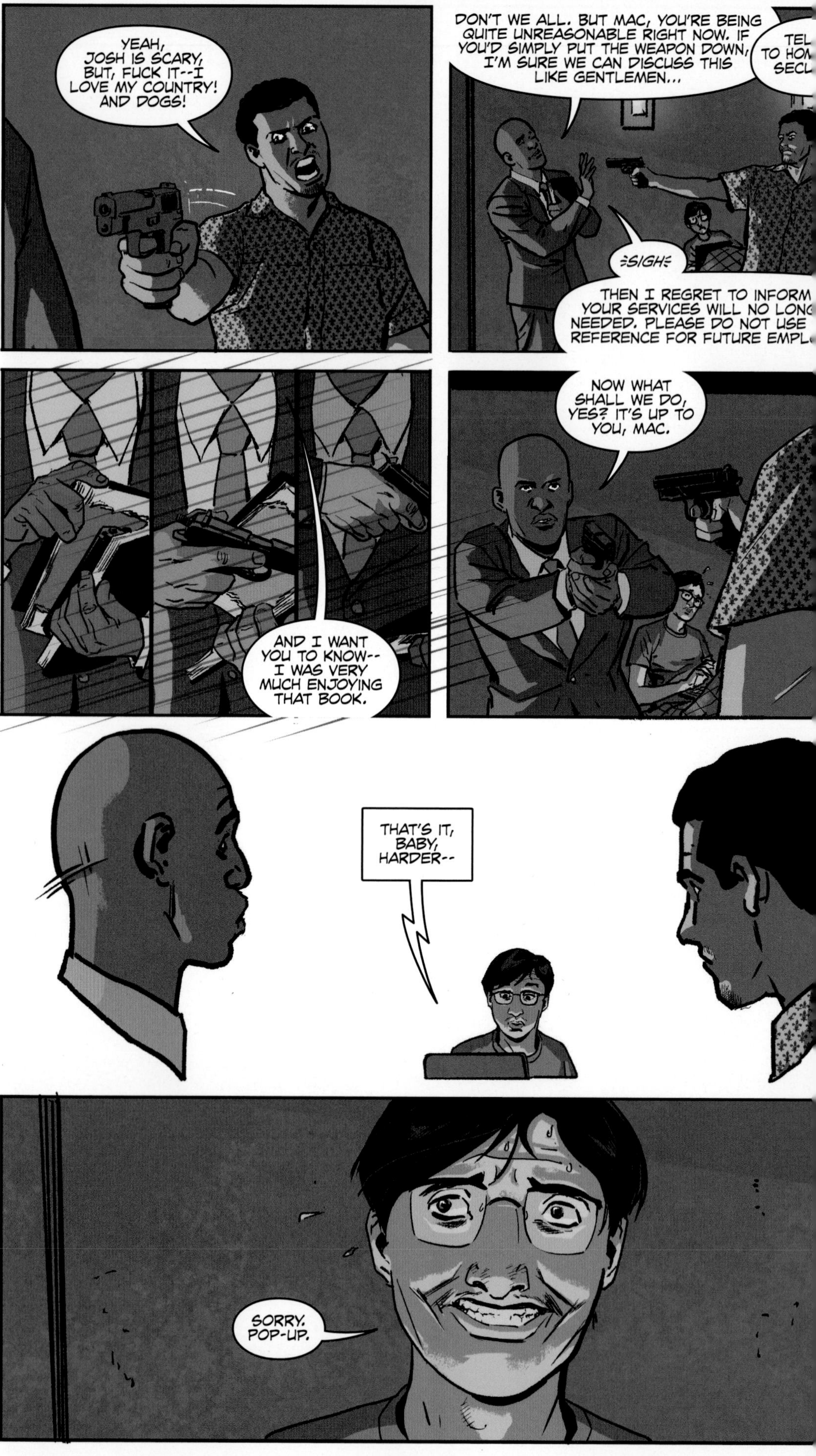
YEAH, JOSH IS SCARY, BUT, FUCK IT--I LOVE MY COUNTRY! AND DOGS!
DON'T WE ALL. BUT MAC, YOU'RE BEING QUITE UNREASONABLE RIGHT NOW. IF YOU'D SIMPLY PUT THE WEAPON DOWN, I'M SURE WE CAN DISCUSS THIS LIKE GENTLEMEN...
TEL TO HOM SECL
=SIGH=
THEN I REGRET TO INFORM YOUR SERVICES WILL NO LONG NEEDED. PLEASE DO NOT USE REFERENCE FOR FUTURE EMPL
AND I WANT YOU TO KNOW-- I WAS VERY MUCH ENJOYING THAT BOOK.
NOW WHAT SHALL WE DO, YES? IT'S UP TO YOU, MAC.
THAT'S IT, BABY, HARDER--
SORRY. POP-UP.

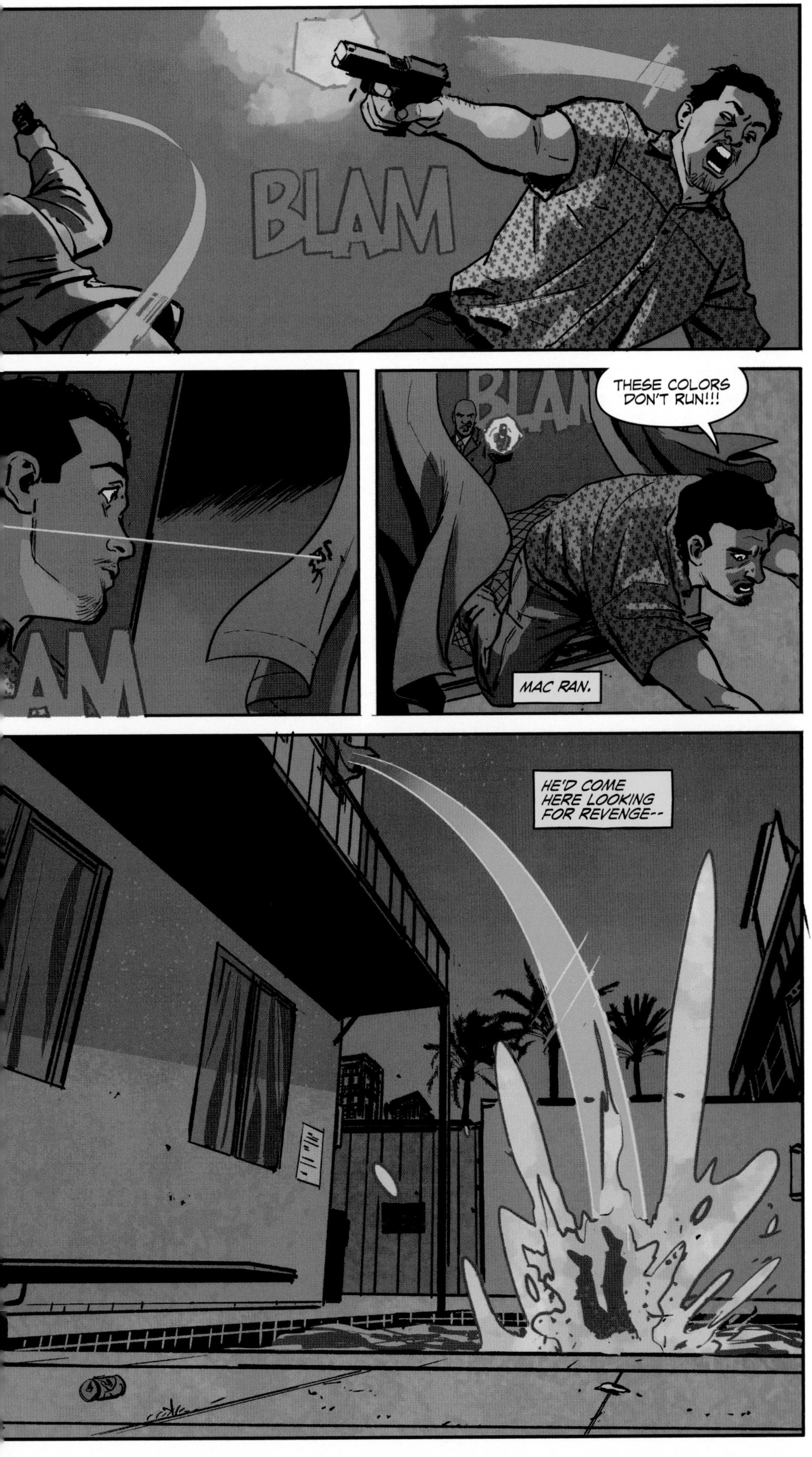
BLAM
BLAM
THESE COLORS DON'T RUN!!!
MAC RAN.
HE'D COME HERE LOOKING FOR REVENGE--

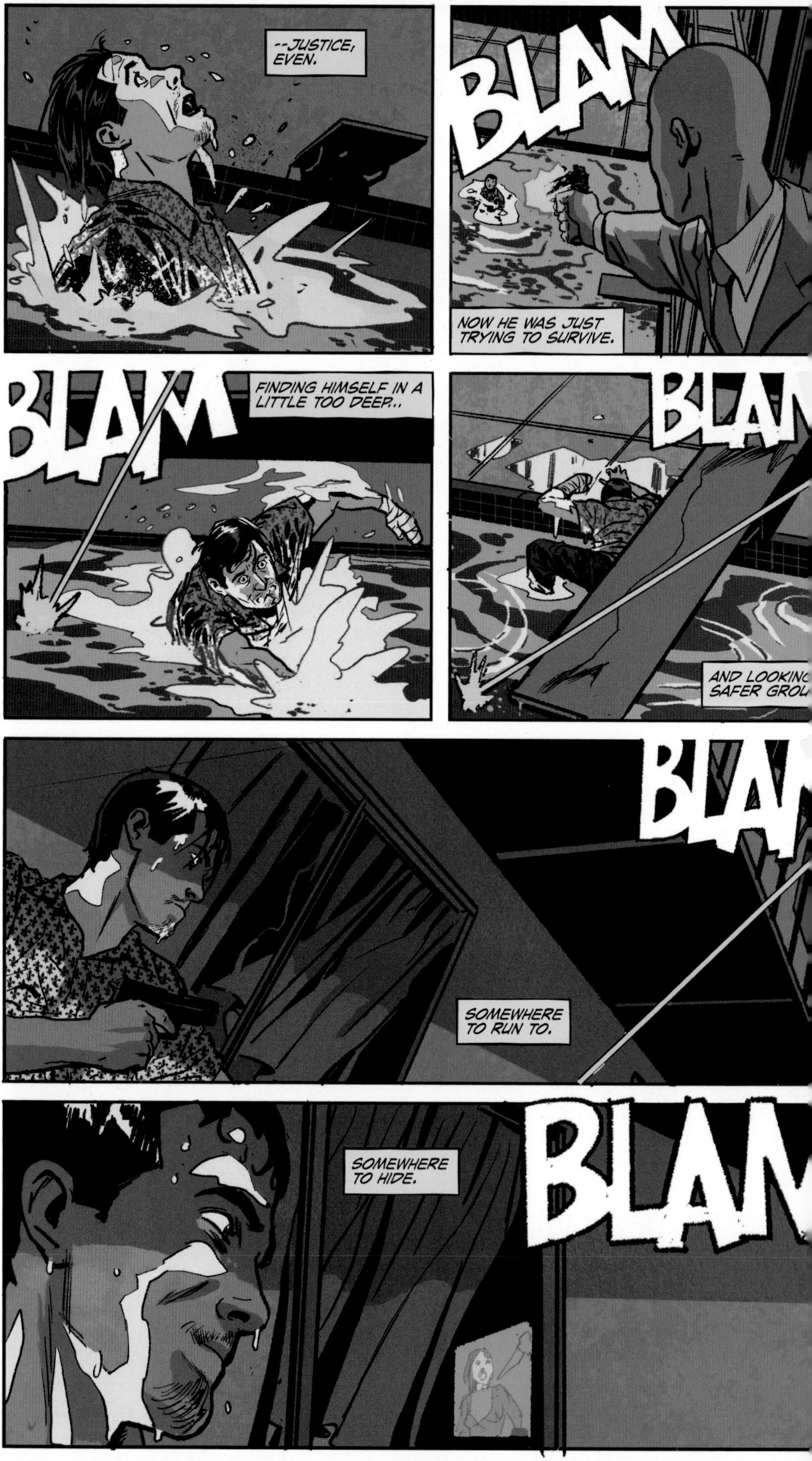
--JUSTICE, EVEN.
BLAM
NOW HE WAS JUST TRYING TO SURVIVE.
BLAM
FINDING HIMSELF IN A LITTLE TOO DEEP...
BLAM
AND LOOKING SAFER GROU
BLAM
SOMEWHERE TO RUN TO.
BLAM
SOMEWHERE TO HIDE.

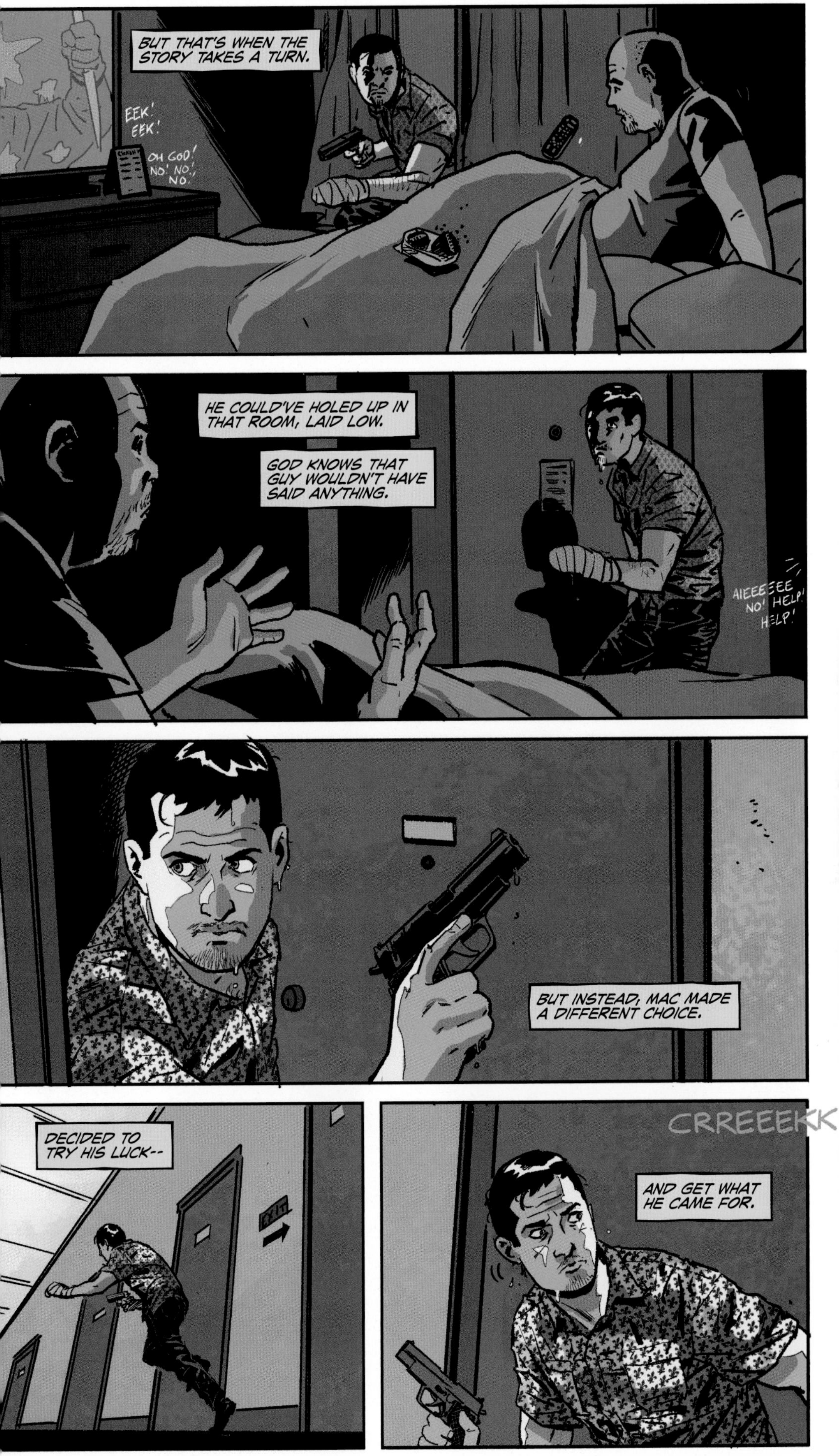
BUT THAT'S WHEN THE STORY TAKES A TURN.
EEK! EEK!
OH GOD! NO! NO! NO!
HE COULD'VE HOLED UP IN THAT ROOM, LAID LOW.
GOD KNOWS THAT GUY WOULDN'T HAVE SAID ANYTHING.
AIEEEEEE NO! HELP! HELP!
BUT INSTEAD, MAC MADE A DIFFERENT CHOICE.
DECIDED TO TRY HIS LUCK--
EXIT
CRREEEKK
AND GET WHAT HE CAME FOR.

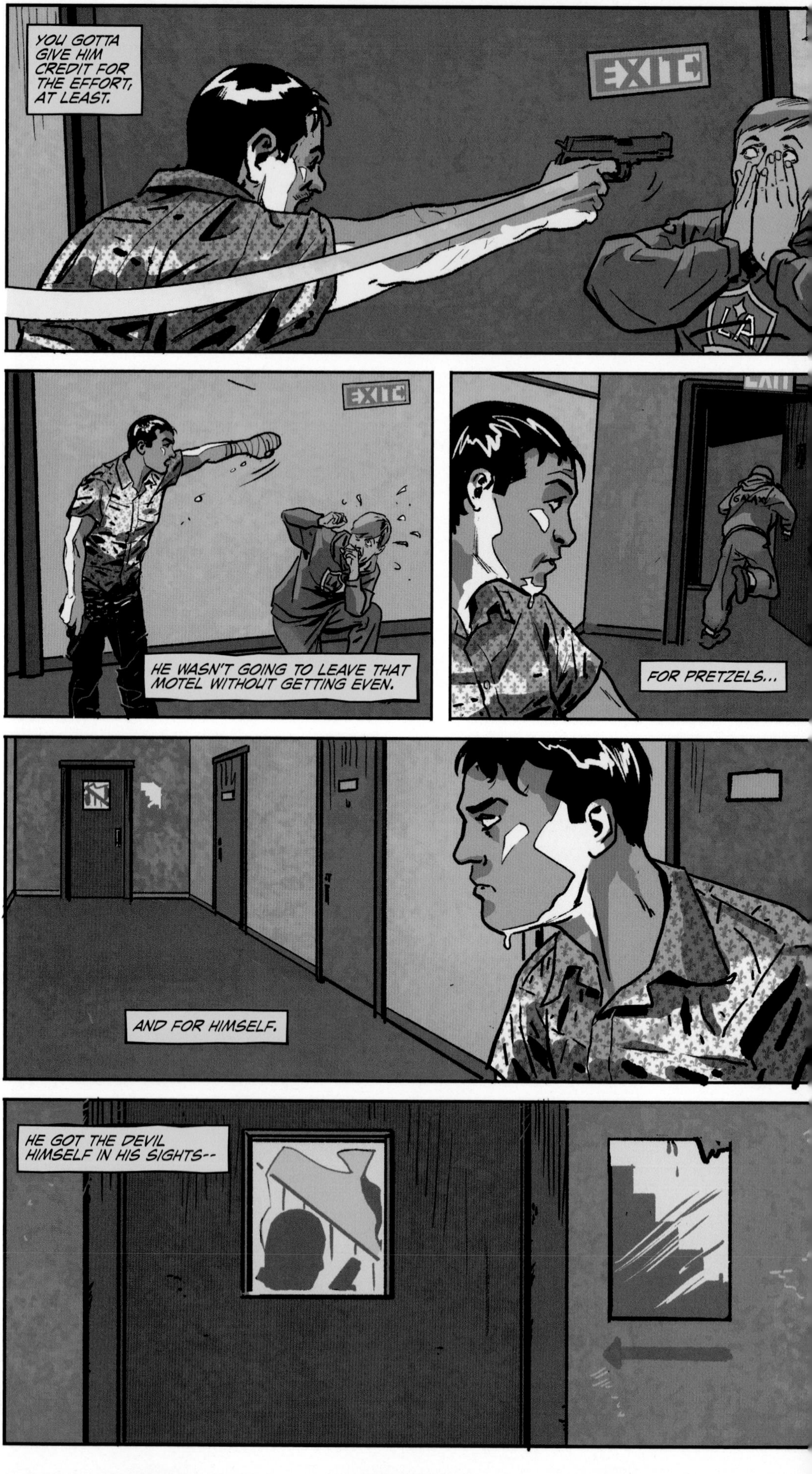
YOU GOTTA GIVE HIM CREDIT FOR THE EFFORT, AT LEAST.
EXIT
EXIT
HE WASN'T GOING TO LEAVE THAT MOTEL WITHOUT GETTING EVEN.
FOR PRETZELS...
AND FOR HIMSELF.
HE GOT THE DEVIL HIMSELF IN HIS SIGHTS--

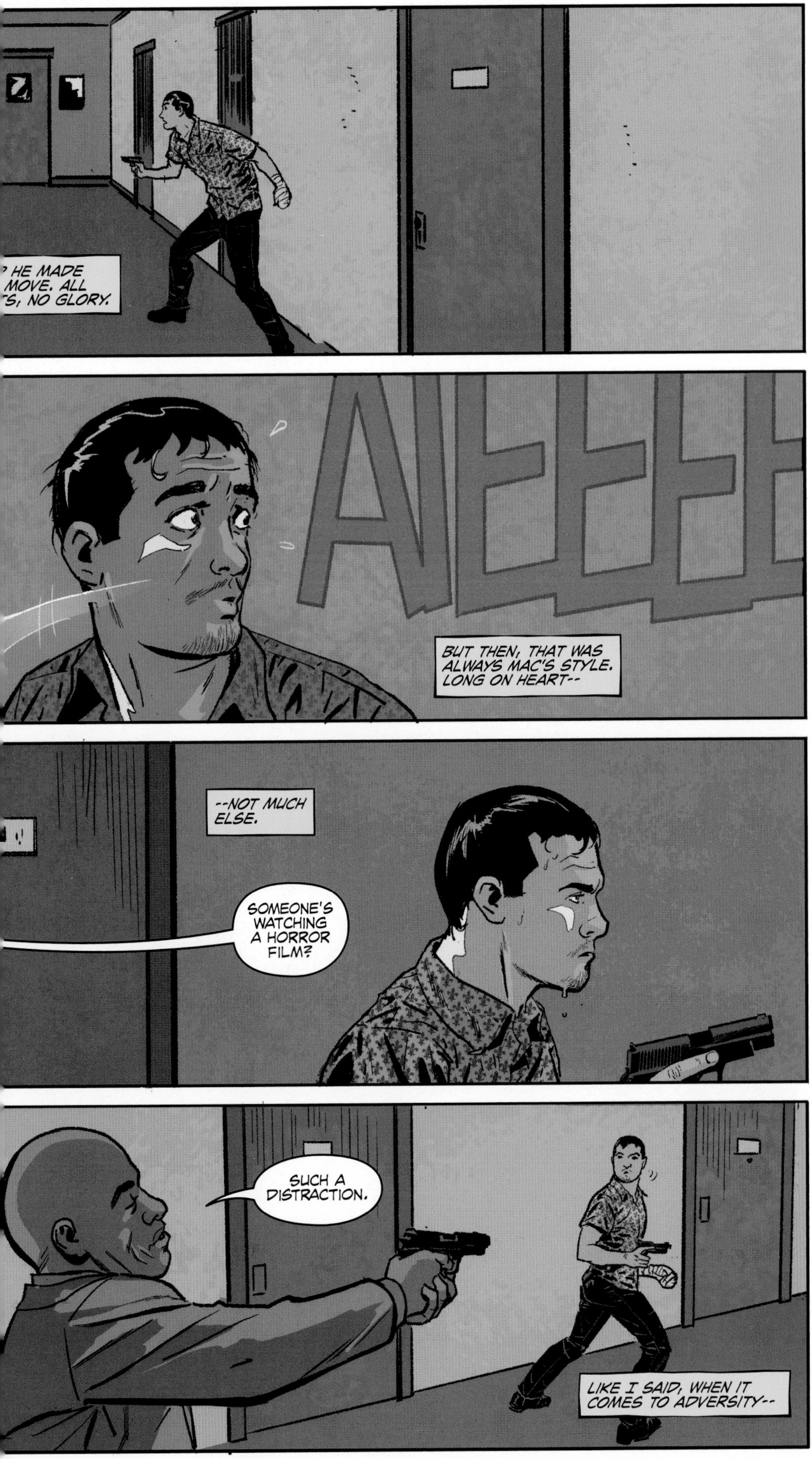
HE MADE MOVE. ALL TS, NO GLORY.
AIEEEE
BUT THEN, THAT WAS ALWAYS MAC'S STYLE. LONG ON HEART--
--NOT MUCH ELSE.
SOMEONE'S WATCHING A HORROR FILM?
SUCH A DISTRACTION.
LIKE I SAID, WHEN IT COMES TO ADVERSITY--

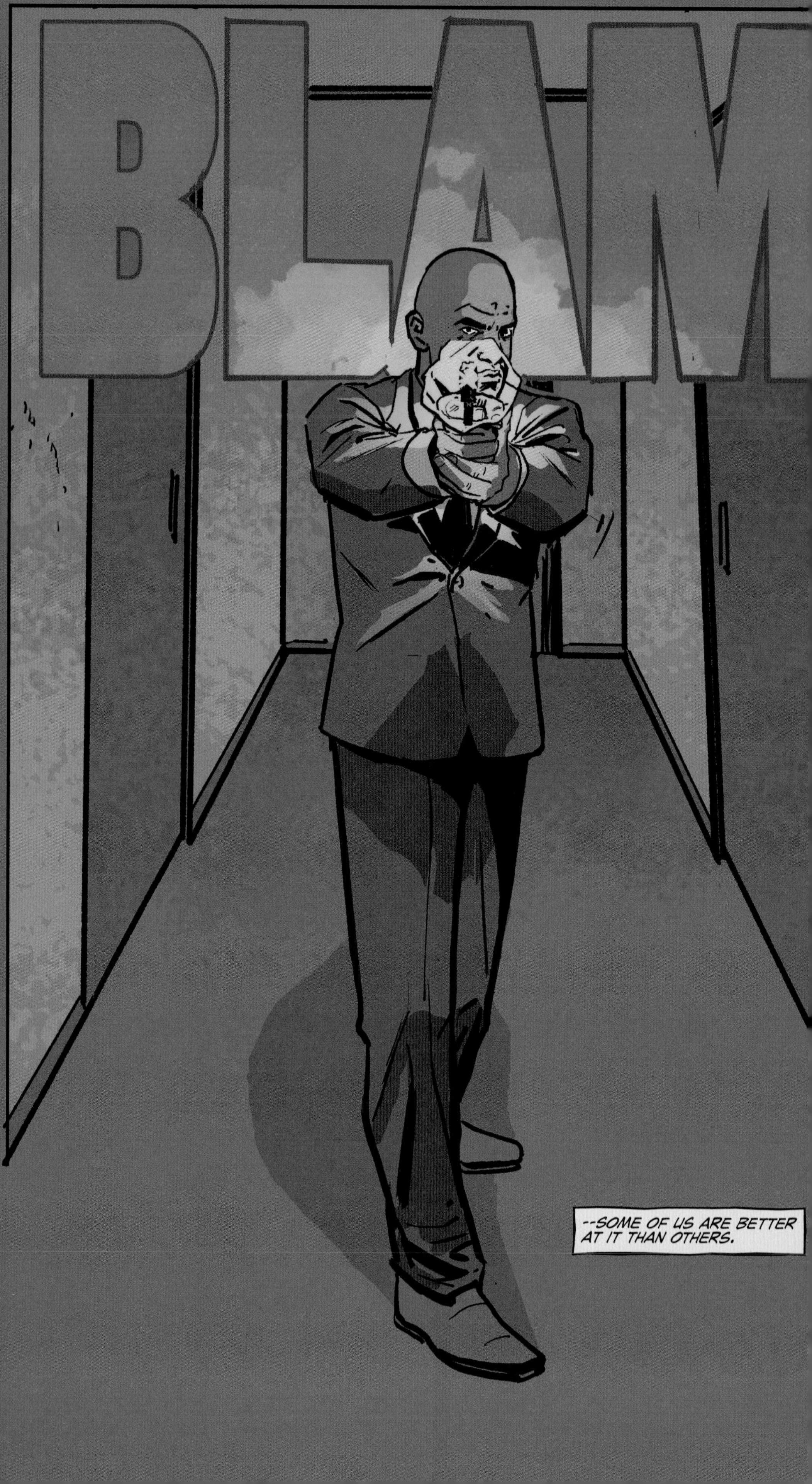
BLAM
--SOME OF US ARE BETTER AT IT THAN OTHERS.

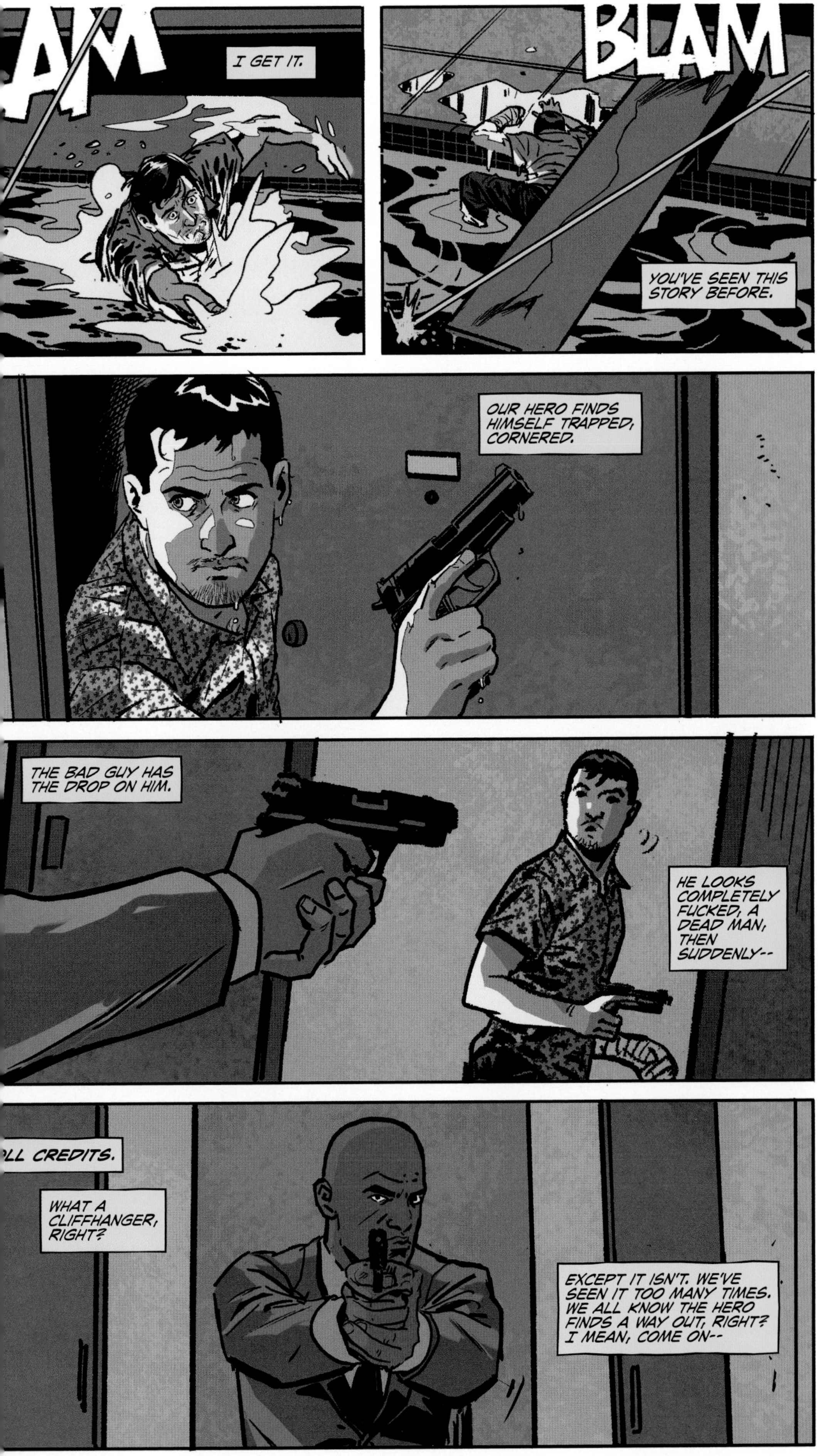
AM
I GET IT.
BLAM
YOU'VE SEEN THIS STORY BEFORE.
OUR HERO FINDS HIMSELF TRAPPED, CORNERED.
THE BAD GUY HAS THE DROP ON HIM.
HE LOOKS COMPLETELY FUCKED, A DEAD MAN, THEN SUDDENLY--
LL CREDITS.
WHAT A CLIFFHANGER, RIGHT?
EXCEPT IT ISN'T. WE'VE SEEN IT TOO MANY TIMES. WE ALL KNOW THE HERO FINDS A WAY OUT, RIGHT? I MEAN, COME ON--

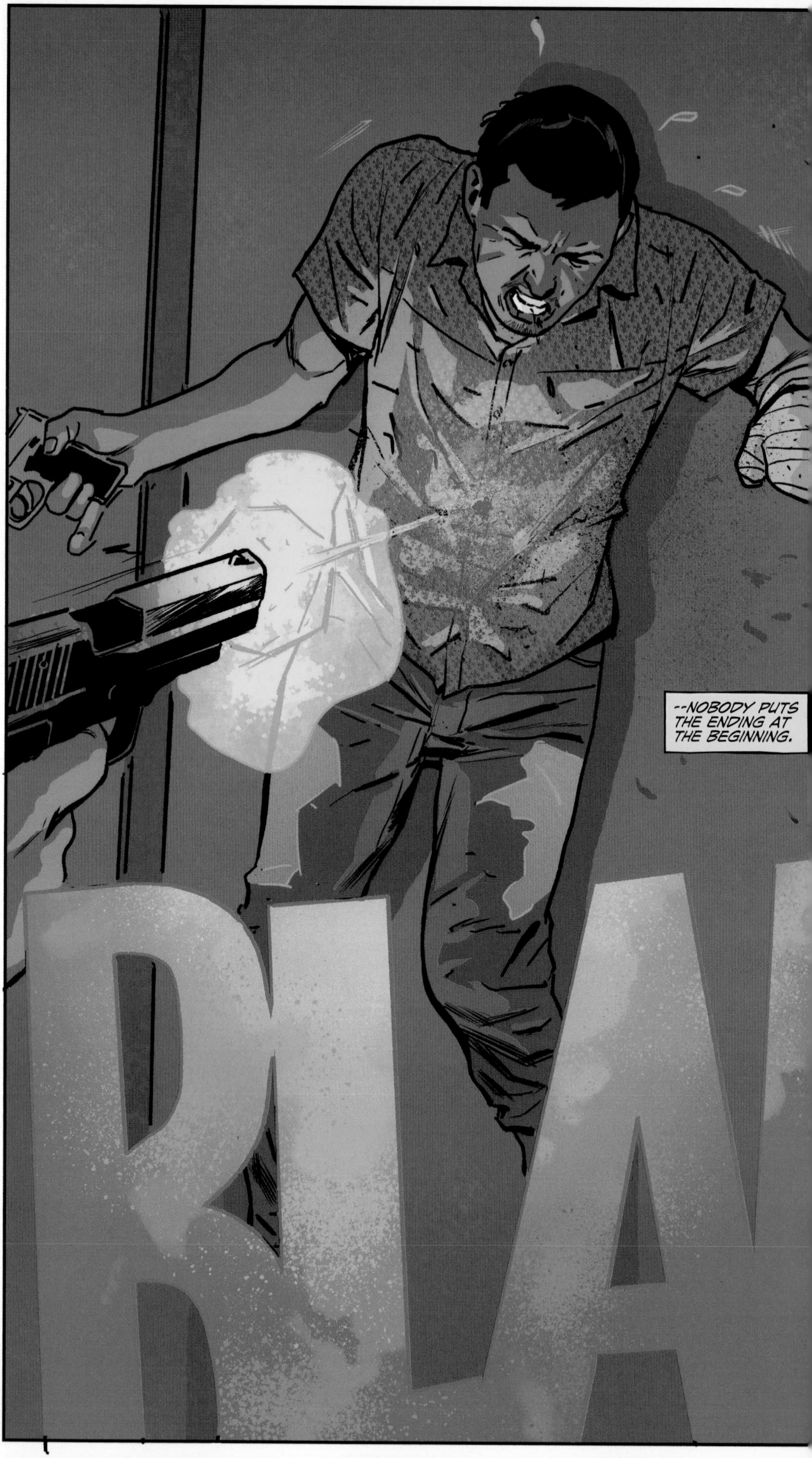
--NOBODY PUTS THE ENDING AT THE BEGINNING.

GOOD DAY.

HI--
[FRO]NT DESK?!!
THERE'S--
[SOME]BODY'S BEEN
[SH]OT IN THE
[H]ALLWAY!!

ALSO, IS IT
TOO LATE FOR ROOM
SERVICE? OH, GREAT,
GREAT. YEAH, ROOM 301.
I JUST WANTED TO GET
THE BURGER, MEDIUM.
AND A COKE.
WHAT'S THE SOUP
TODAY?

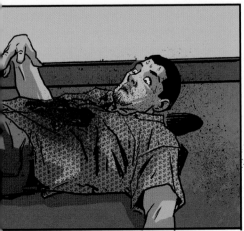

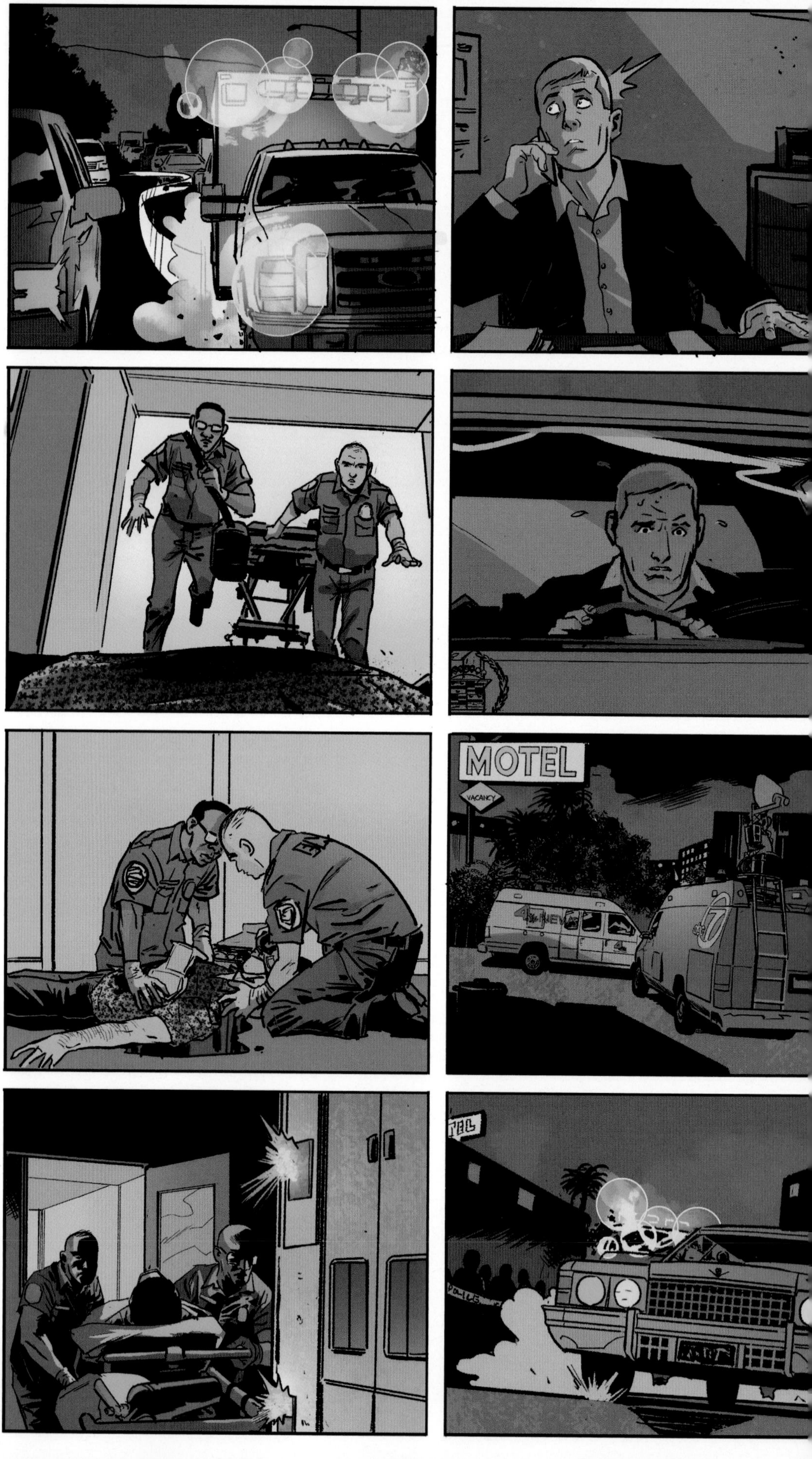
MOTEL
VACANCY

SURPRISE.

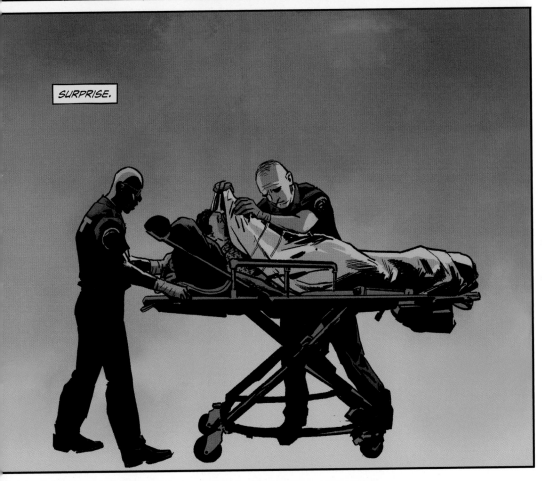

THE

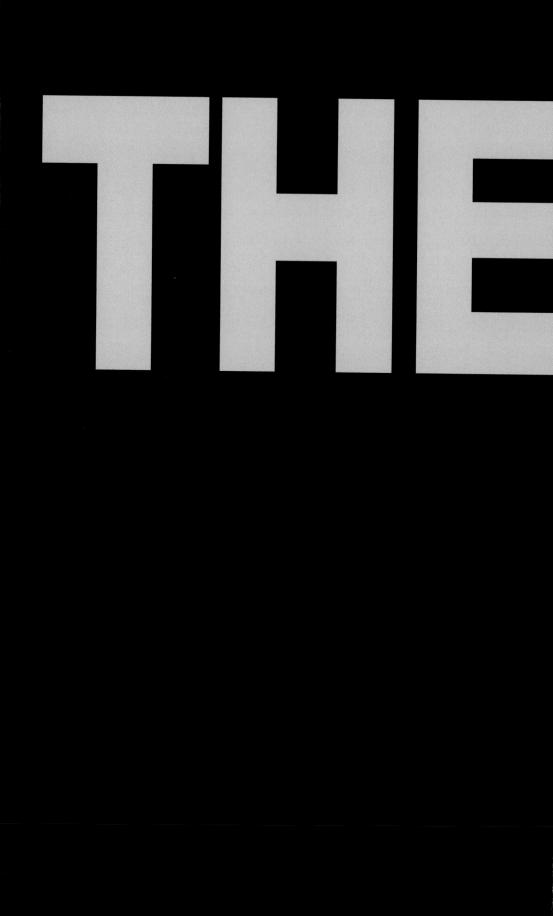

FIX

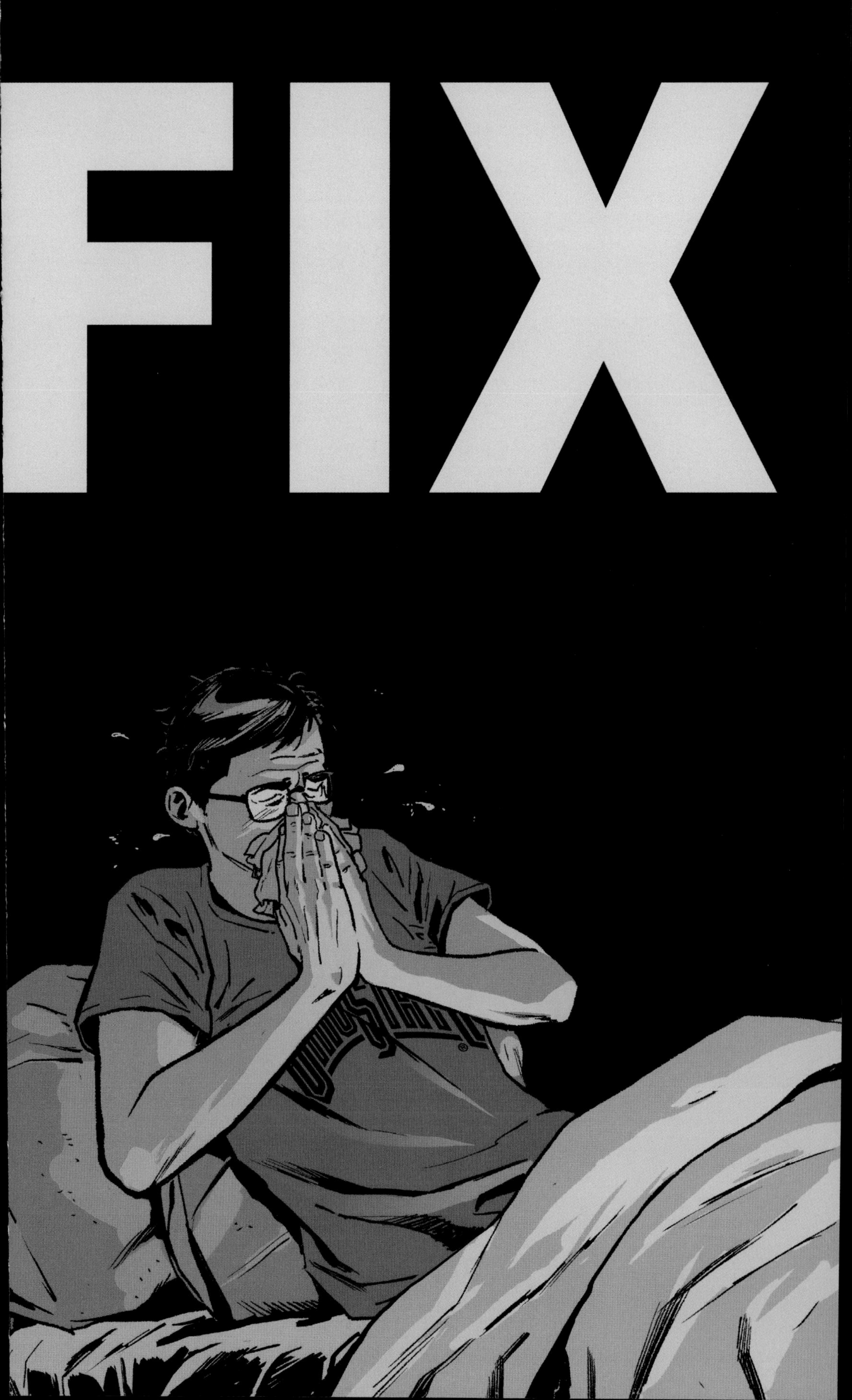

I STILL CAN'T BELIEVE THIS.
MAC IS DEAD.
MY PARTNER IS DEAD...
MY BEST FRIEND IS DEAD...

ROY...

I'M SORRY. REALLY. HE WAS A GOOD COP.

LL-- WASN'T IALLY OOD OP.

HE WAS... PRETTY CORRUPT, AND EVEN IF HE WASN'T--

--HE'D ACTUALLY STILL BE PRETTY TERRIBLE AT THE JOB.

YEAH.

HE DID LOVE THAT DOG, THOUGH.

YEAH.

LOOK-- I'VE ALREADY DONE THE ID. BUT, FAMILY, LOVED ONES--

I'M ON IT.

GOOD. I GOTTA GET TO THE MAYOR'S OFFICE, KID IS LOSING HIS GODDAMN MIND ABOUT THIS.

I'LL EMAIL YOU THE COVER STORY. HE WAS INVESTIGATING AN UNRELATED HOMICIDE, GOT A LEAD THE PERP MIGHT'VE BEEN STAYING HERE--

WAIT--*COVER STORY?*

YEAH. OBVIOUSLY WE HAVE TO KEEP JOSH OUT OF THIS--

THE FUCK WE DO, CHERYL. WE BOTH KNOW WHO DID THIS.

AND I'M NOT JUST GONNA LET IT SLIDE.

WHICH IS BIG TALK, I KNOW--

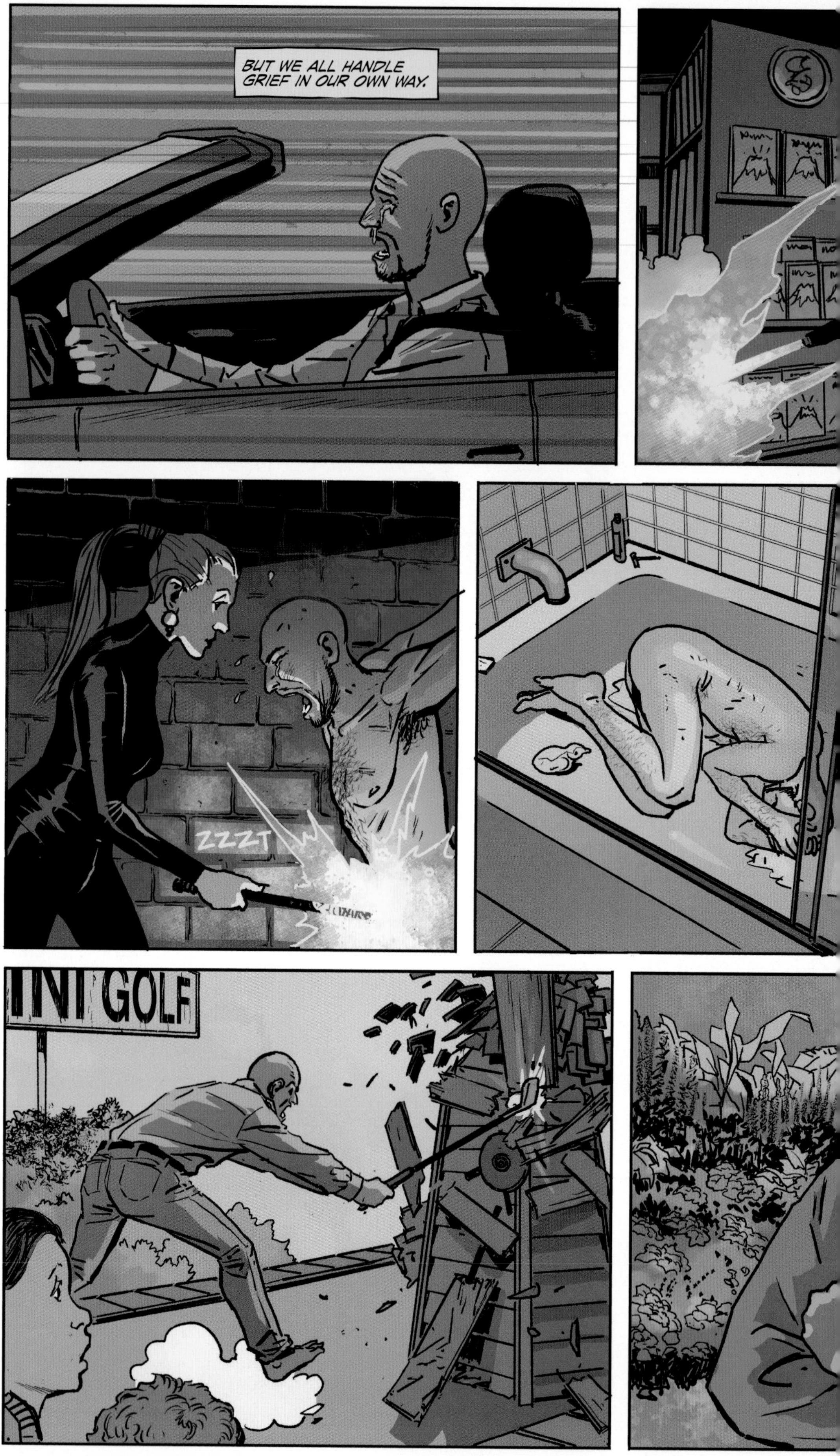
BUT WE ALL HANDLE GRIEF IN OUR OWN WAY.
ZZZT
INI GOLF

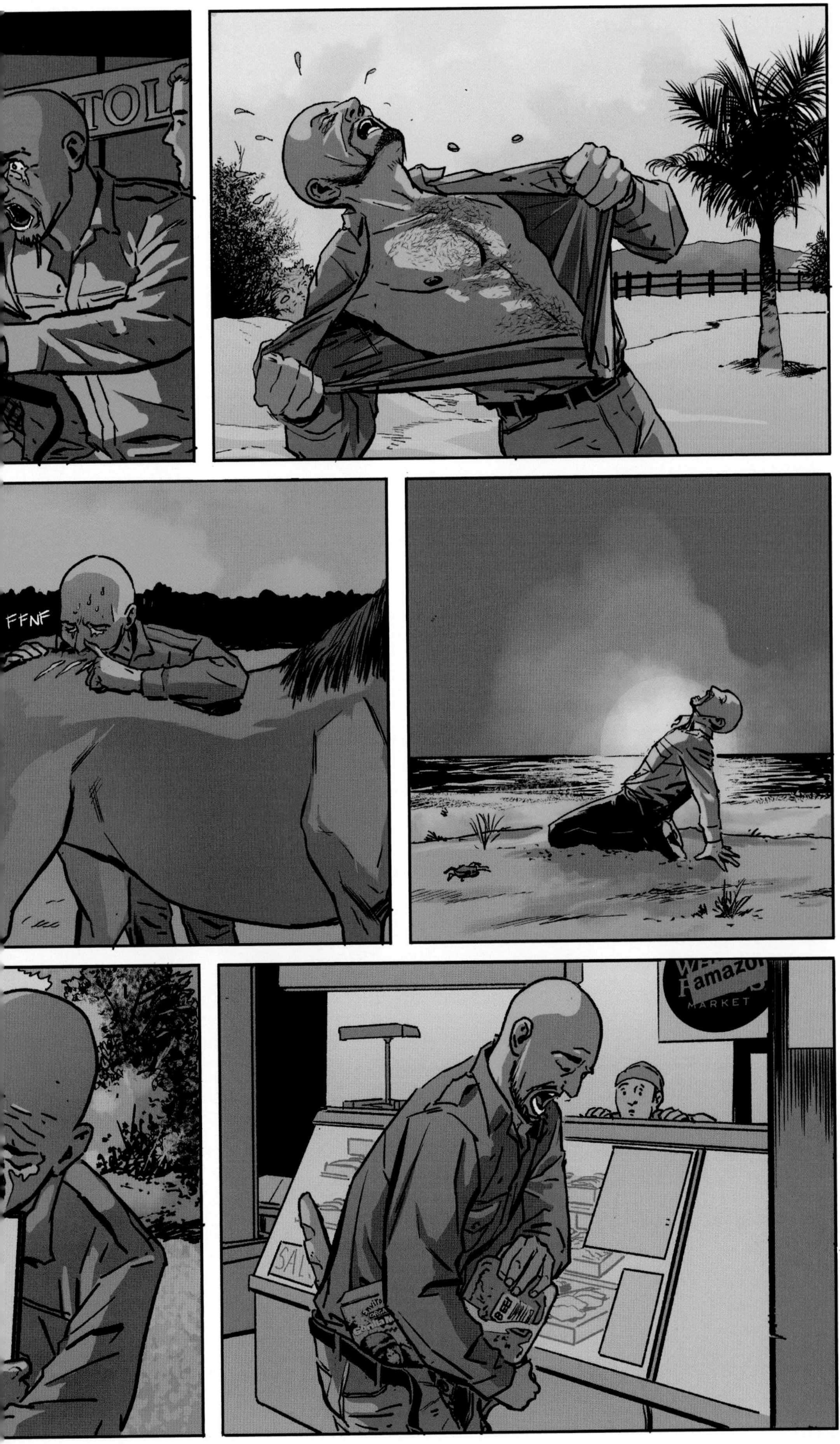
TOL
FFNF
amazon
MARKET
SAL

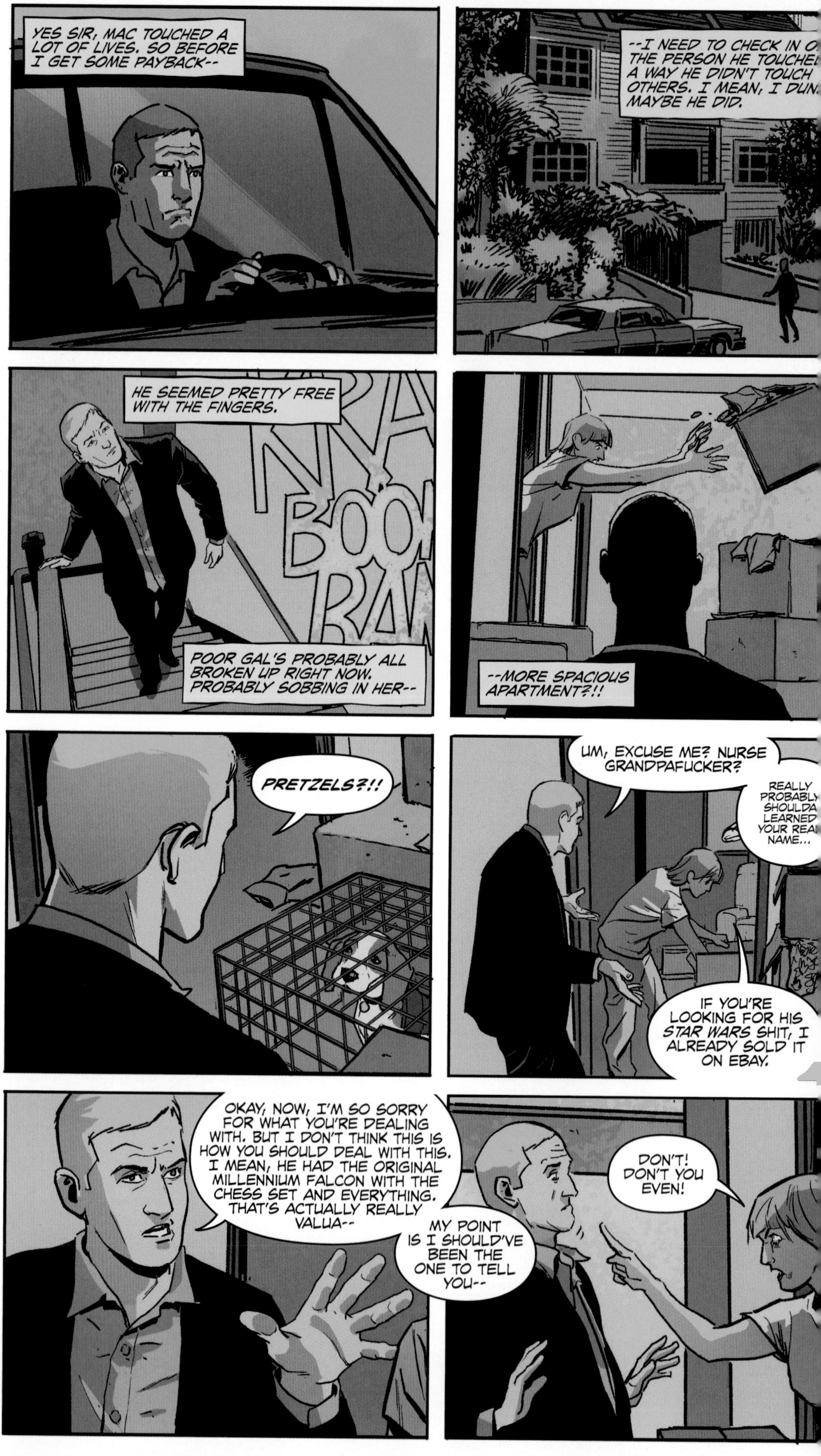
YES SIR, MAC TOUCHED A LOT OF LIVES. SO BEFORE I GET SOME PAYBACK--
--I NEED TO CHECK IN O THE PERSON HE TOUCHE A WAY HE DIDN'T TOUCH OTHERS. I MEAN, I DUN MAYBE HE DID.
HE SEEMED PRETTY FREE WITH THE FINGERS.
BOOM
POOR GAL'S PROBABLY ALL BROKEN UP RIGHT NOW. PROBABLY SOBBING IN HER--
--MORE SPACIOUS APARTMENT?!!
PRETZELS?!!
UM, EXCUSE ME? NURSE GRANDPAFUCKER?
REALLY PROBABLY SHOULDA LEARNED YOUR REA NAME...
IF YOU'RE LOOKING FOR HIS *STAR WARS* SHIT, I ALREADY SOLD IT ON EBAY.
OKAY, NOW, I'M SO SORRY FOR WHAT YOU'RE DEALING WITH. BUT I DON'T THINK THIS IS HOW YOU SHOULD DEAL WITH THIS. I MEAN, HE HAD THE ORIGINAL MILLENNIUM FALCON WITH THE CHESS SET AND EVERYTHING. THAT'S ACTUALLY REALLY VALUA--
MY POINT IS I SHOULD'VE BEEN THE ONE TO TELL YOU--
DON'T! DON'T YOU EVEN!

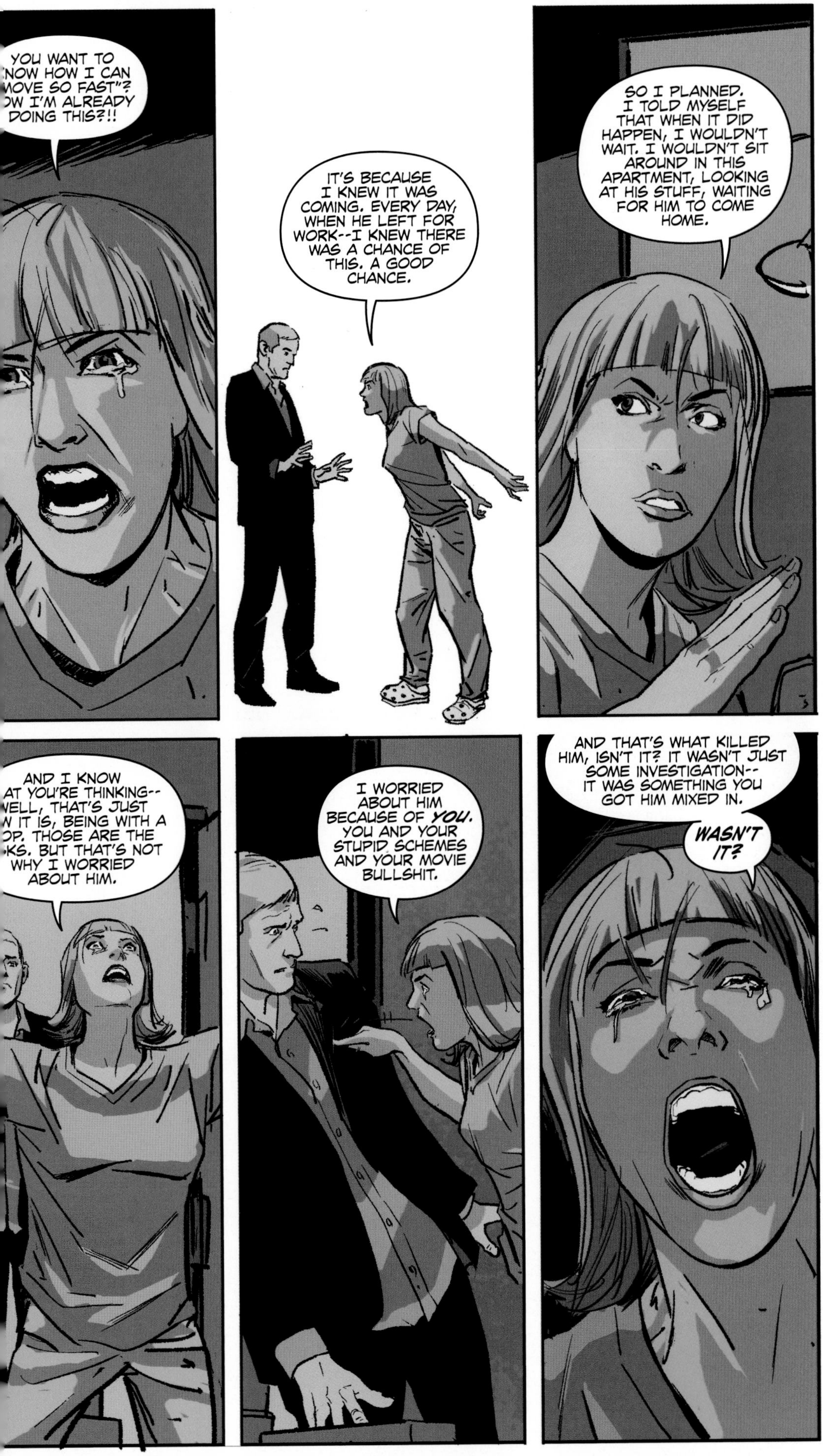
YOU WANT TO NOW HOW I CAN MOVE SO FAST"? OW I'M ALREADY DOING THIS?!!
IT'S BECAUSE I KNEW IT WAS COMING. EVERY DAY, WHEN HE LEFT FOR WORK--I KNEW THERE WAS A CHANCE OF THIS. A GOOD CHANCE.
SO I PLANNED. I TOLD MYSELF THAT WHEN IT DID HAPPEN, I WOULDN'T WAIT. I WOULDN'T SIT AROUND IN THIS APARTMENT, LOOKING AT HIS STUFF, WAITING FOR HIM TO COME HOME.
AND I KNOW AT YOU'RE THINKING-- WELL, THAT'S JUST W IT IS, BEING WITH A OP. THOSE ARE THE KS. BUT THAT'S NOT WHY I WORRIED ABOUT HIM.
I WORRIED ABOUT HIM BECAUSE OF *YOU*. YOU AND YOUR STUPID SCHEMES AND YOUR MOVIE BULLSHIT.
AND THAT'S WHAT KILLED HIM, ISN'T IT? IT WASN'T JUST SOME INVESTIGATION-- IT WAS SOMETHING YOU GOT HIM MIXED IN.
WASN'T IT?

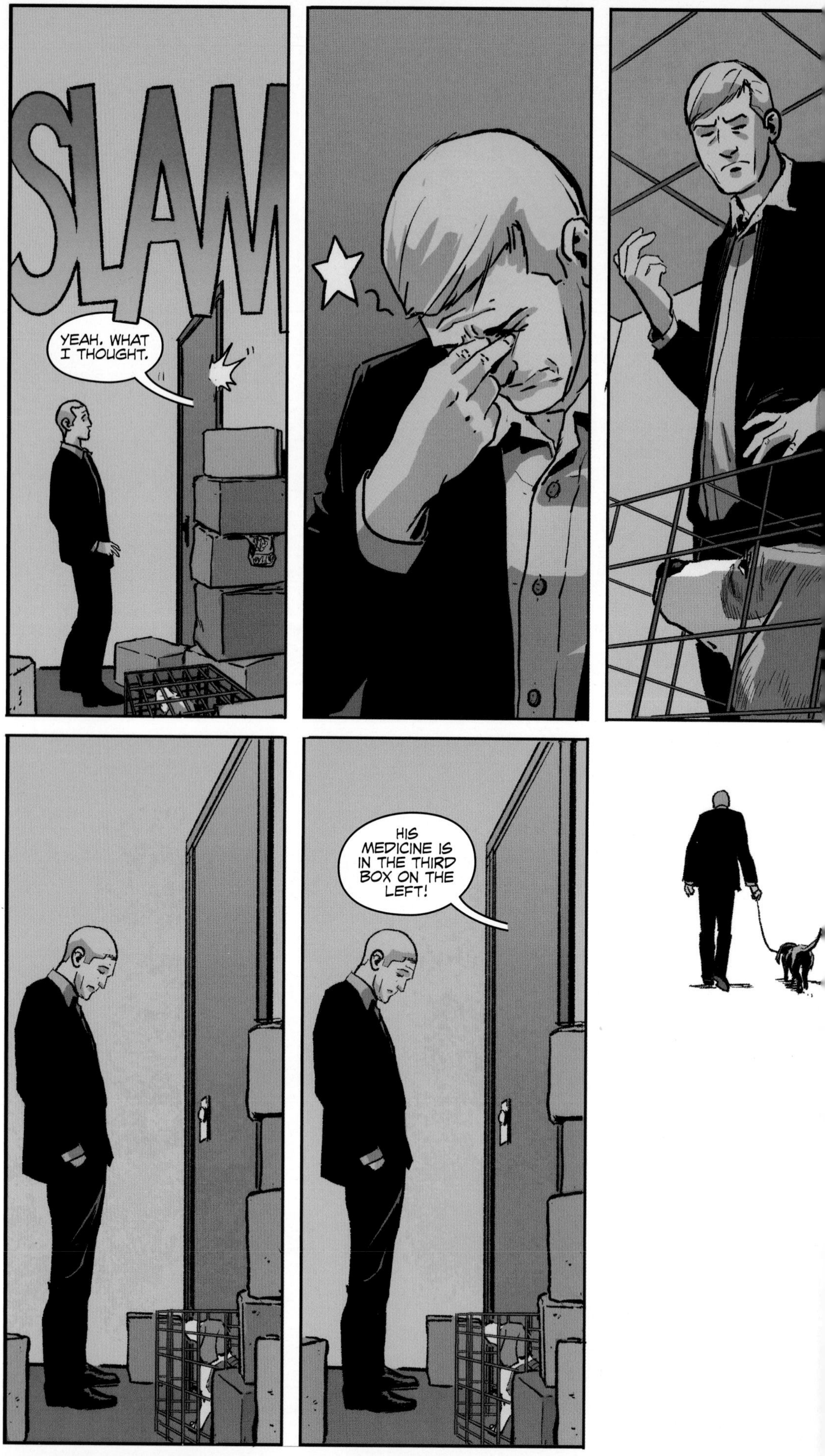
SLAM
YEAH. WHAT I THOUGHT.
HIS MEDICINE IS IN THE THIRD BOX ON THE LEFT!

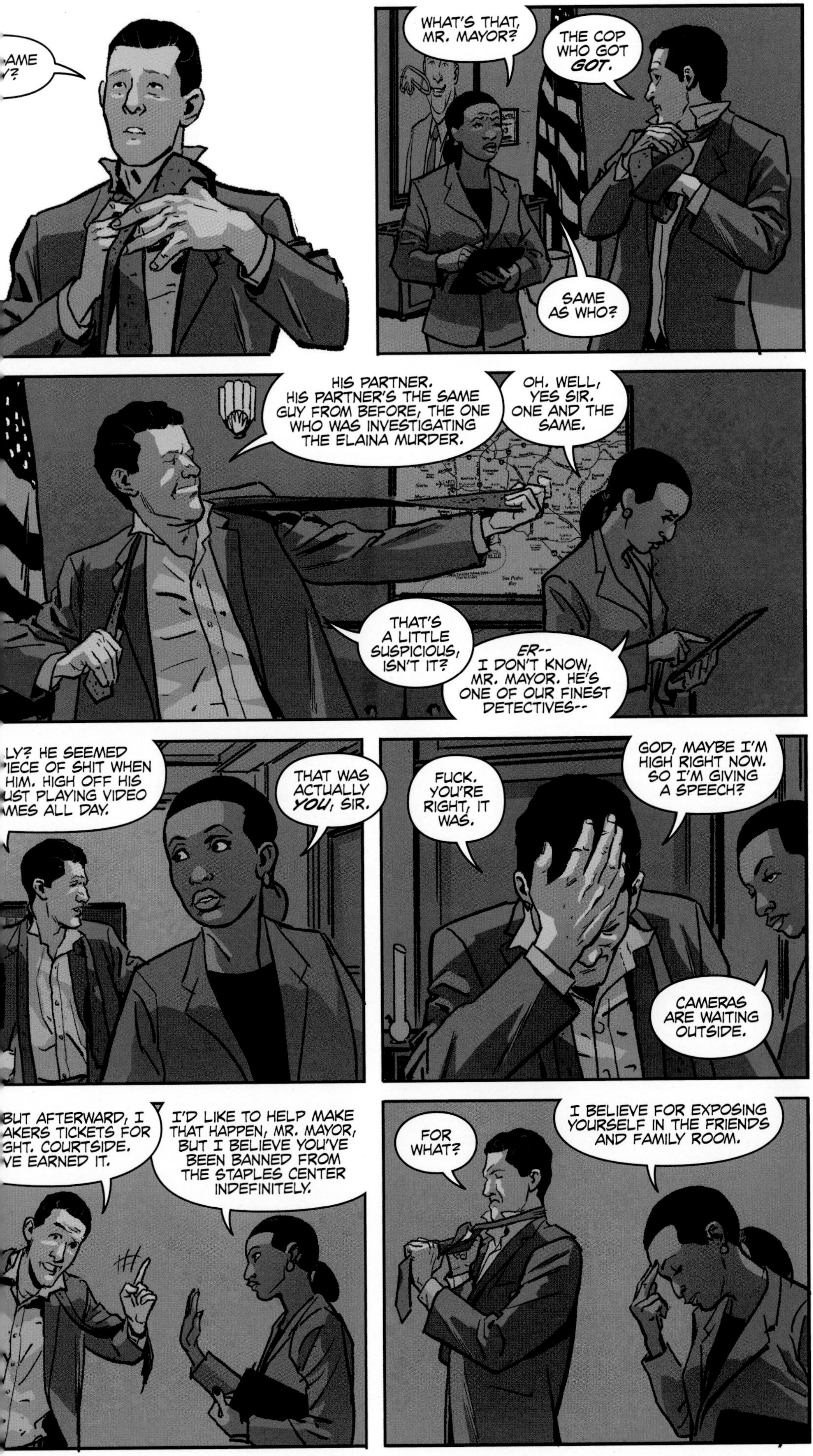

AME
Y?
WHAT'S THAT, MR. MAYOR?
THE COP WHO GOT *GOT*.
SAME AS WHO?
HIS PARTNER. HIS PARTNER'S THE SAME GUY FROM BEFORE, THE ONE WHO WAS INVESTIGATING THE ELAINA MURDER.
OH. WELL, YES SIR. ONE AND THE SAME.
THAT'S A LITTLE SUSPICIOUS, ISN'T IT?
ER-- I DON'T KNOW, MR. MAYOR. HE'S ONE OF OUR FINEST DETECTIVES--
LY? HE SEEMED
IECE OF SHIT WHEN
HIM. HIGH OFF HIS
UST PLAYING VIDEO
MES ALL DAY.
THAT WAS ACTUALLY *YOU*, SIR.
FUCK. YOU'RE RIGHT, IT WAS.
GOD, MAYBE I'M HIGH RIGHT NOW. SO I'M GIVING A SPEECH?
CAMERAS ARE WAITING OUTSIDE.
BUT AFTERWARD, I
AKERS TICKETS FOR
GHT. COURTSIDE.
VE EARNED IT.
I'D LIKE TO HELP MAKE THAT HAPPEN, MR. MAYOR, BUT I BELIEVE YOU'VE BEEN BANNED FROM THE STAPLES CENTER INDEFINITELY.
FOR WHAT?
I BELIEVE FOR EXPOSING YOURSELF IN THE FRIENDS AND FAMILY ROOM.

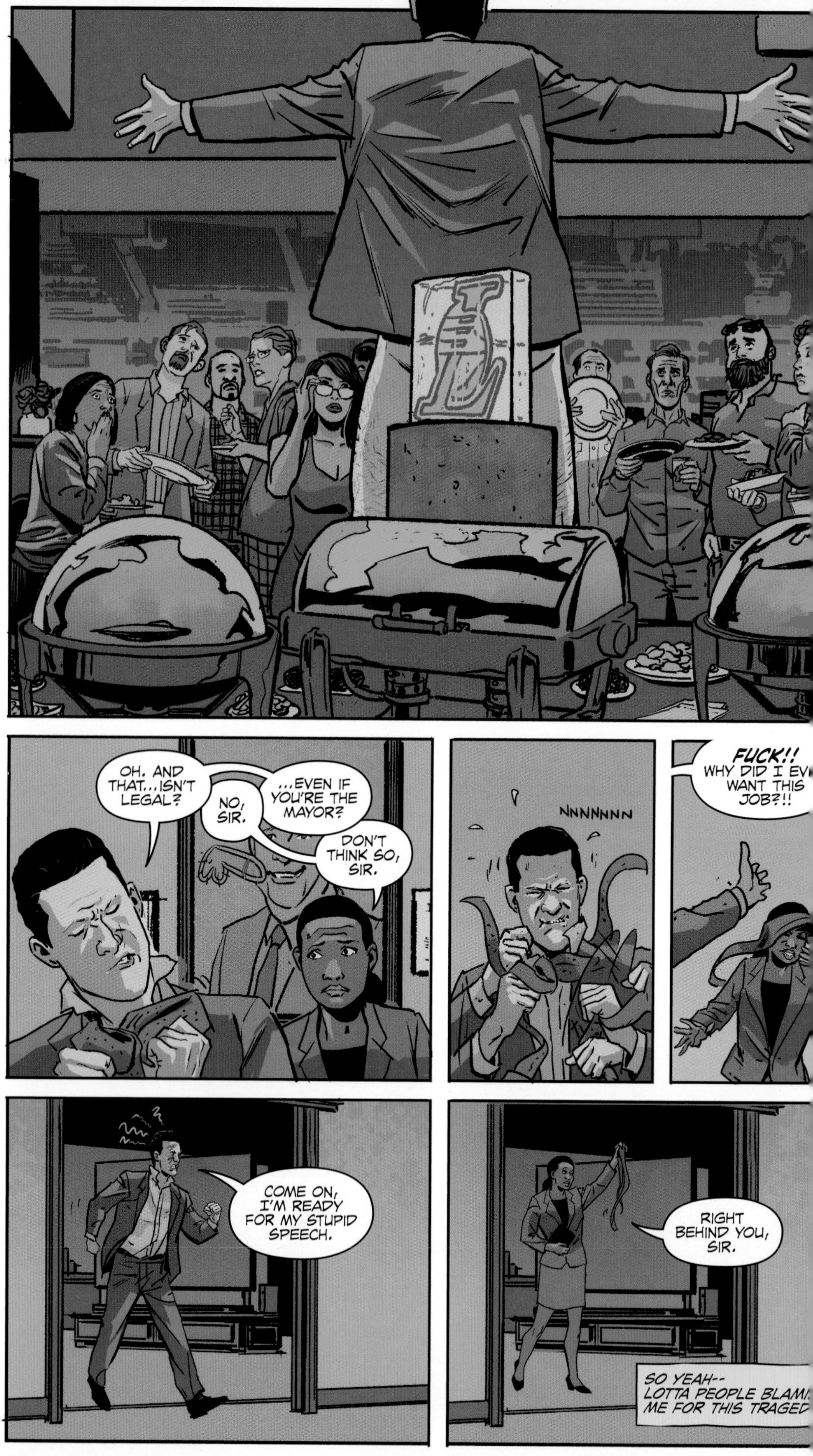

OH. AND THAT...ISN'T LEGAL?
NO, SIR.
...EVEN IF YOU'RE THE MAYOR?
DON'T THINK SO, SIR.
NNNNNNN
FUCK!! WHY DID I EV WANT THIS JOB?!!
COME ON, I'M READY FOR MY STUPID SPEECH.
RIGHT BEHIND YOU, SIR.
SO YEAH-- LOTTA PEOPLE BLAM ME FOR THIS TRAGED

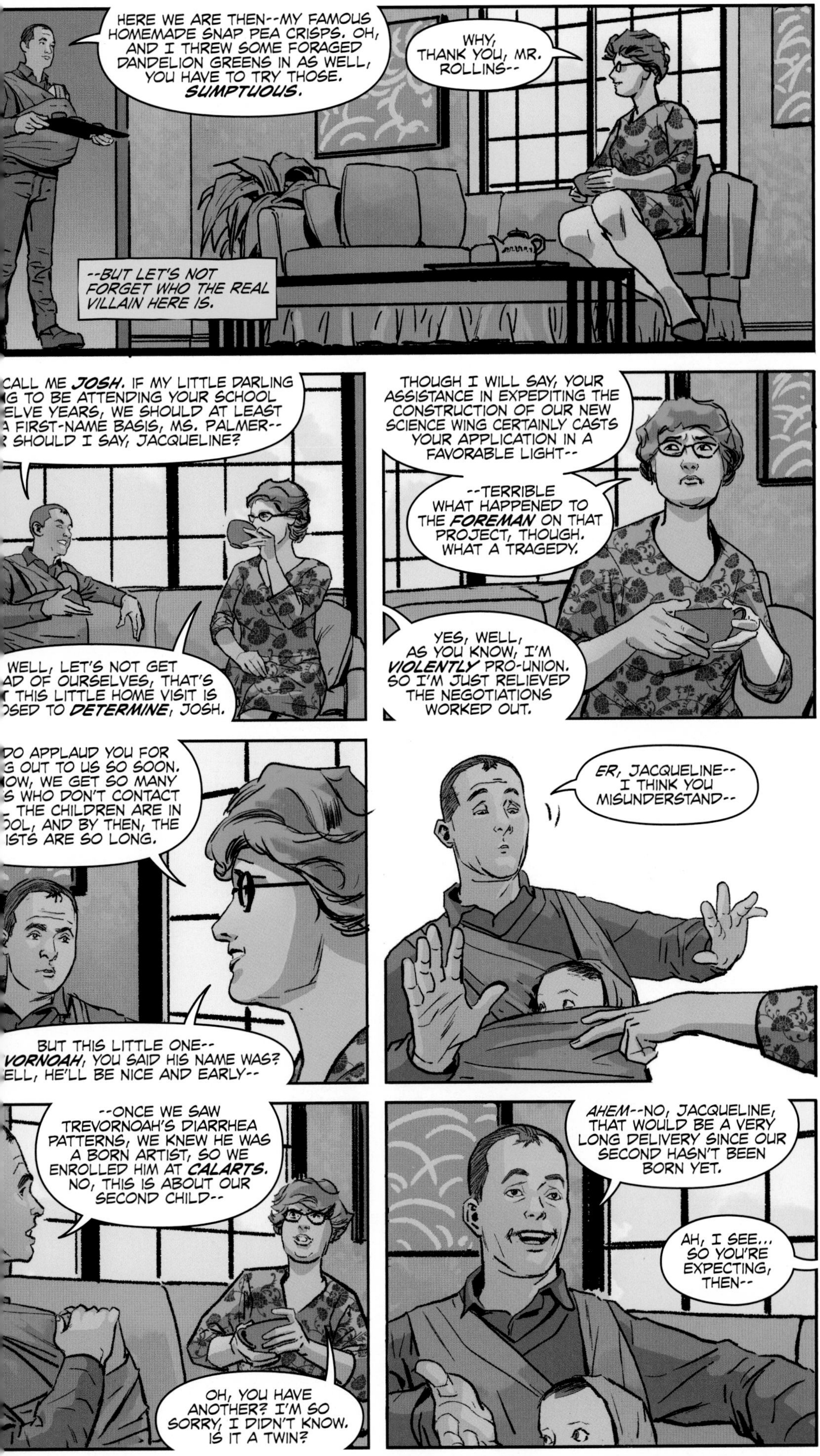
HERE WE ARE THEN--MY FAMOUS HOMEMADE SNAP PEA CRISPS. OH, AND I THREW SOME FORAGED DANDELION GREENS IN AS WELL, YOU HAVE TO TRY THOSE. SUMPTUOUS.
WHY, THANK YOU, MR. ROLLINS--
--BUT LET'S NOT FORGET WHO THE REAL VILLAIN HERE IS.
CALL ME JOSH. IF MY LITTLE DARLING G TO BE ATTENDING YOUR SCHOOL ELVE YEARS, WE SHOULD AT LEAST A FIRST-NAME BASIS, MS. PALMER-- SHOULD I SAY, JACQUELINE?
WELL, LET'S NOT GET AD OF OURSELVES, THAT'S T THIS LITTLE HOME VISIT IS OSED TO DETERMINE, JOSH.
THOUGH I WILL SAY, YOUR ASSISTANCE IN EXPEDITING THE CONSTRUCTION OF OUR NEW SCIENCE WING CERTAINLY CASTS YOUR APPLICATION IN A FAVORABLE LIGHT--
--TERRIBLE WHAT HAPPENED TO THE FOREMAN ON THAT PROJECT, THOUGH. WHAT A TRAGEDY.
YES, WELL, AS YOU KNOW, I'M VIOLENTLY PRO-UNION. SO I'M JUST RELIEVED THE NEGOTIATIONS WORKED OUT.
DO APPLAUD YOU FOR G OUT TO US SO SOON. OW, WE GET SO MANY S WHO DON'T CONTACT . THE CHILDREN ARE IN OOL, AND BY THEN, THE ISTS ARE SO LONG.
BUT THIS LITTLE ONE-- VORNOAH, YOU SAID HIS NAME WAS? ELL, HE'LL BE NICE AND EARLY--
ER, JACQUELINE-- I THINK YOU MISUNDERSTAND--
--ONCE WE SAW TREVORNOAH'S DIARRHEA PATTERNS, WE KNEW HE WAS A BORN ARTIST, SO WE ENROLLED HIM AT CALARTS. NO, THIS IS ABOUT OUR SECOND CHILD--
OH, YOU HAVE ANOTHER? I'M SO SORRY, I DIDN'T KNOW. IS IT A TWIN?
AHEM--NO, JACQUELINE, THAT WOULD BE A VERY LONG DELIVERY SINCE OUR SECOND HASN'T BEEN BORN YET.
AH, I SEE... SO YOU'RE EXPECTING, THEN--

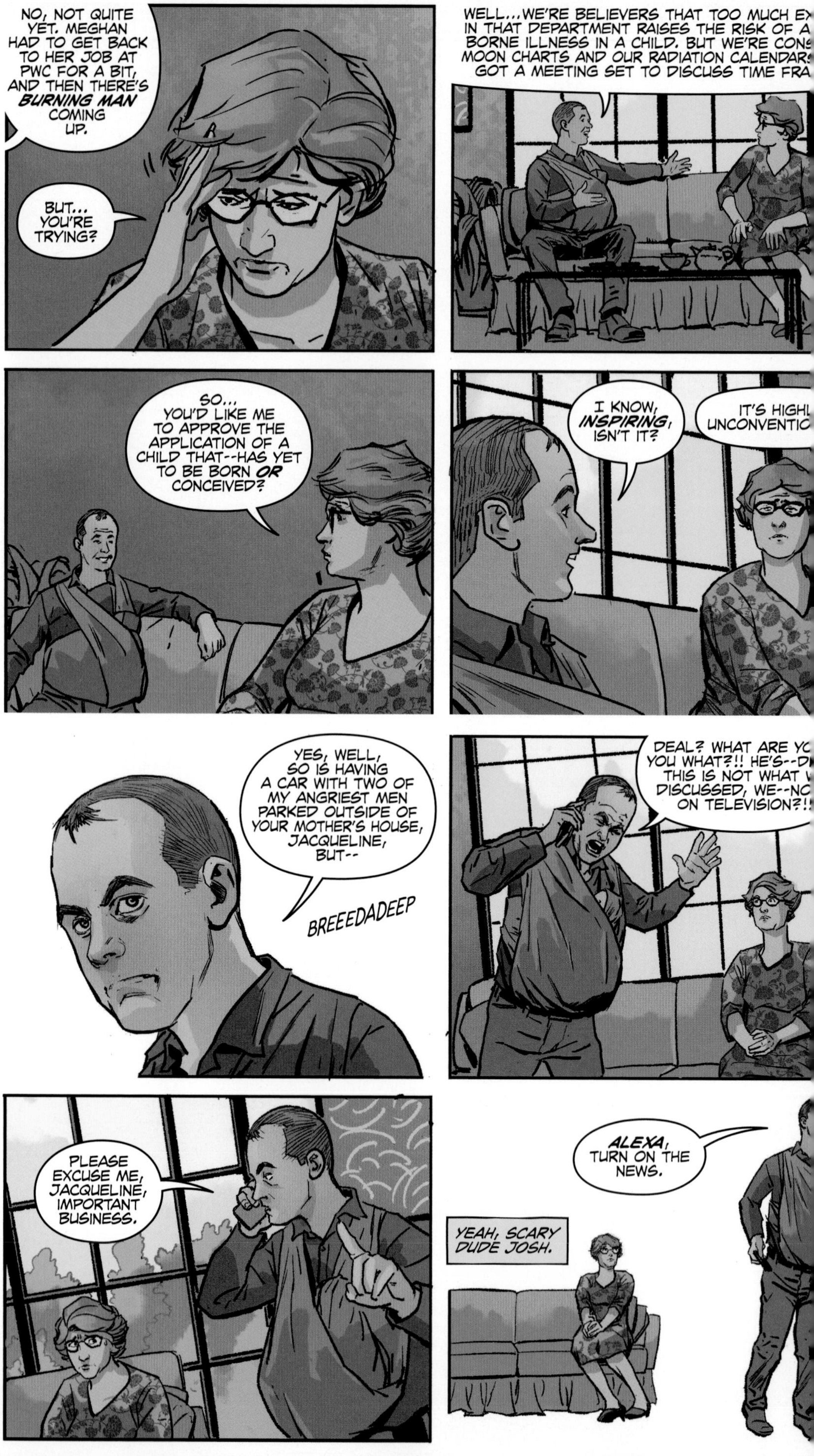

NO, NOT QUITE YET. MEGHAN HAD TO GET BACK TO HER JOB AT PWC FOR A BIT, AND THEN THERE'S *BURNING MAN* COMING UP.
BUT... YOU'RE TRYING?
WELL...WE'RE BELIEVERS THAT TOO MUCH EX IN THAT DEPARTMENT RAISES THE RISK OF A BORNE ILLNESS IN A CHILD. BUT WE'RE CONS MOON CHARTS AND OUR RADIATION CALENDARS GOT A MEETING SET TO DISCUSS TIME FRA
SO... YOU'D LIKE ME TO APPROVE THE APPLICATION OF A CHILD THAT--HAS YET TO BE BORN *OR* CONCEIVED?
I KNOW, *INSPIRING*, ISN'T IT?
IT'S HIGHL UNCONVENTIO
YES, WELL, SO IS HAVING A CAR WITH TWO OF MY ANGRIEST MEN PARKED OUTSIDE OF YOUR MOTHER'S HOUSE, JACQUELINE, BUT--
BREEEDADEEP
DEAL? WHAT ARE YO YOU WHAT?!! HE'S--D THIS IS NOT WHAT W DISCUSSED, WE--NO ON TELEVISION?!!
PLEASE EXCUSE ME, JACQUELINE, IMPORTANT BUSINESS.
ALEXA, TURN ON THE NEWS.
YEAH, SCARY DUDE JOSH.

TRUTH IS, I HAVE NO IDEA WHAT TO DO.

LOOKING AT PRETZELS' ADORABLE SAD EYES JUST MAKES IT WORSE.

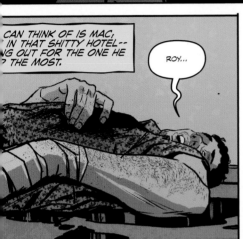

CAN THINK OF IS MAC, IN THAT SHITTY HOTEL-- NG OUT FOR THE ONE HE THE MOST.

ROY...

OR MORE LIKELY--

PORNHUB...

I TELL MYSELF I JUST GOTTA REGROUP, COME UP WITH A PLAN.

POLICE SERVICES

BUT YOU KNOW WHAT THEY SAY ABOUT WHILE YOU'RE MAKING PLANS--

HAT'S WHEN REAL E IS HAPPENING.

SO I'M CALLING TODAY FOR THE CREATION OF AN ORGANIZED CRIME STRIKE FORCE--

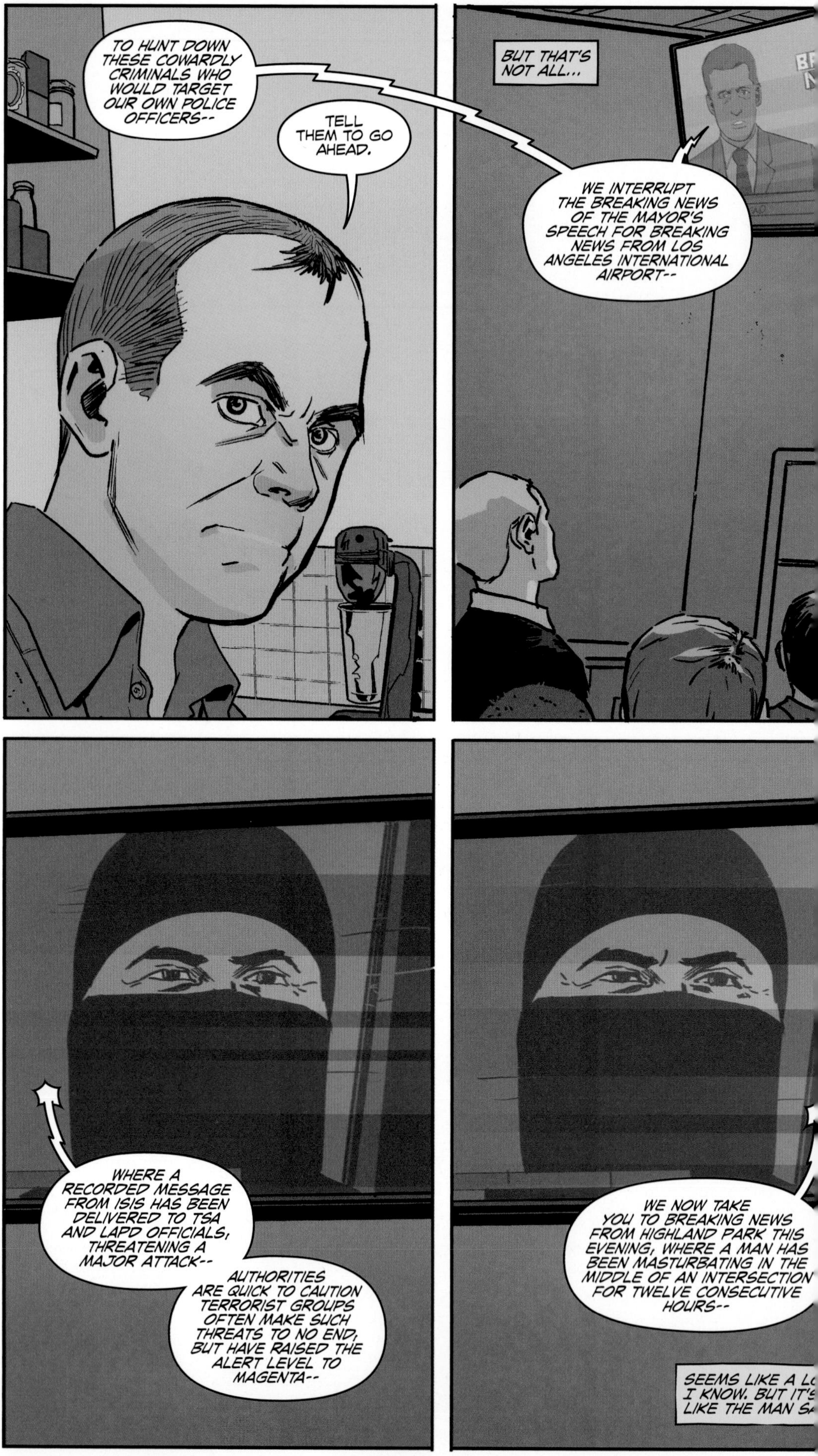

TO HUNT DOWN THESE COWARDLY CRIMINALS WHO WOULD TARGET OUR OWN POLICE OFFICERS--
TELL THEM TO GO AHEAD.
BUT THAT'S NOT ALL...
WE INTERRUPT THE BREAKING NEWS OF THE MAYOR'S SPEECH FOR BREAKING NEWS FROM LOS ANGELES INTERNATIONAL AIRPORT--
WHERE A RECORDED MESSAGE FROM ISIS HAS BEEN DELIVERED TO TSA AND LAPD OFFICIALS, THREATENING A MAJOR ATTACK--
AUTHORITIES ARE QUICK TO CAUTION TERRORIST GROUPS OFTEN MAKE SUCH THREATS TO NO END, BUT HAVE RAISED THE ALERT LEVEL TO MAGENTA--
WE NOW TAKE YOU TO BREAKING NEWS FROM HIGHLAND PARK THIS EVENING, WHERE A MAN HAS BEEN MASTURBATING IN THE MIDDLE OF AN INTERSECTION FOR TWELVE CONSECUTIVE HOURS--

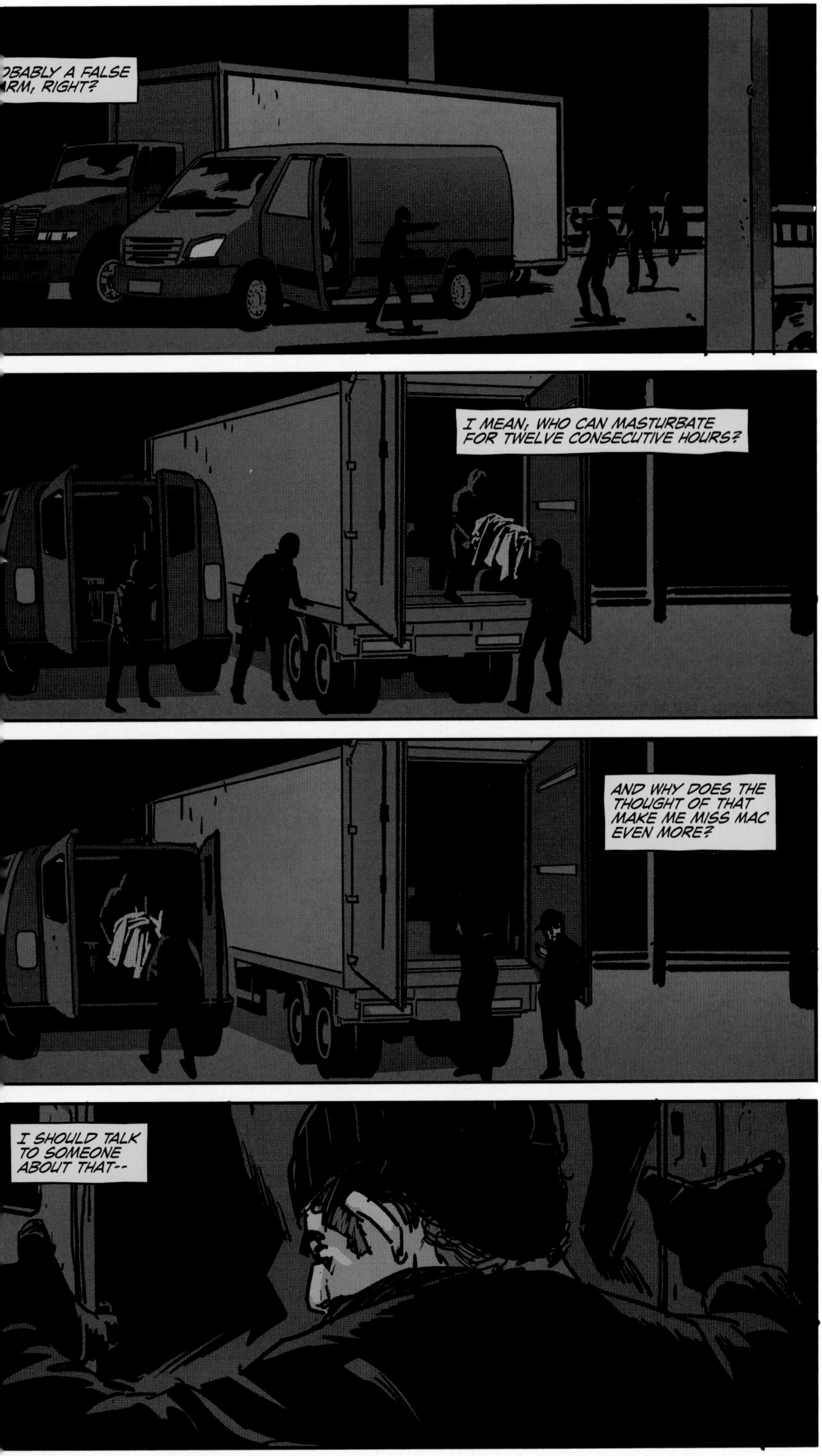

OBABLY A FALSE
ARM, RIGHT?
I MEAN, WHO CAN MASTURBATE FOR TWELVE CONSECUTIVE HOURS?
AND WHY DOES THE THOUGHT OF THAT MAKE ME MISS MAC EVEN MORE?
I SHOULD TALK TO SOMEONE ABOUT THAT--

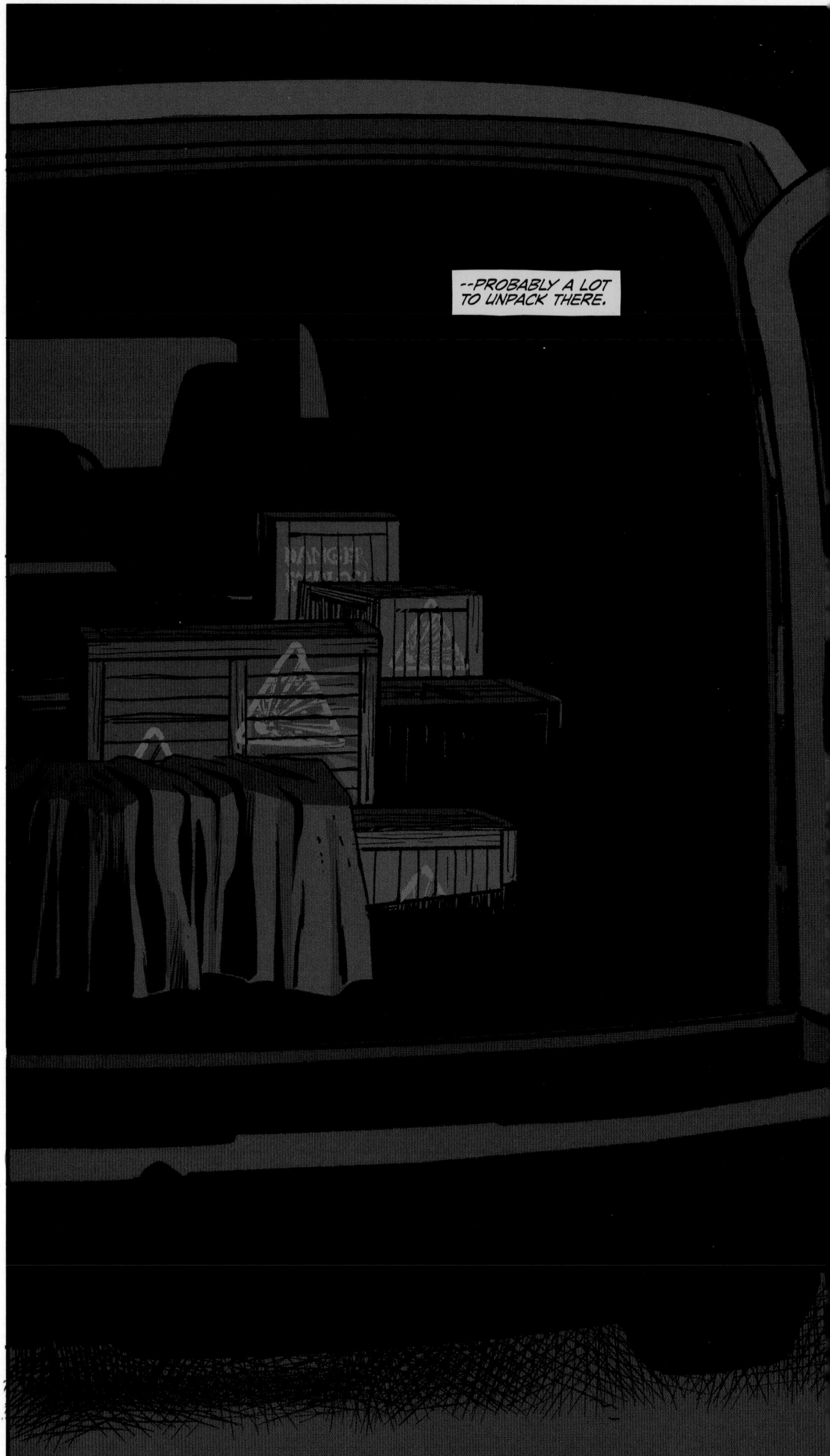
--PROBABLY A LOT TO UNPACK THERE.

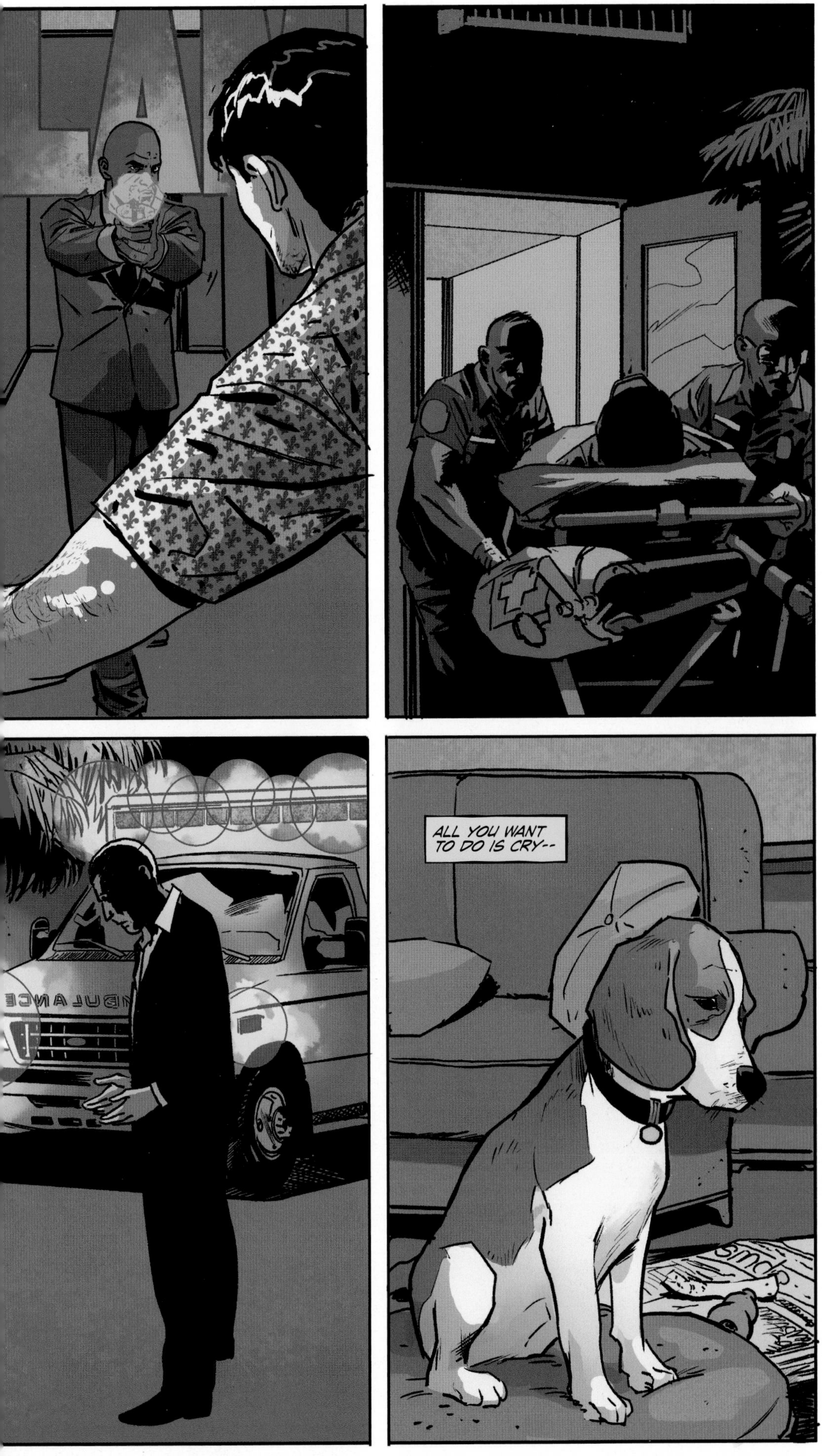
ALL YOU WANT TO DO IS CRY--

--BUT SOMETIMES THAT HAS TO WAIT.
BREAKING NEWS OUT OF LOS ANGELES INTERNATIONAL AIRPORT TONIGHT, AS A CAR BOMB EXPLODED IN A PARKING STRUCTURE NEAR TERMINAL 2--
PARAMEDIC
CROSS POLICE LINE DO NOT CROSS POLICE LINE DO NOT CROSS
2780155
--SEVERAL TERRORIST ORGANIZATIONS ARE ALREADY CLAIMING RESPONSIBILITY--
--EMERGENCY RESPONDERS ARE ALREADY ON THE SCENE--

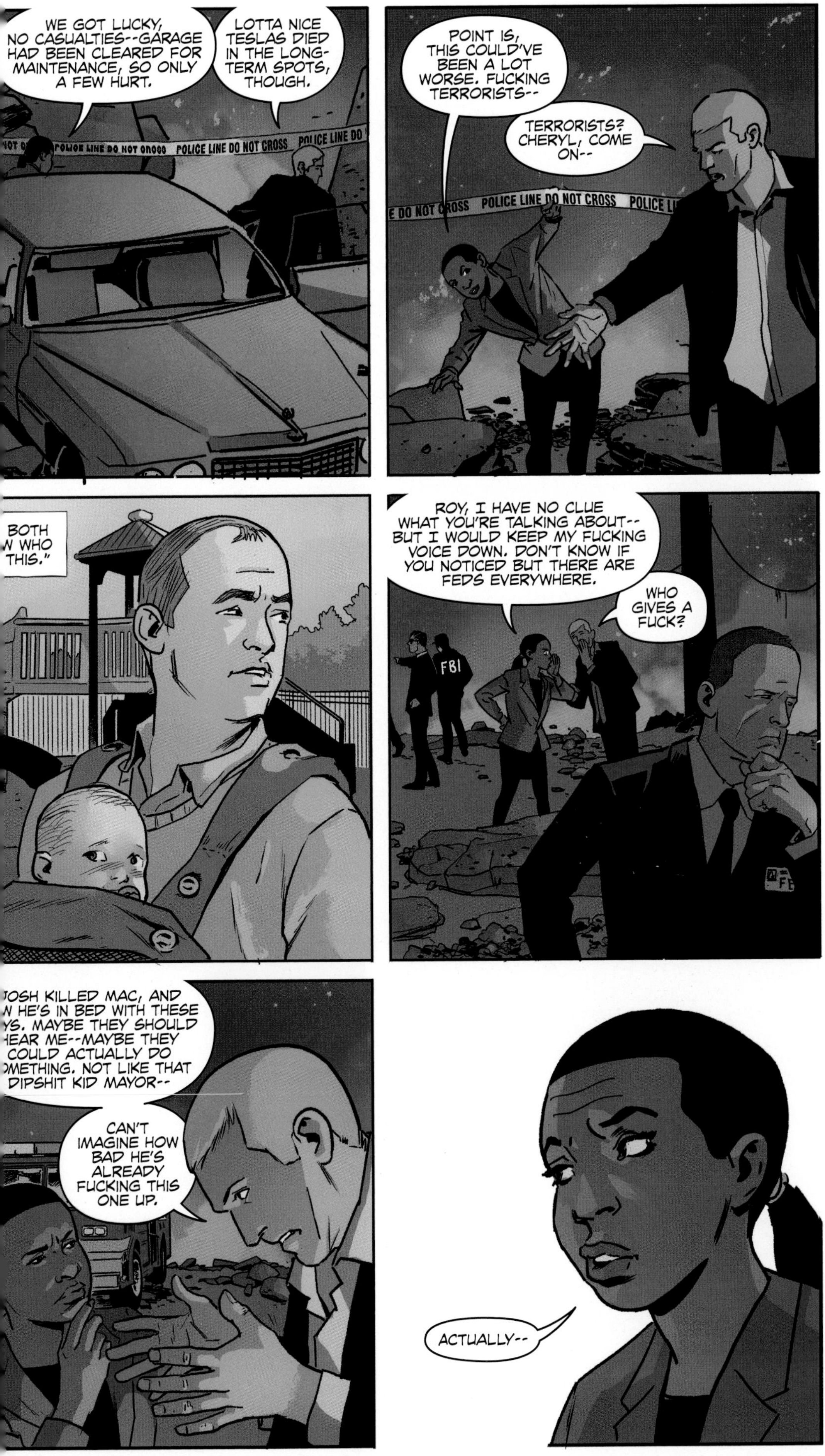
WE GOT LUCKY, NO CASUALTIES--GARAGE HAD BEEN CLEARED FOR MAINTENANCE, SO ONLY A FEW HURT.
LOTTA NICE TESLAS DIED IN THE LONG-TERM SPOTS, THOUGH.
POLICE LINE DO NOT CROSS
POINT IS, THIS COULD'VE BEEN A LOT WORSE. FUCKING TERRORISTS--
TERRORISTS? CHERYL, COME ON--
POLICE LINE DO NOT CROSS
BOTH
W WHO
THIS."
ROY, I HAVE NO CLUE WHAT YOU'RE TALKING ABOUT--BUT I WOULD KEEP MY FUCKING VOICE DOWN. DON'T KNOW IF YOU NOTICED BUT THERE ARE FEDS EVERYWHERE.
WHO GIVES A FUCK?
FBI
JOSH KILLED MAC, AND N HE'S IN BED WITH THESE YS. MAYBE THEY SHOULD HEAR ME--MAYBE THEY COULD ACTUALLY DO OMETHING. NOT LIKE THAT DIPSHIT KID MAYOR--
CAN'T IMAGINE HOW BAD HE'S ALREADY FUCKING THIS ONE UP.
ACTUALLY--

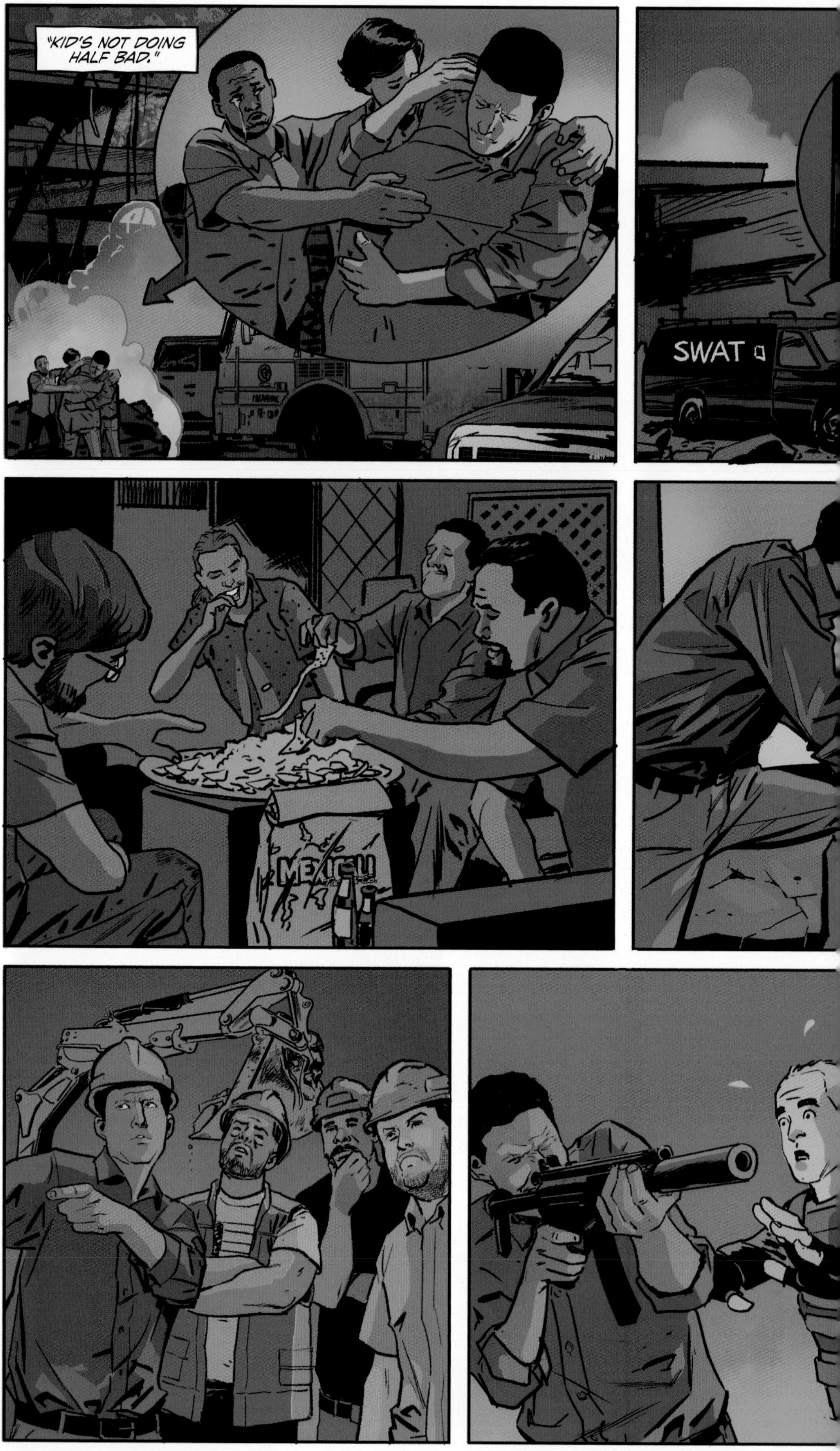
"KID'S NOT DOING HALF BAD."
SWAT
MEXICALI

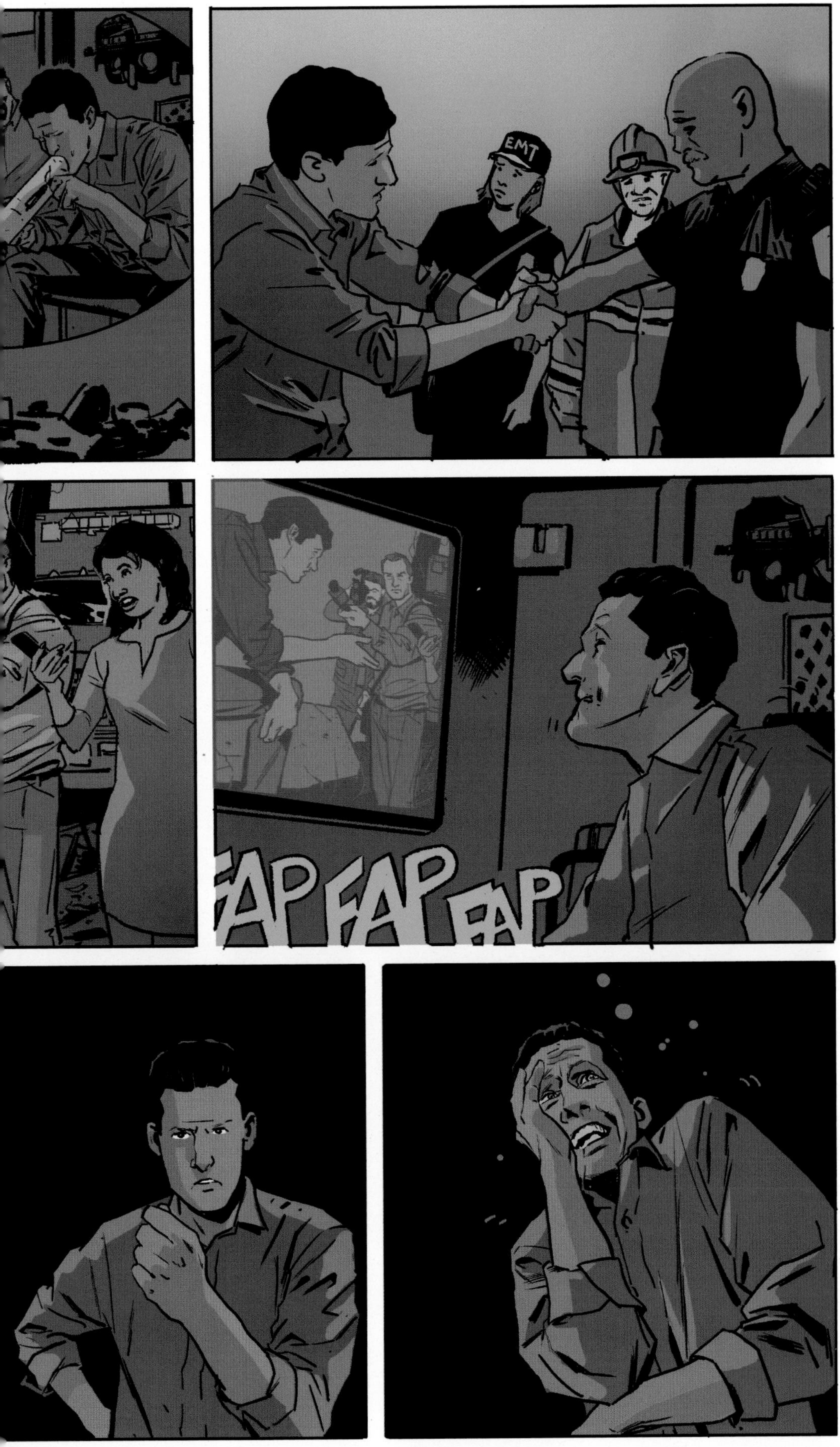
EMT
FAP FAP FAP

THE

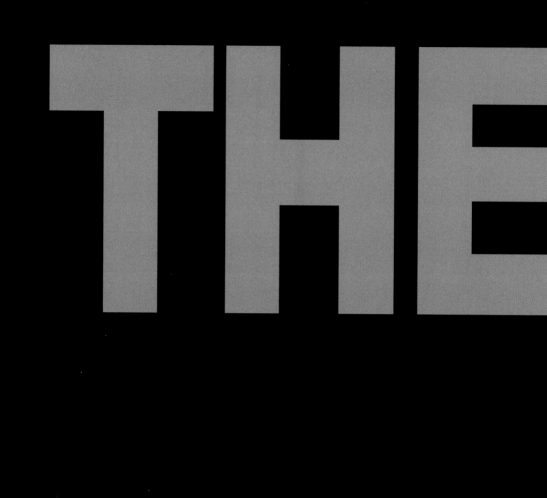

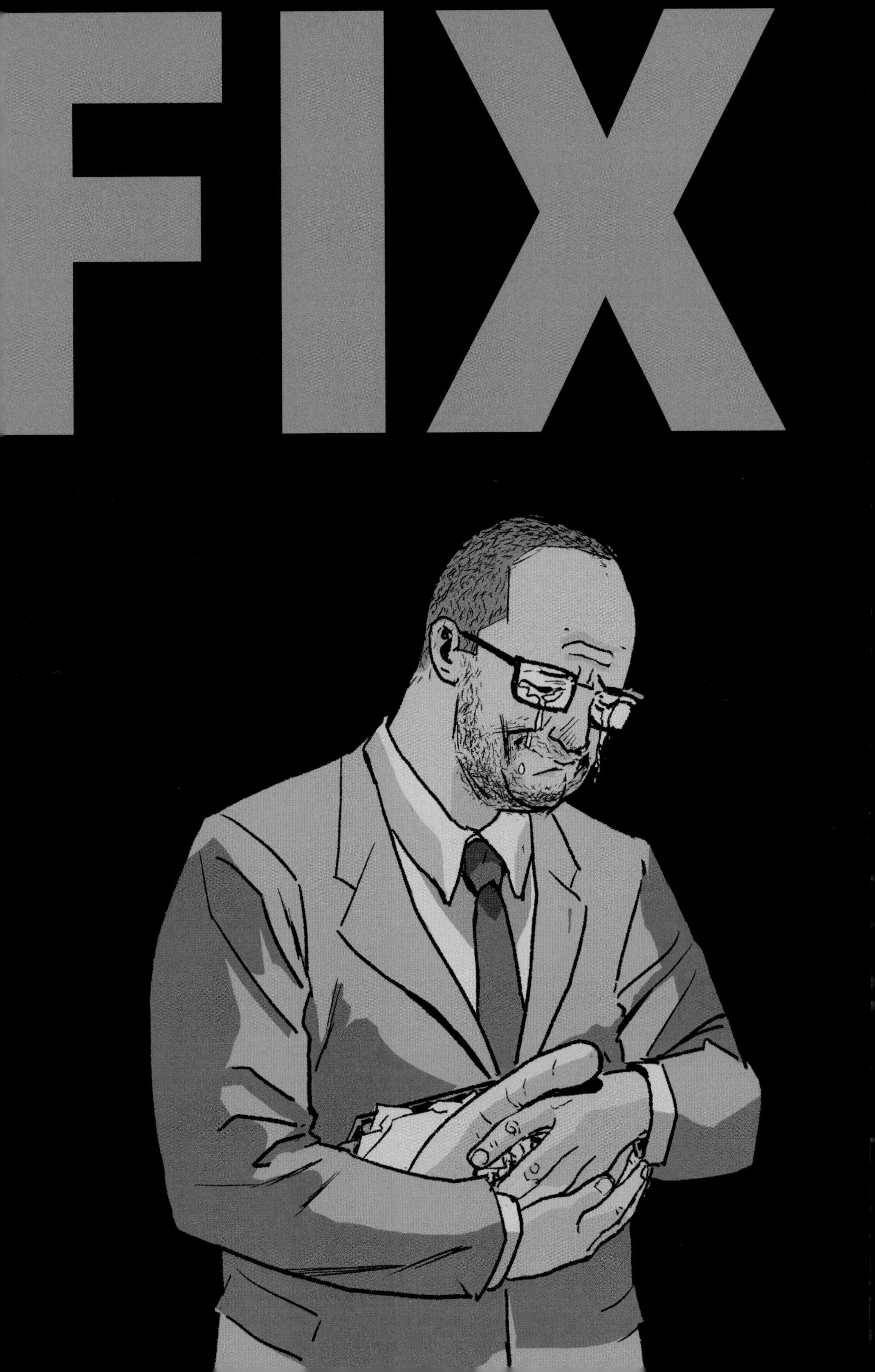
FIX

THIS IS BAD, DEAL. VERY BAD.

I UNDERSTAND YOU'RE QUITE UPSET, JOSH. BUT PLEASE, TRY TO RELAX--

YOU KNOW WHAT A SILENT KILLER STRESS CAN BE.

HOW CAN I NOT BE STRESSED? I BROUGHT YOU IN BECAUSE YOUR REPUTATION FOR EFFICIENCY WAS UNPARALLELED. YOUR COMMENTS ON GLASSDOOR WERE ALL VERY GLOWING.

AND MUCH DESE I SHOULD POINT THE AIRPORT OPE WAS A SMASH SUCCESS.

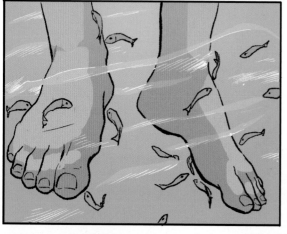

YES, IT'S THE BIT THAT FOLLOWED THAT I'M STRUGGLING WITH--WHY AGAIN DID YOU SHOOT A POLICE OFFICER ON MY PAYROLL?

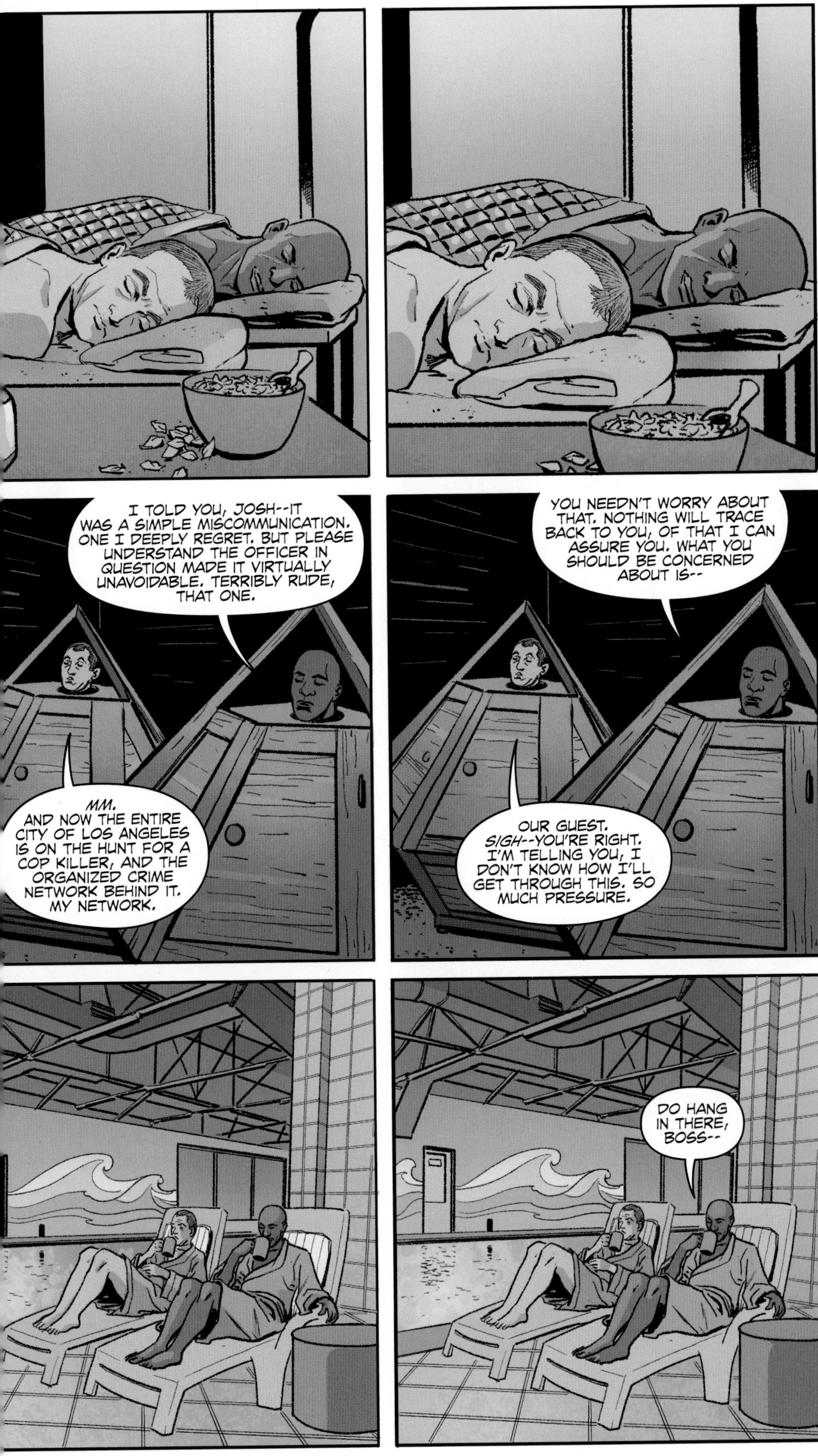
I TOLD YOU, JOSH--IT WAS A SIMPLE MISCOMMUNICATION. ONE I DEEPLY REGRET. BUT PLEASE UNDERSTAND THE OFFICER IN QUESTION MADE IT VIRTUALLY UNAVOIDABLE. TERRIBLY RUDE, THAT ONE.
MM. AND NOW THE ENTIRE CITY OF LOS ANGELES IS ON THE HUNT FOR A COP KILLER, AND THE ORGANIZED CRIME NETWORK BEHIND IT. MY NETWORK.
YOU NEEDN'T WORRY ABOUT THAT. NOTHING WILL TRACE BACK TO YOU, OF THAT I CAN ASSURE YOU. WHAT YOU SHOULD BE CONCERNED ABOUT IS--
OUR GUEST. *SIGH*--YOU'RE RIGHT. I'M TELLING YOU, I DON'T KNOW HOW I'LL GET THROUGH THIS. SO MUCH PRESSURE.
DO HANG IN THERE, BOSS--

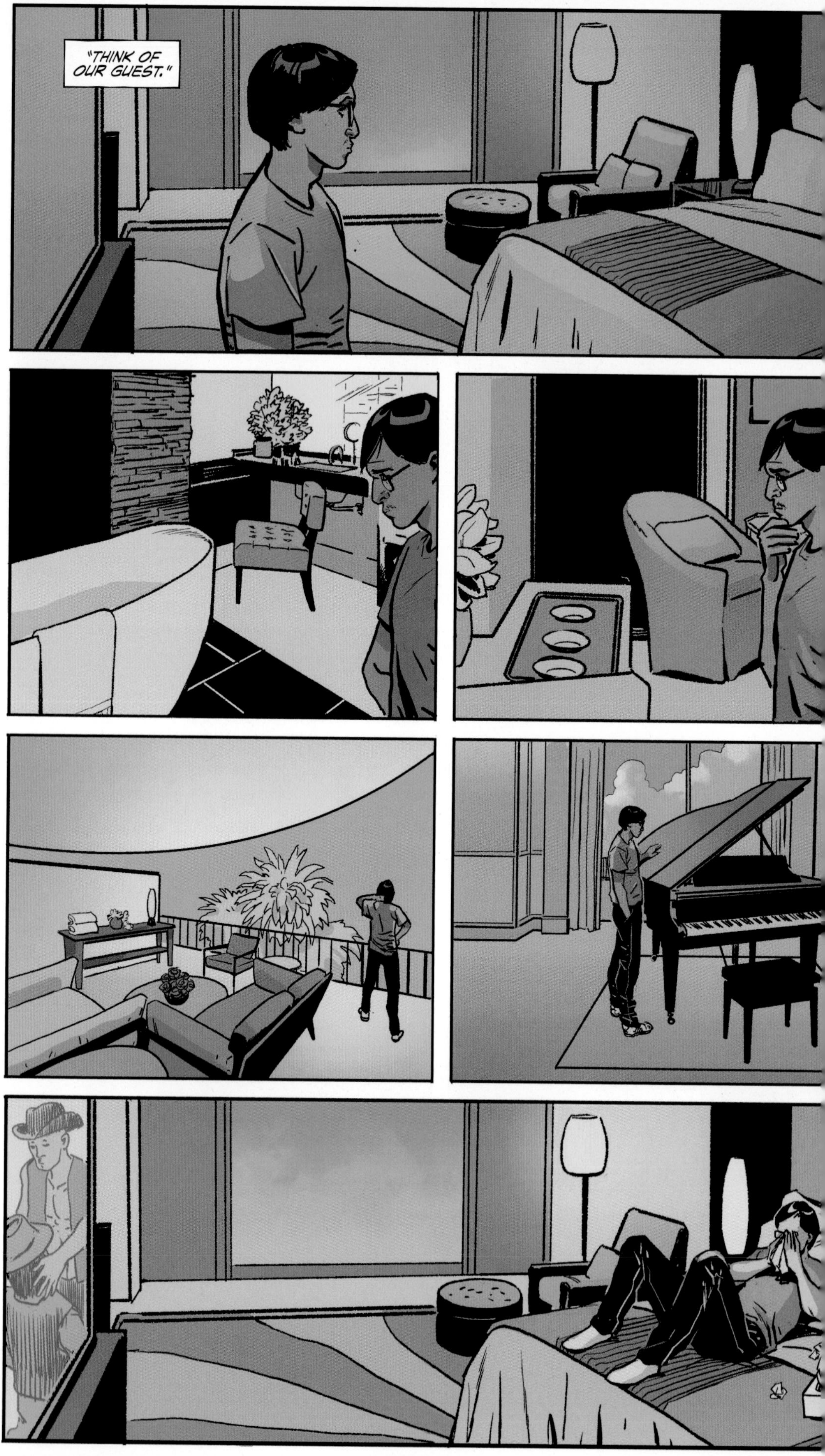
"THINK OF OUR GUEST."

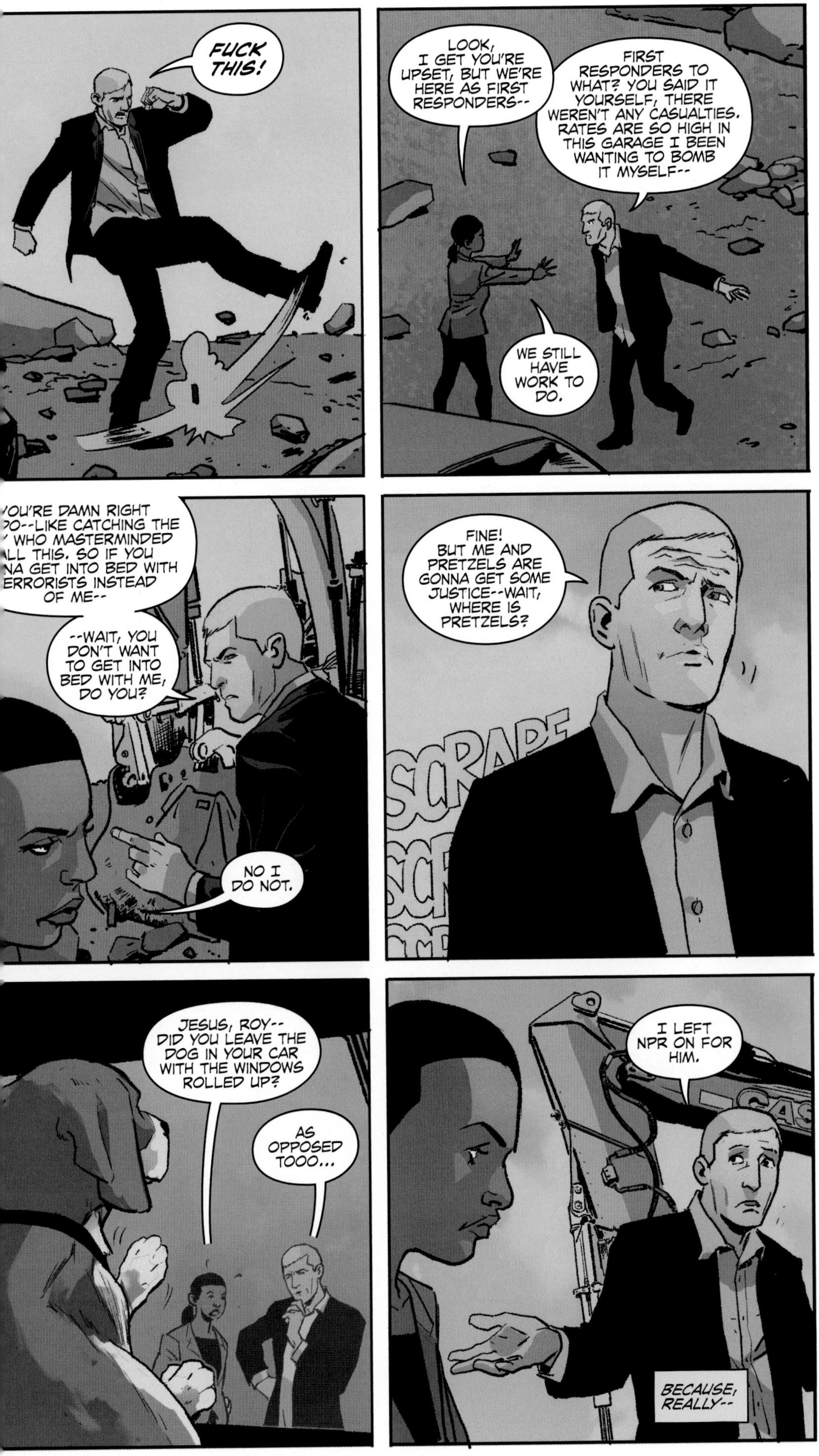
FUCK THIS!
LOOK, I GET YOU'RE UPSET, BUT WE'RE HERE AS FIRST RESPONDERS--
FIRST RESPONDERS TO WHAT? YOU SAID IT YOURSELF, THERE WEREN'T ANY CASUALTIES. RATES ARE SO HIGH IN THIS GARAGE I BEEN WANTING TO BOMB IT MYSELF--
WE STILL HAVE WORK TO DO.
OU'RE DAMN RIGHT DO--LIKE CATCHING THE WHO MASTERMINDED LL THIS. SO IF YOU NA GET INTO BED WITH ERRORISTS INSTEAD OF ME--
--WAIT, YOU DON'T WANT TO GET INTO BED WITH ME, DO YOU?
NO I DO NOT.
FINE! BUT ME AND PRETZELS ARE GONNA GET SOME JUSTICE--WAIT, WHERE IS PRETZELS?
SCRAPE
JESUS, ROY-- DID YOU LEAVE THE DOG IN YOUR CAR WITH THE WINDOWS ROLLED UP?
AS OPPOSED TOOO...
I LEFT NPR ON FOR HIM.
BECAUSE, REALLY--

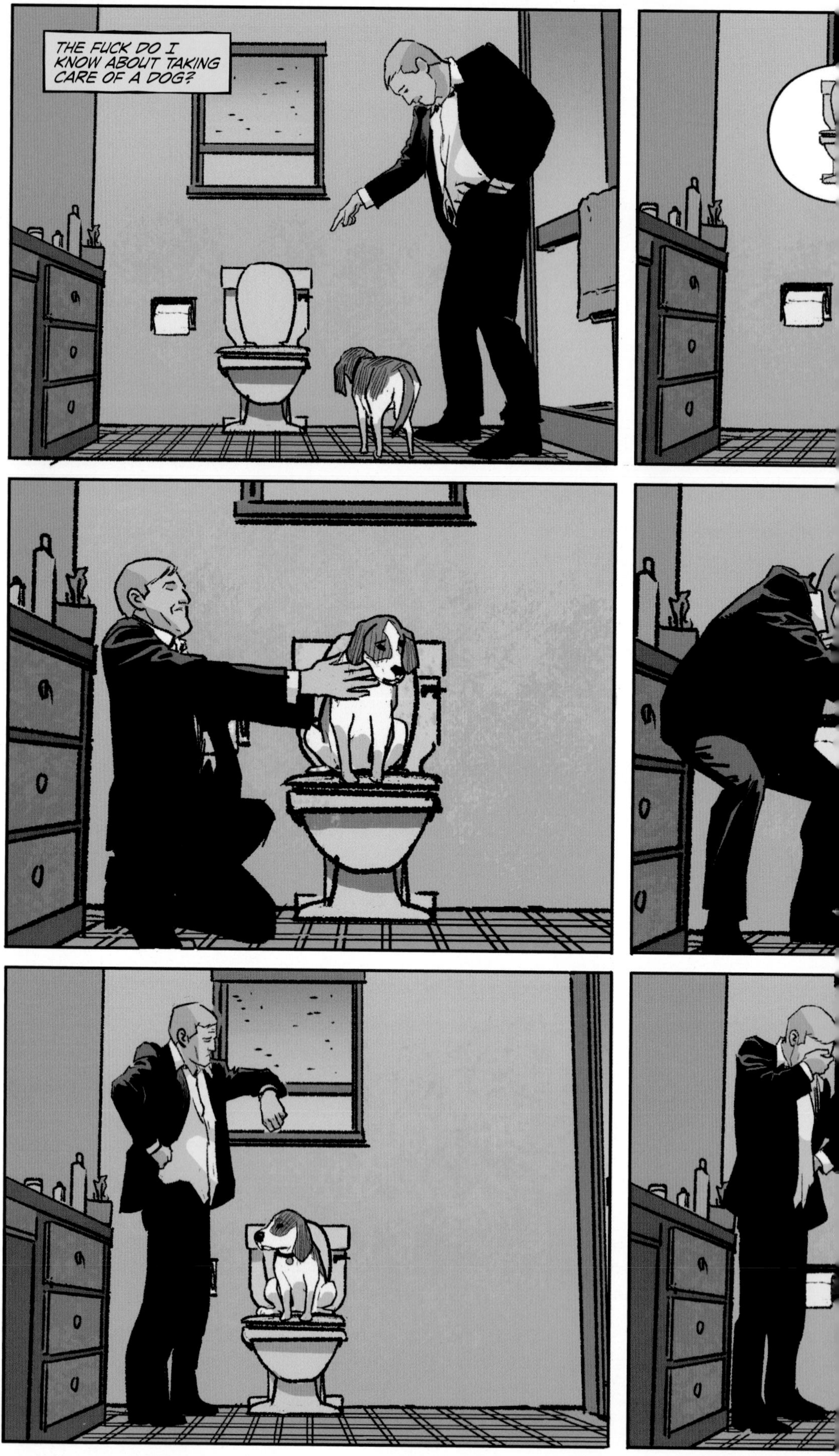
THE FUCK DO I KNOW ABOUT TAKING CARE OF A DOG?

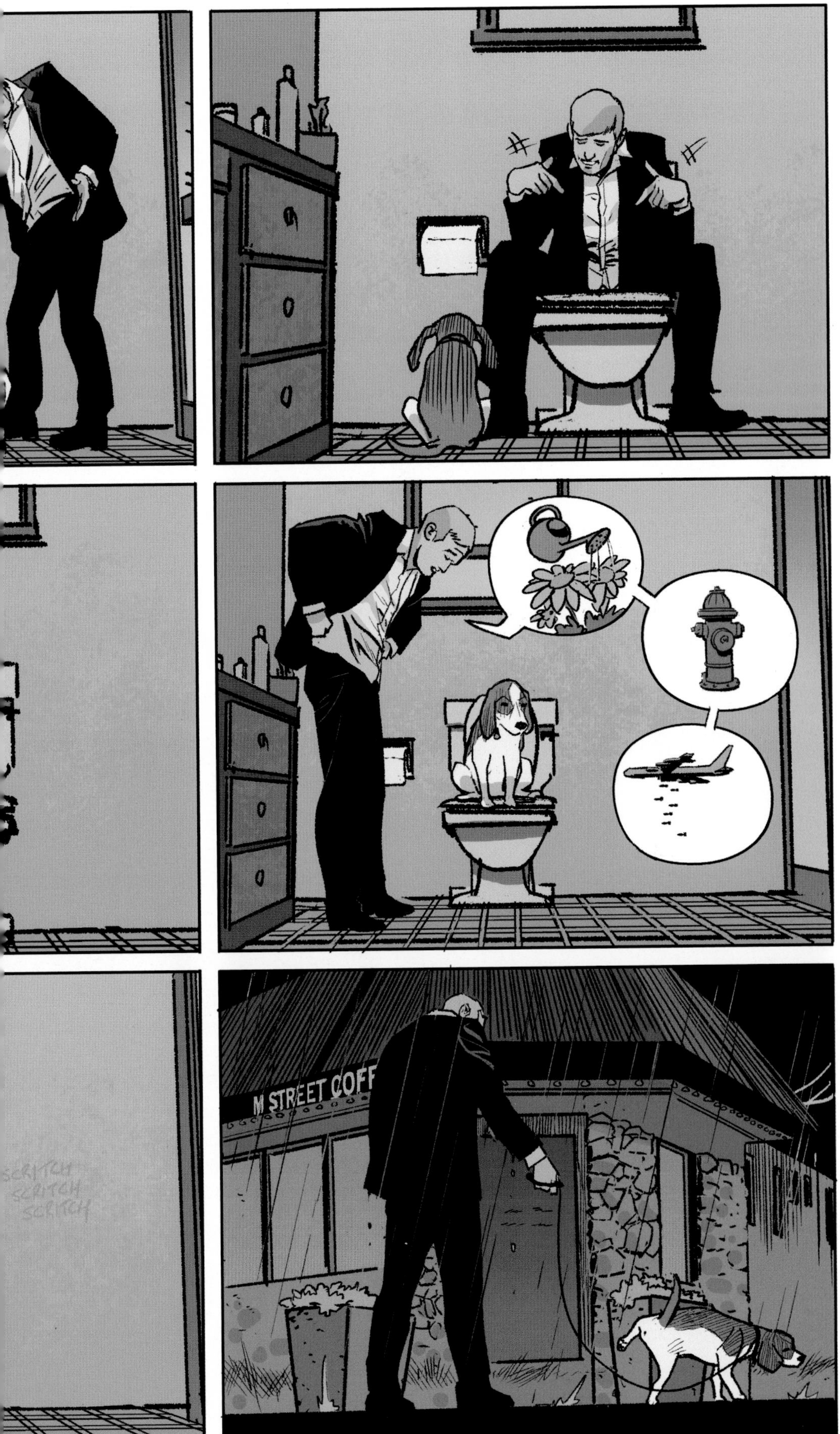
M STREET COFF
SCRITCH
SCRITCH
SCRITCH

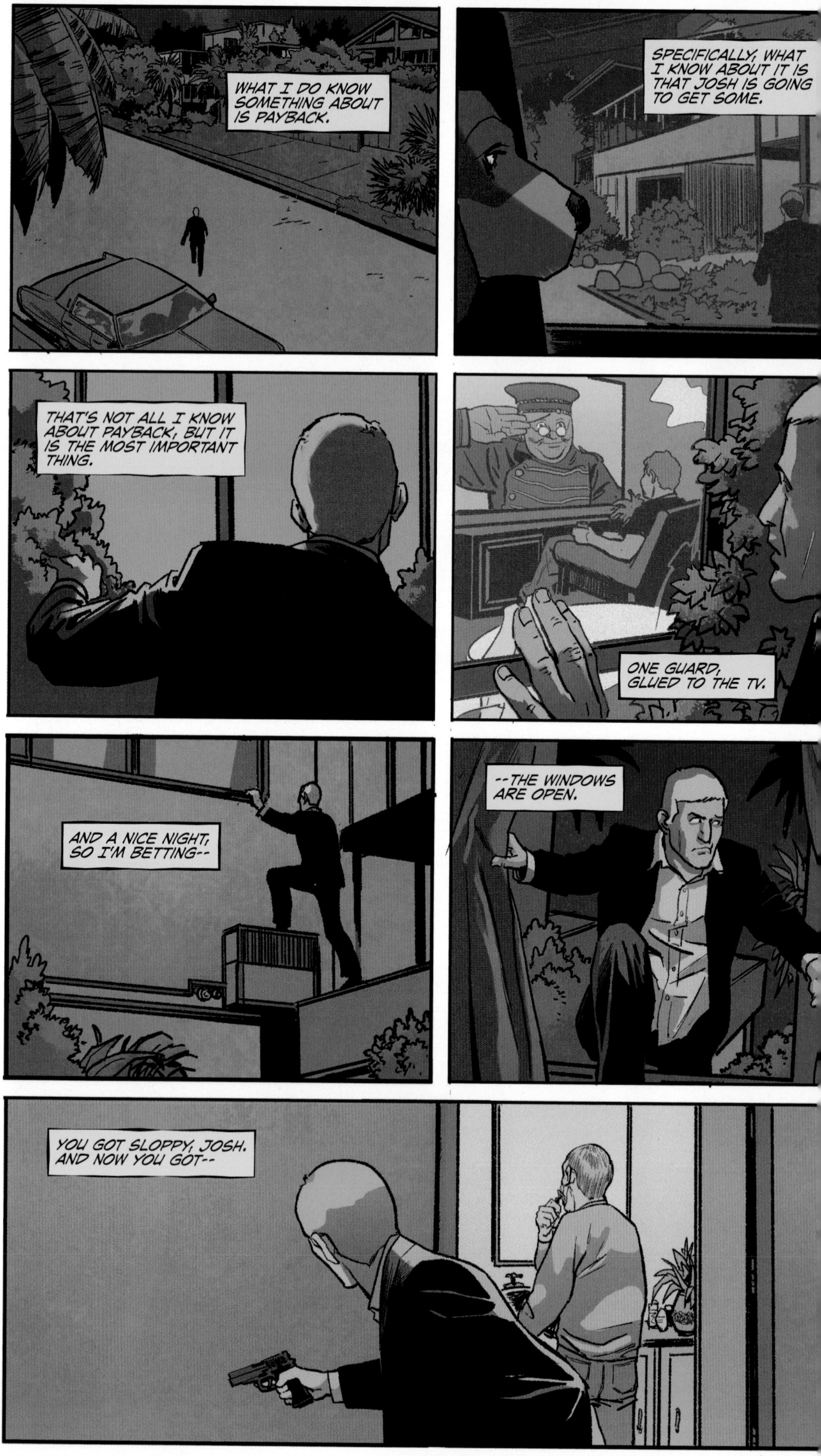
WHAT I DO KNOW SOMETHING ABOUT IS PAYBACK.
SPECIFICALLY, WHAT I KNOW ABOUT IT IS THAT JOSH IS GOING TO GET SOME.
THAT'S NOT ALL I KNOW ABOUT PAYBACK, BUT IT IS THE MOST IMPORTANT THING.
ONE GUARD, GLUED TO THE TV.
AND A NICE NIGHT, SO I'M BETTING--
--THE WINDOWS ARE OPEN.
YOU GOT SLOPPY, JOSH. AND NOW YOU GOT--

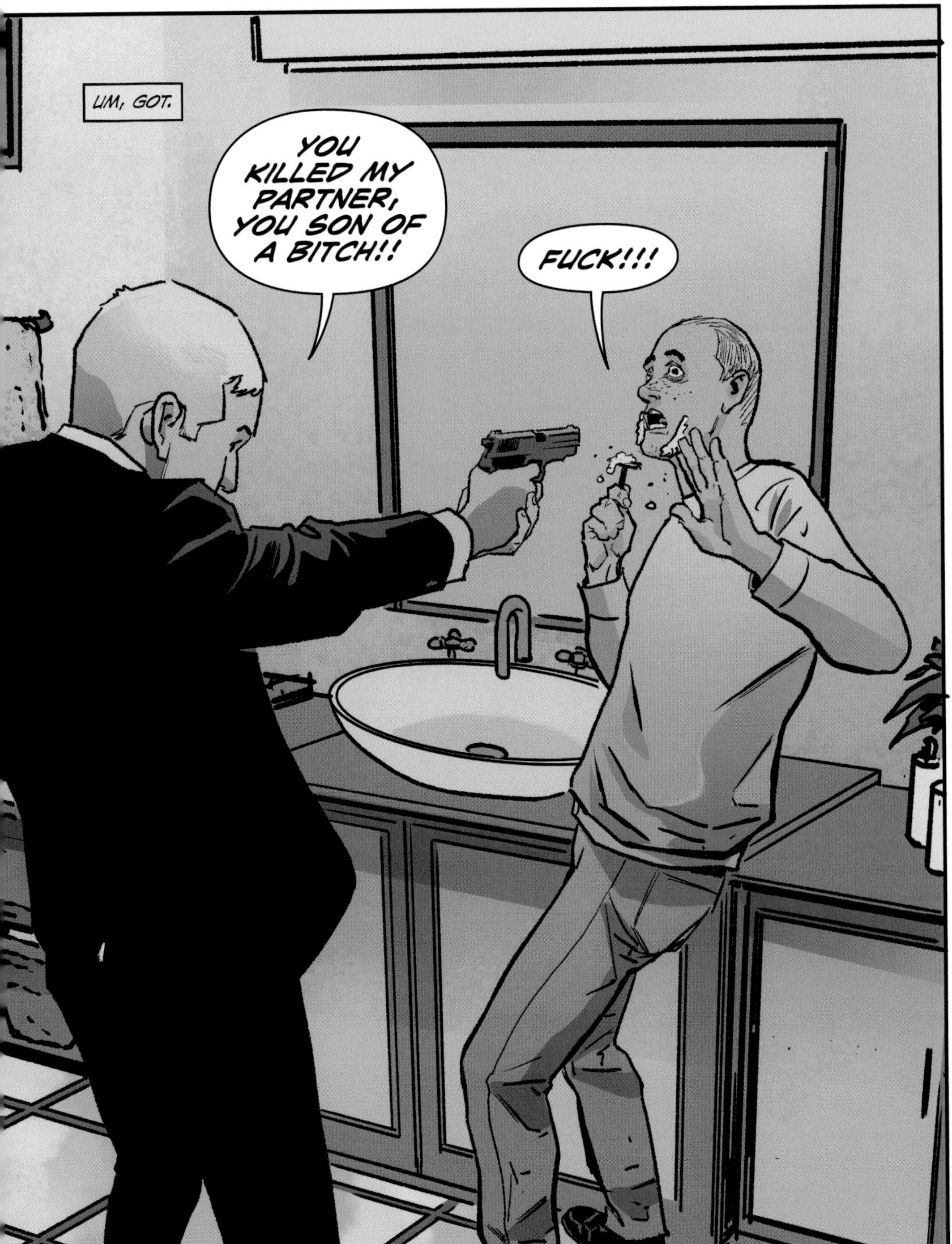
UM, GOT.
YOU KILLED MY PARTNER, YOU SON OF A BITCH!!
FUCK!!!

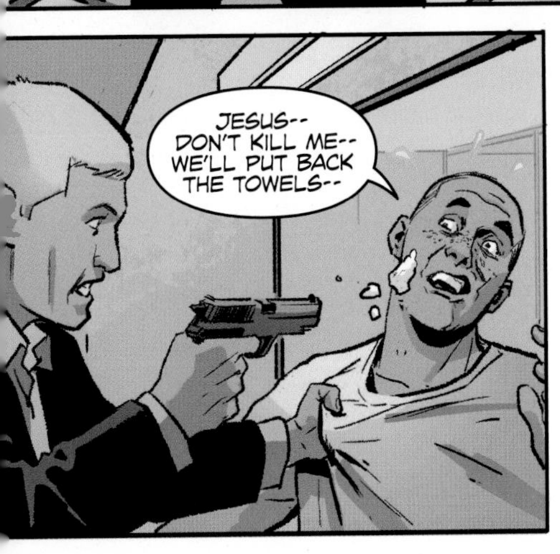
JESUS-- DON'T KILL ME-- WE'LL PUT BACK THE TOWELS--

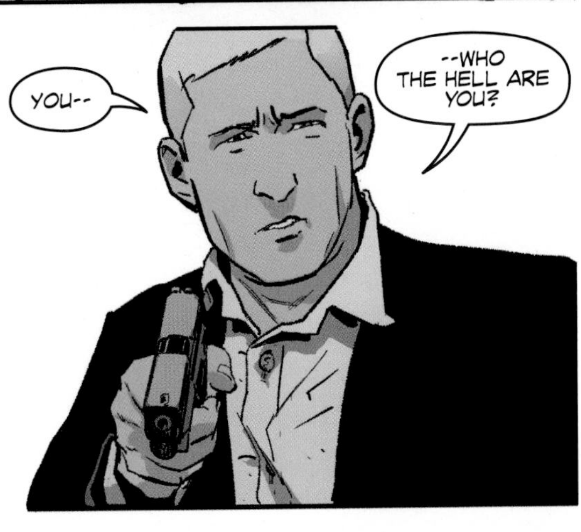
YOU--
--WHO THE HELL ARE YOU?

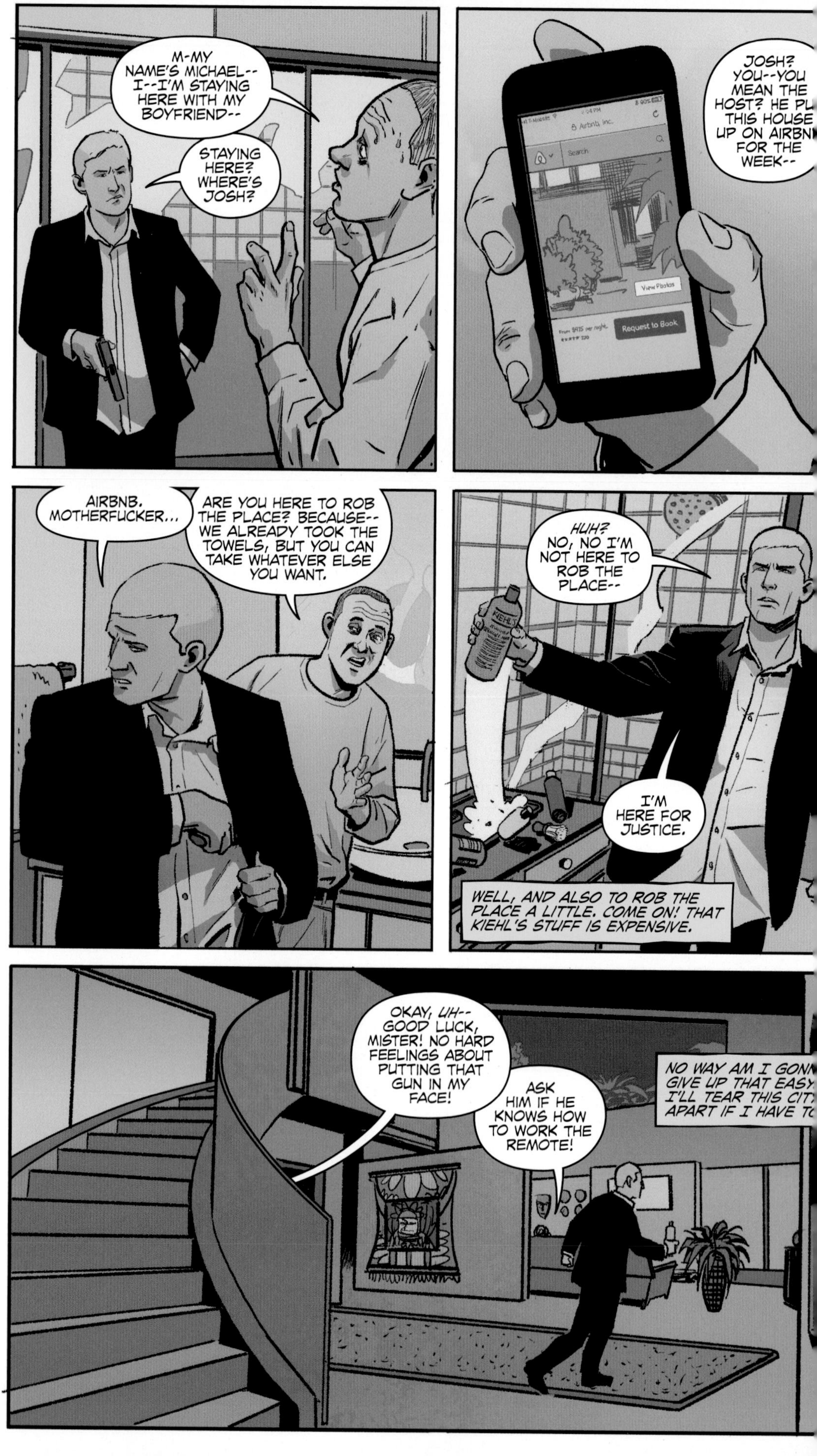

M-MY NAME'S MICHAEL-- I--I'M STAYING HERE WITH MY BOYFRIEND--
STAYING HERE? WHERE'S JOSH?
Airbnb, Inc.
View Photos
Request to Book
JOSH? YOU--YOU MEAN THE HOST? HE PU THIS HOUSE UP ON AIRBN FOR THE WEEK--
AIRBNB. MOTHERFUCKER...
ARE YOU HERE TO ROB THE PLACE? BECAUSE-- WE ALREADY TOOK THE TOWELS, BUT YOU CAN TAKE WHATEVER ELSE YOU WANT.
HUH? NO, NO I'M NOT HERE TO ROB THE PLACE--
I'M HERE FOR JUSTICE.
WELL, AND ALSO TO ROB THE PLACE A LITTLE. COME ON! THAT KIEHL'S STUFF IS EXPENSIVE.
OKAY, UH-- GOOD LUCK, MISTER! NO HARD FEELINGS ABOUT PUTTING THAT GUN IN MY FACE!
ASK HIM IF HE KNOWS HOW TO WORK THE REMOTE!
NO WAY AM I GONN GIVE UP THAT EASY I'LL TEAR THIS CIT APART IF I HAVE T

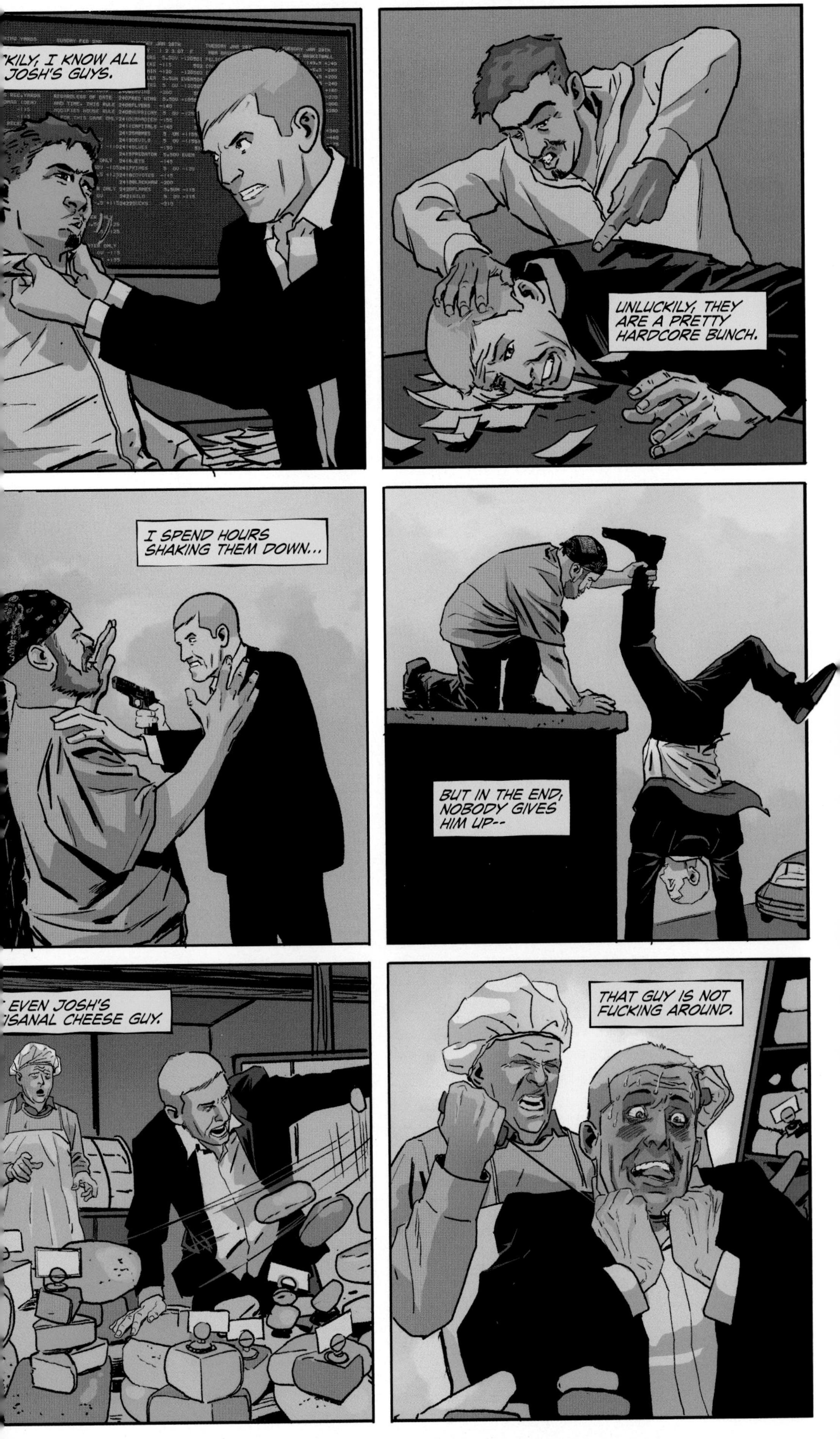
KILY, I KNOW ALL JOSH'S GUYS.
UNLUCKILY, THEY ARE A PRETTY HARDCORE BUNCH.
I SPEND HOURS SHAKING THEM DOWN...
BUT IN THE END, NOBODY GIVES HIM UP--
EVEN JOSH'S TISANAL CHEESE GUY.
THAT GUY IS NOT FUCKING AROUND.

--I'VE CHECKED EVERY SAFEHOUSE, EVERY PAYOUT, DONOVAN. THERE'S NO SIGN OF JOSH ANYWHERE.

IT'S BULLSHIT, TOTAL BULLSHIT.

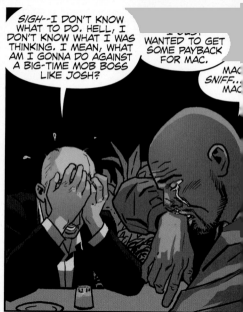

SIGH--I DON'T KNOW WHAT TO DO. HELL, I DON'T KNOW WHAT I WAS THINKING. I MEAN, WHAT AM I GONNA DO AGAINST A BIG-TIME MOB BOSS LIKE JOSH?

...JUST WANTED TO GET SOME PAYBACK FOR MAC.

MAC. SNIFF... MAC.

S'OKAY, MAN--

NO, I KNOW, IT'S JUST--I ALWAYS REALLY PREFERRED HIM, YOU KNOW? I MEAN, YOU'RE FINE, ROY, BUT MAC-- MAC, I ACTUALLY LIKED--

I KNOW.

IT'S NOT FAIR, MAC! DESERVED BE THAN THIS! DESERVE ANYTHING Y WANTED!

LIKE A PONY! OR TRUE LOVE! OR TRUE LOVE WITH A PONY! BECAUSE THAT SHOULD BE OKAY IF IT'S WHAT YOU AND THE PONY WANT!

I HOPE YOU CAN HEAR ME UP IN HEAVEN, MAC! I HOPE YOU'RE FUCKING THAT PONY NOW...OR THAT PONY'S FUCKING YOU-- IT'S YOUR CHOICE!

OKAY, EASY MAN--

NO!

WHAT-- WHAT ARE YOU--

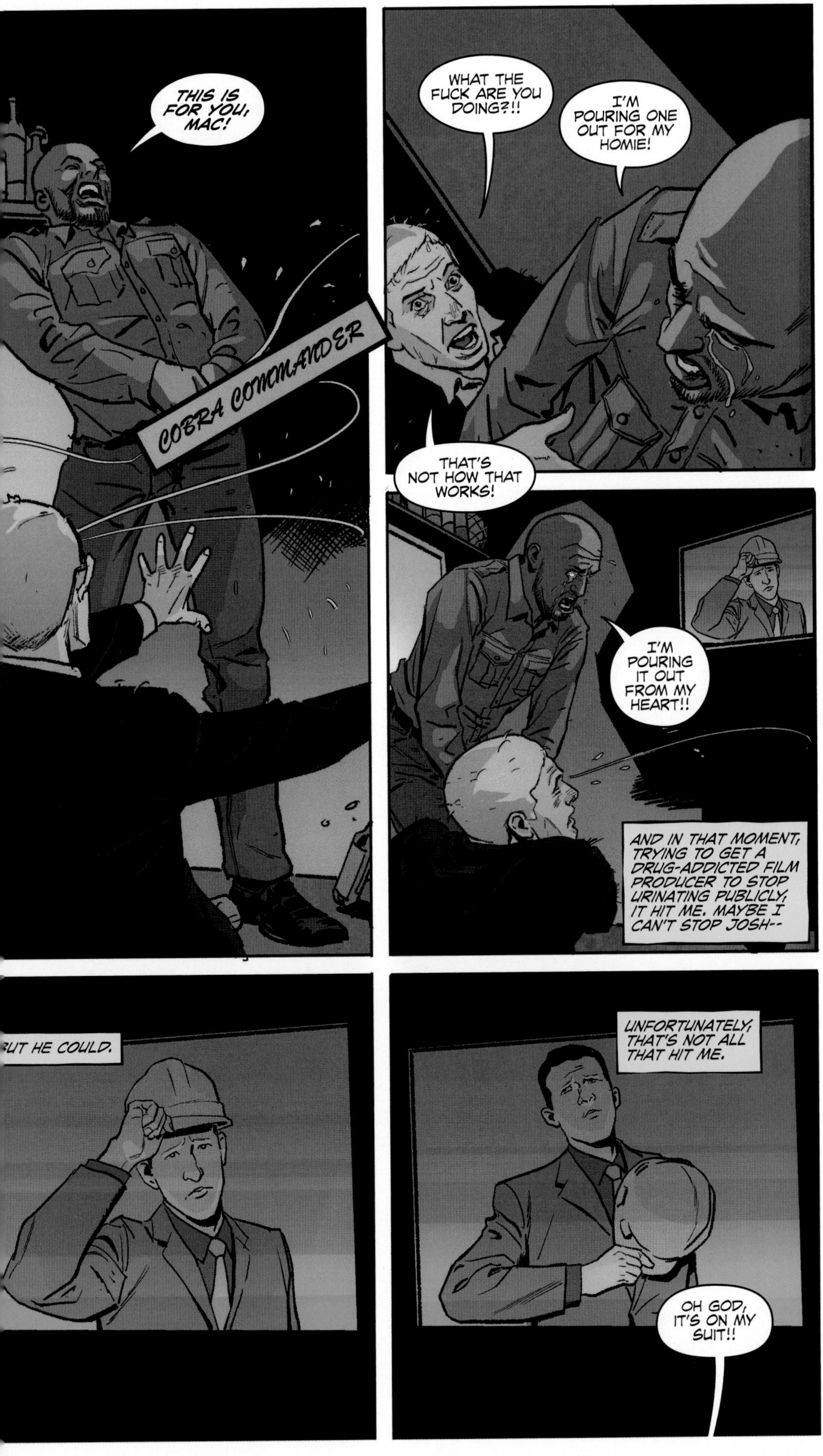
THIS IS FOR YOU, MAC!
COBRA COMMANDER
WHAT THE FUCK ARE YOU DOING?!!
I'M POURING ONE OUT FOR MY HOMIE!
THAT'S NOT HOW THAT WORKS!
I'M POURING IT OUT FROM MY HEART!!
AND IN THAT MOMENT, TRYING TO GET A DRUG-ADDICTED FILM PRODUCER TO STOP URINATING PUBLICLY, IT HIT ME. MAYBE I CAN'T STOP JOSH--
BUT HE COULD.
UNFORTUNATELY, THAT'S NOT ALL THAT HIT ME.
OH GOD, IT'S ON MY SUIT!!

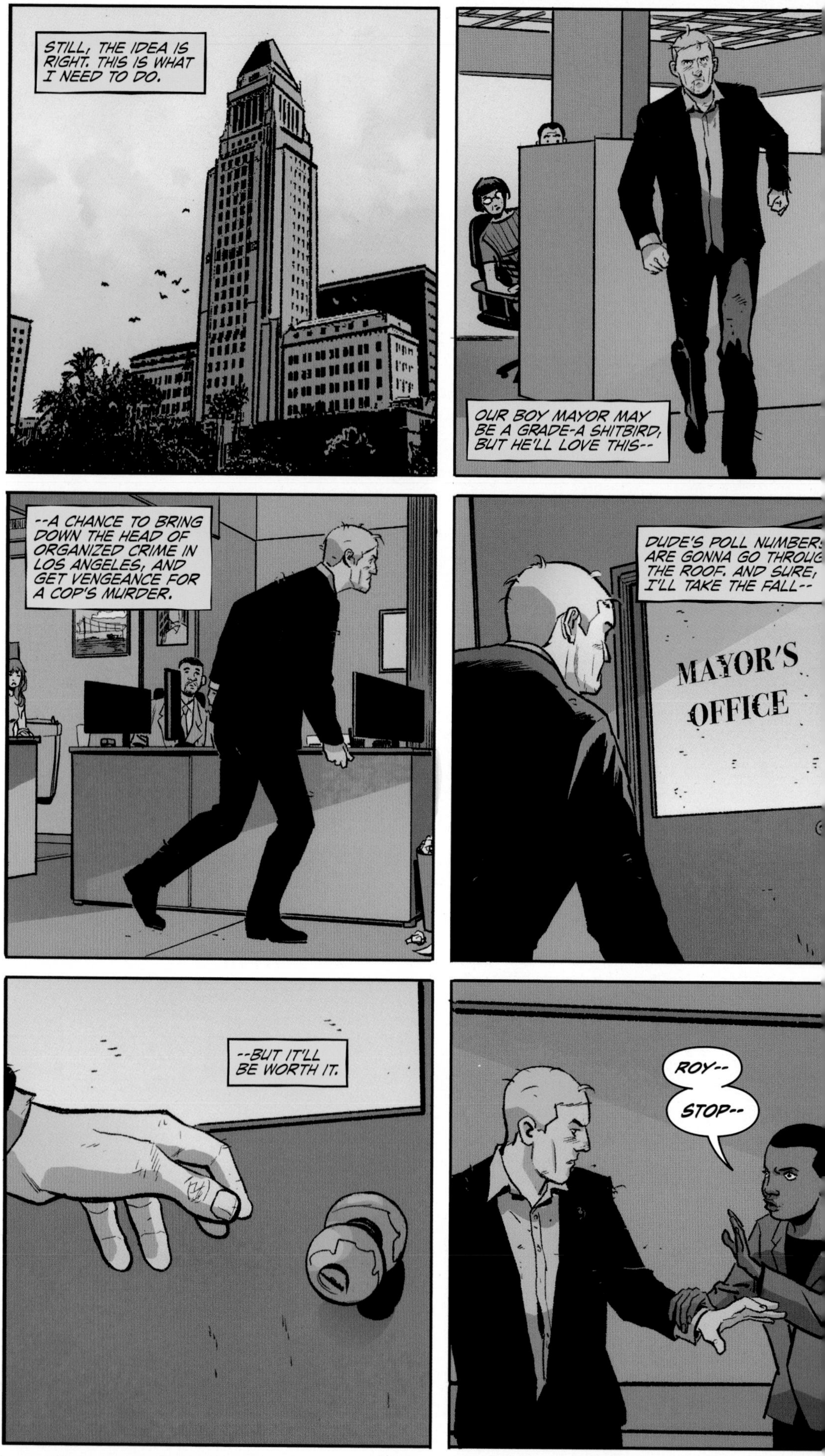
STILL, THE IDEA IS RIGHT. THIS IS WHAT I NEED TO DO.
OUR BOY MAYOR MAY BE A GRADE-A SHITBIRD, BUT HE'LL LOVE THIS--
--A CHANCE TO BRING DOWN THE HEAD OF ORGANIZED CRIME IN LOS ANGELES, AND GET VENGEANCE FOR A COP'S MURDER.
DUDE'S POLL NUMBERS ARE GONNA GO THROUG THE ROOF. AND SURE, I'LL TAKE THE FALL--
MAYOR'S OFFICE
--BUT IT'LL BE WORTH IT.
ROY--
STOP--

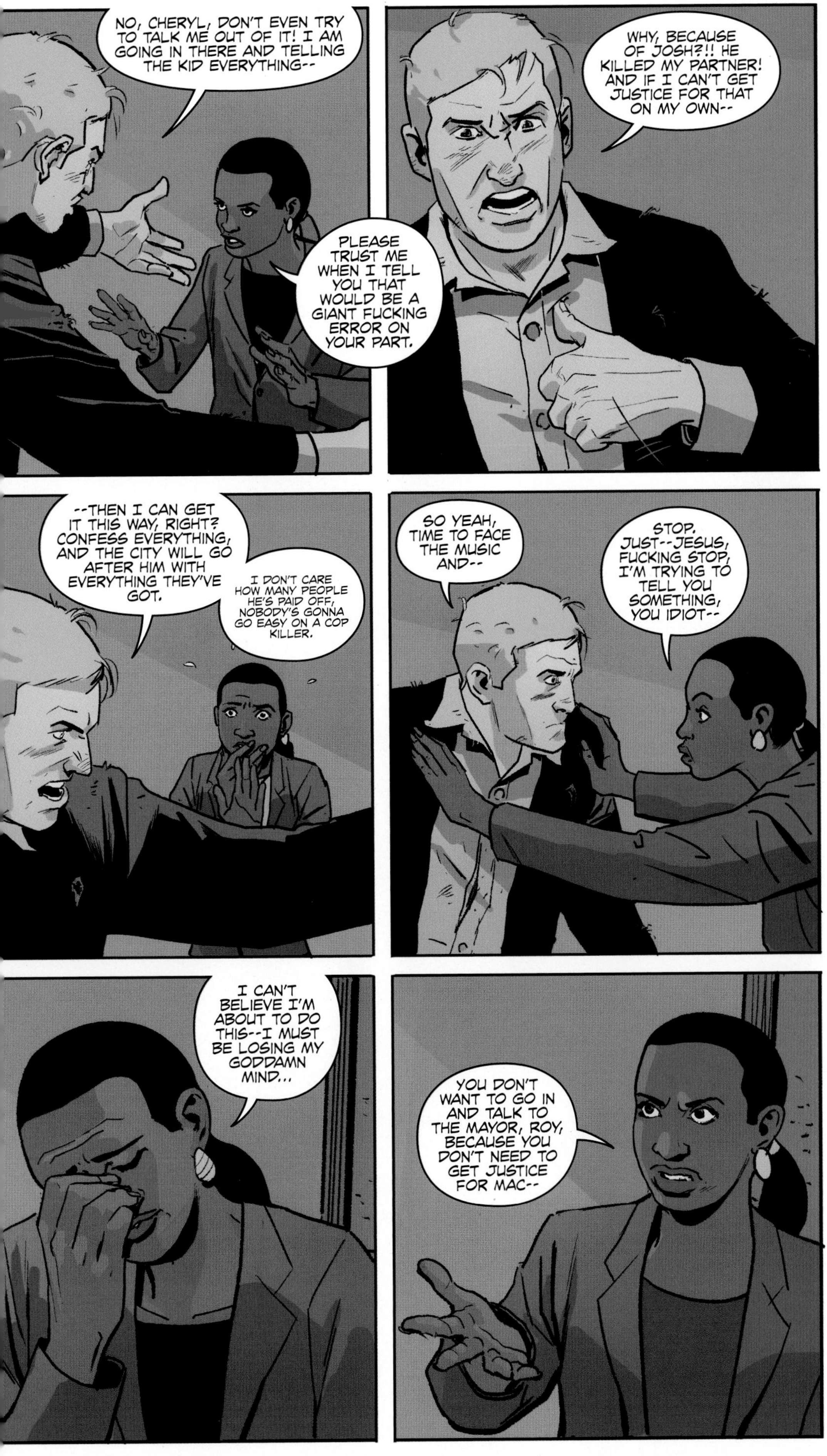
NO, CHERYL, DON'T EVEN TRY TO TALK ME OUT OF IT! I AM GOING IN THERE AND TELLING THE KID EVERYTHING--
PLEASE TRUST ME WHEN I TELL YOU THAT WOULD BE A GIANT FUCKING ERROR ON YOUR PART.
WHY, BECAUSE OF JOSH?!! HE KILLED MY PARTNER! AND IF I CAN'T GET JUSTICE FOR THAT ON MY OWN--
--THEN I CAN GET IT THIS WAY, RIGHT? CONFESS EVERYTHING, AND THE CITY WILL GO AFTER HIM WITH EVERYTHING THEY'VE GOT.
I DON'T CARE HOW MANY PEOPLE HE'S PAID OFF, NOBODY'S GONNA GO EASY ON A COP KILLER.
SO YEAH, TIME TO FACE THE MUSIC AND--
STOP. JUST--JESUS, FUCKING STOP, I'M TRYING TO TELL YOU SOMETHING, YOU IDIOT--
I CAN'T BELIEVE I'M ABOUT TO DO THIS--I MUST BE LOSING MY GODDAMN MIND...
YOU DON'T WANT TO GO IN AND TALK TO THE MAYOR, ROY, BECAUSE YOU DON'T NEED TO GET JUSTICE FOR MAC--

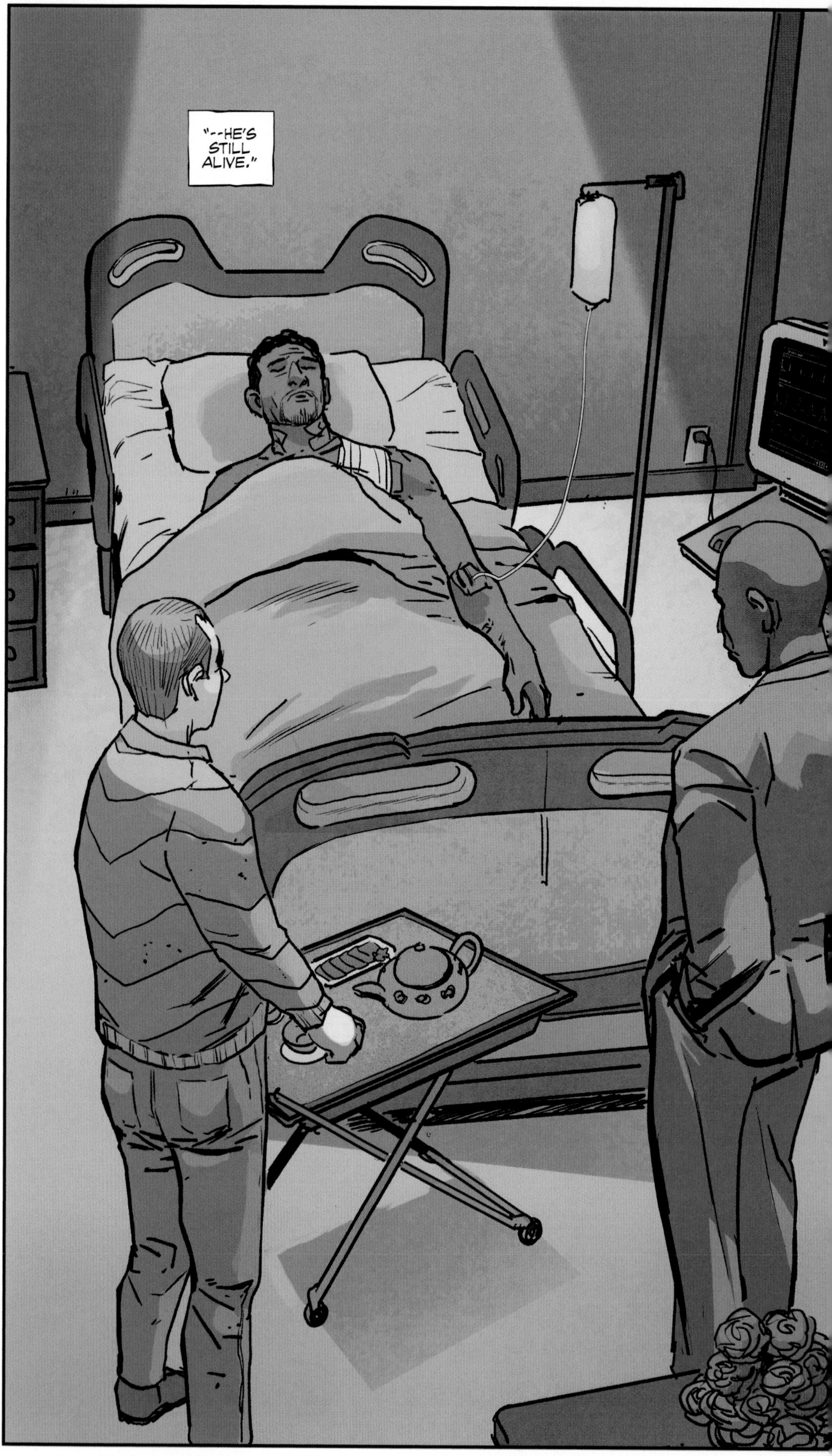
"--HE'S STILL ALIVE."

THE FIX

pin-ups by Steve Lieber, Cassie Anderson, Cat Farris, Maria Frantz, Dan Schkade, Jeff Parker, Benjamin Dewey & Ron Chan

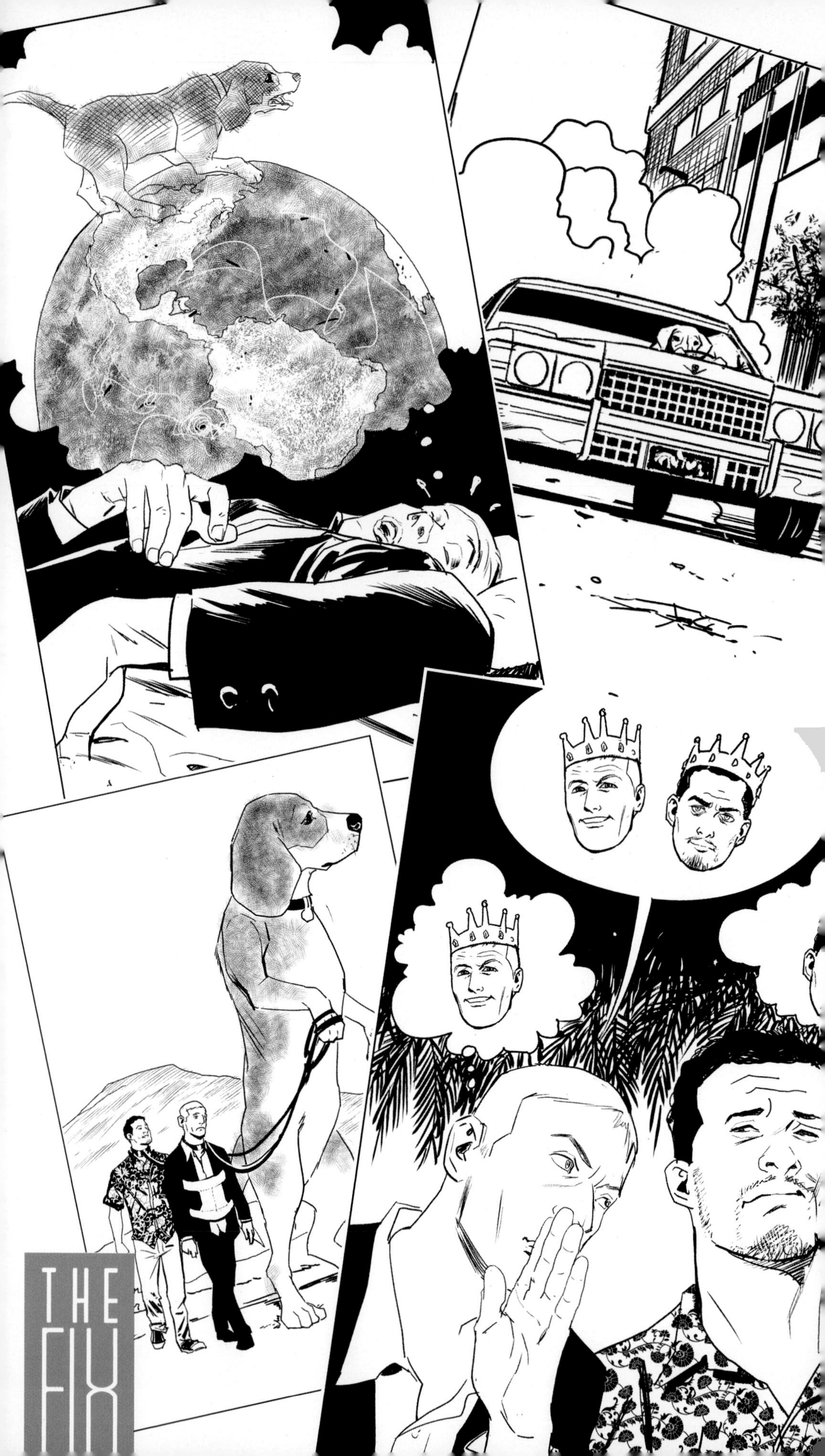
THE FIX

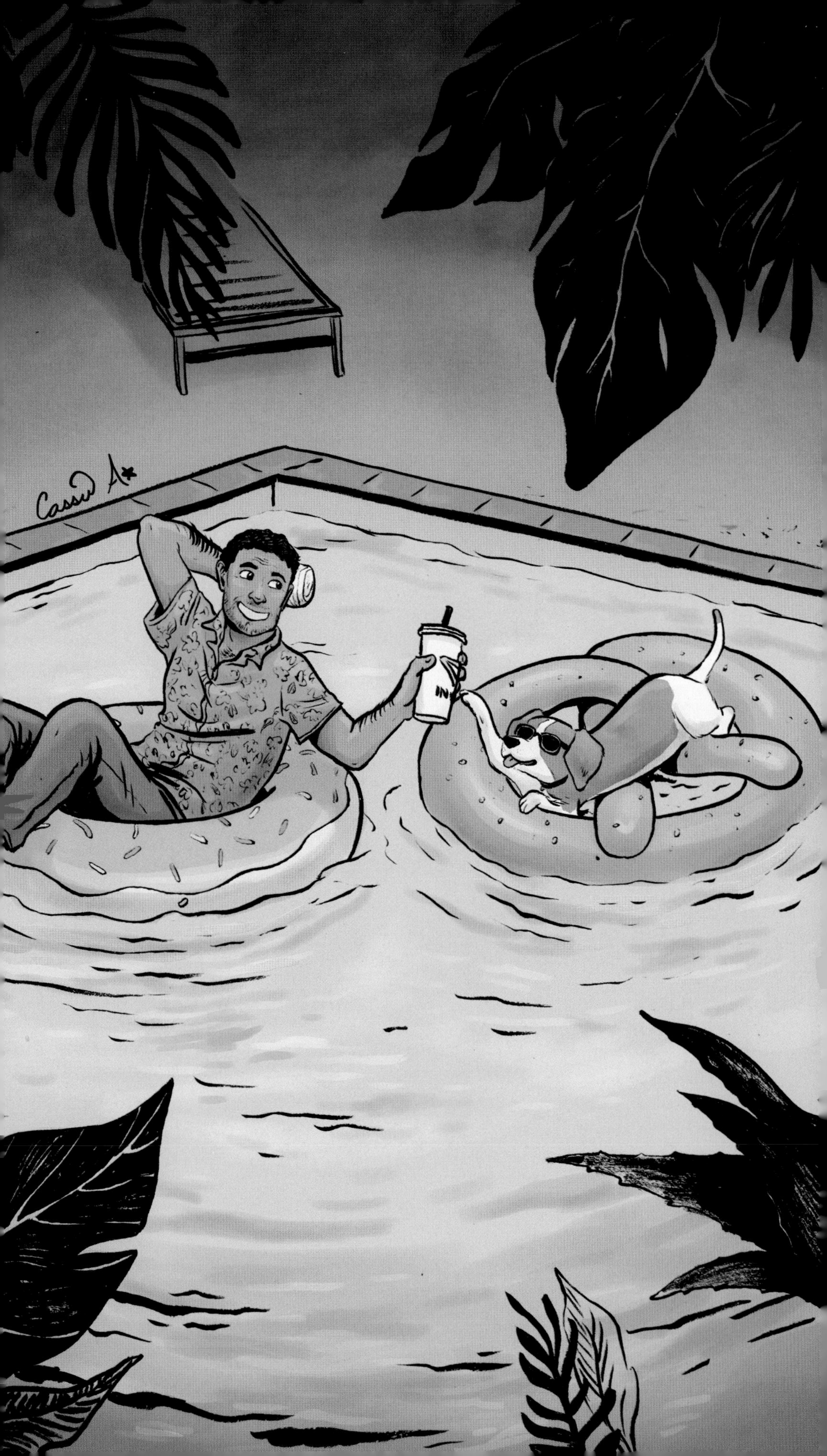

$

THE FIX

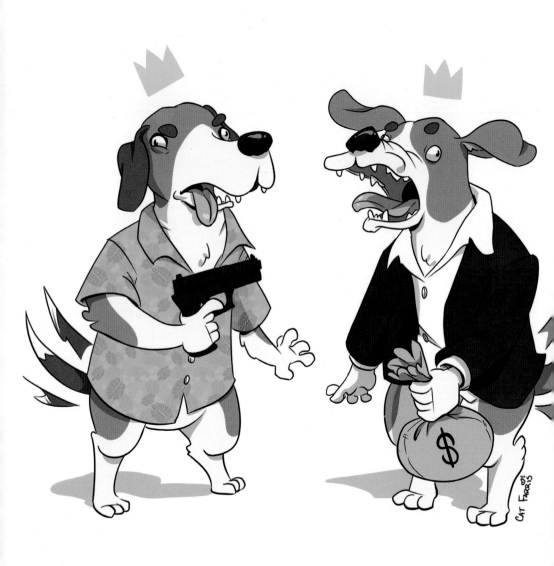

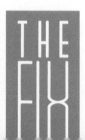

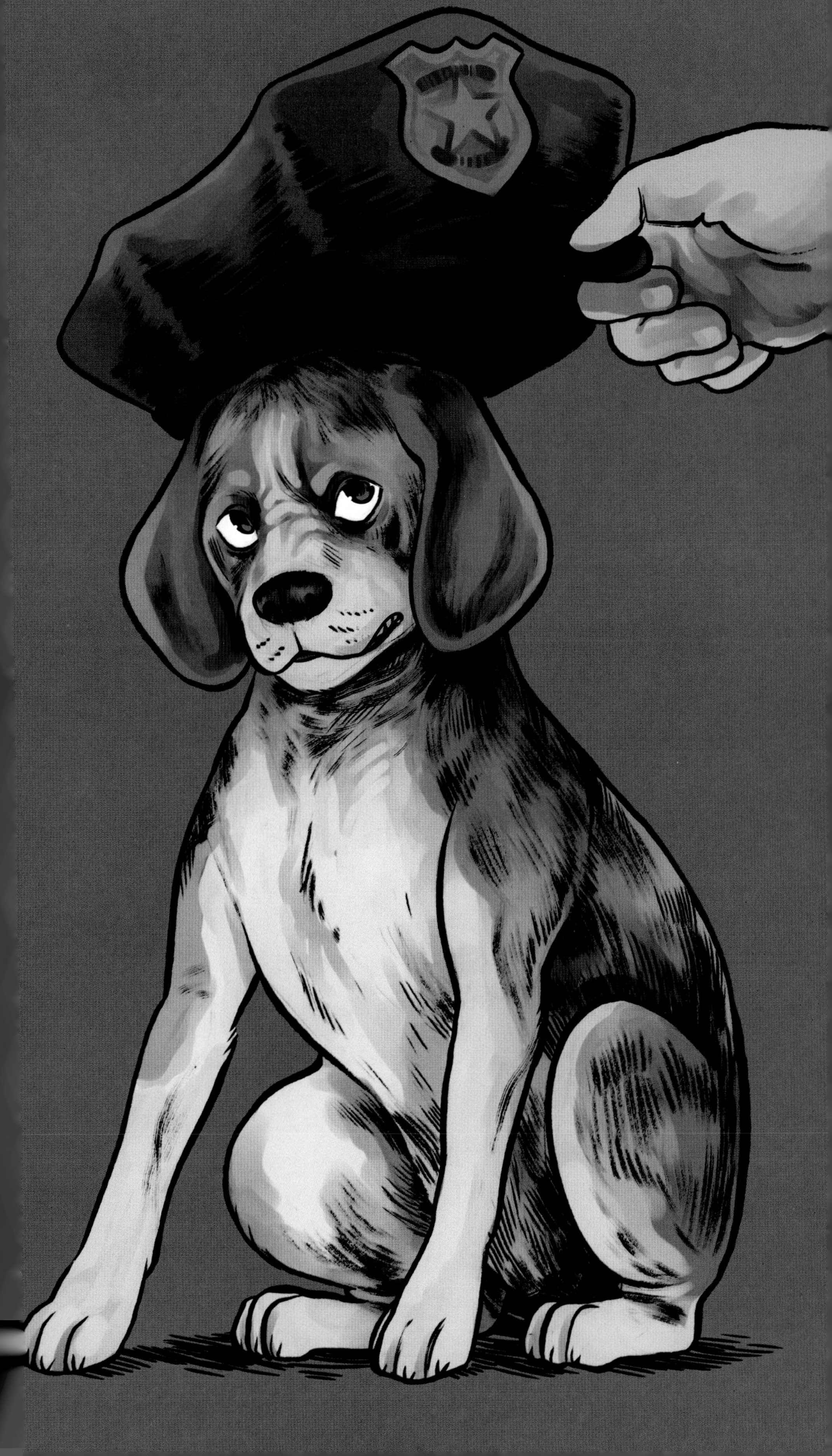

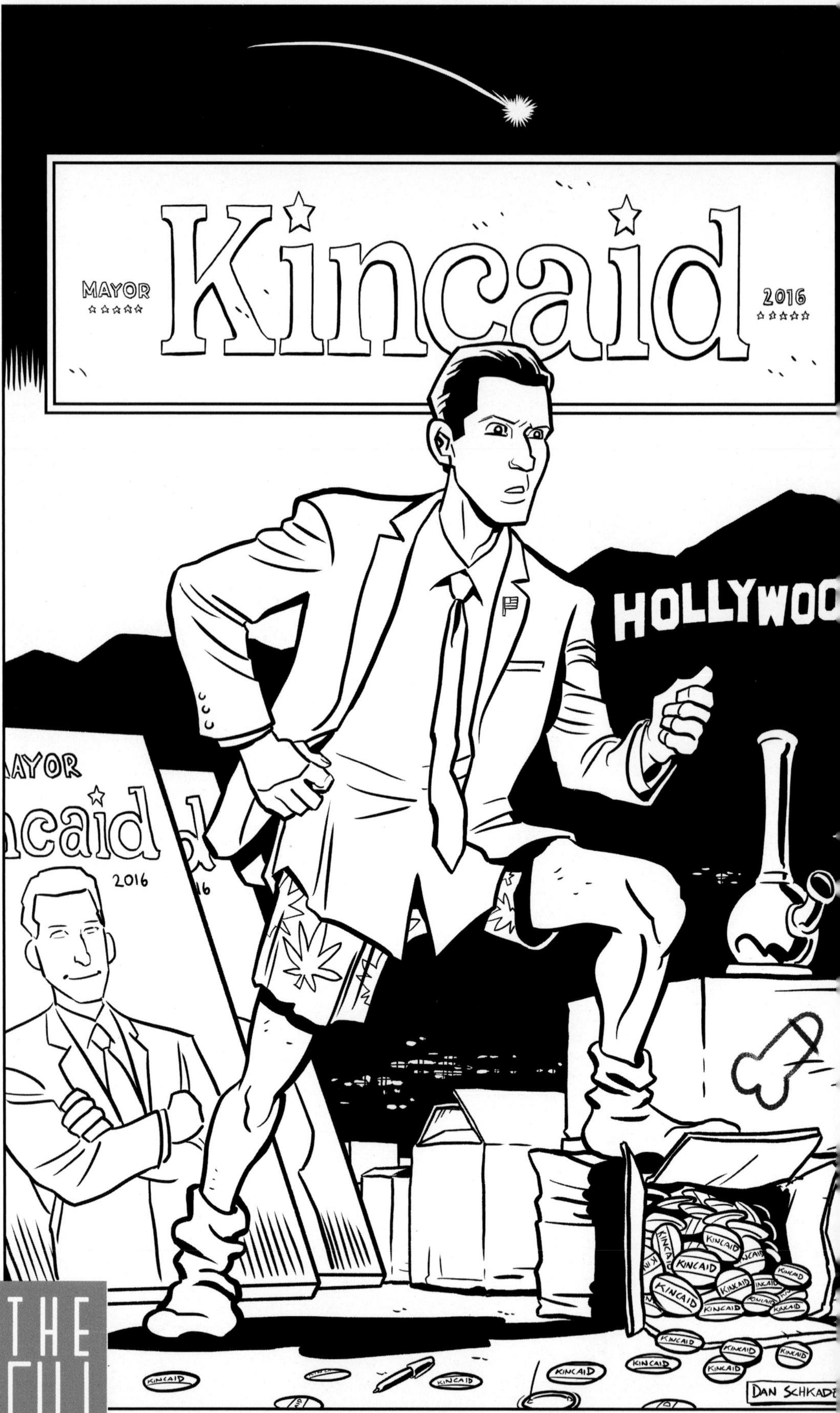

MAYOR
Kincaid
2016
HOLLYWOO
AYOR
ncaid
2016
KINCAID
DAN SCHKADE

THE FIX

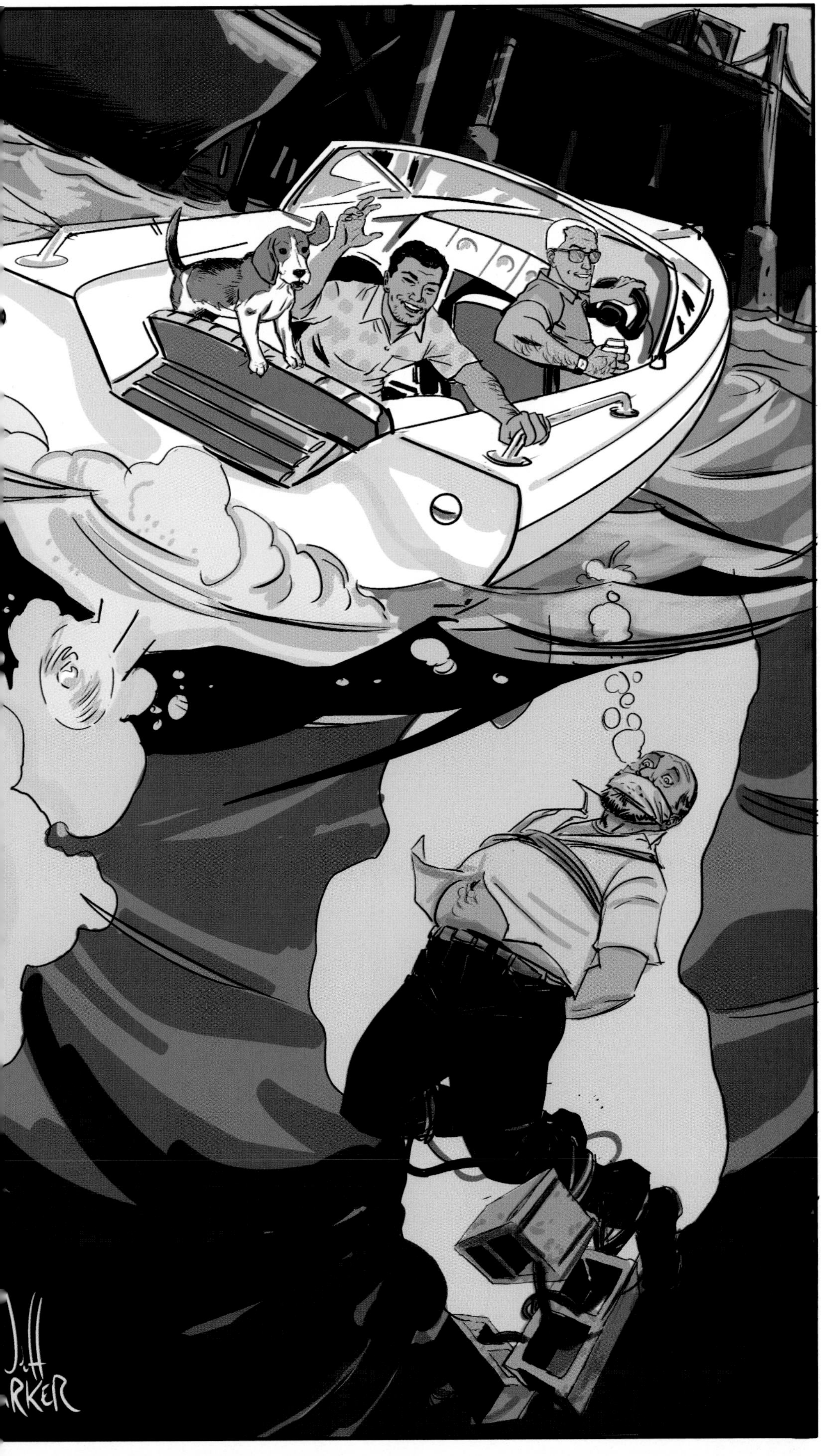

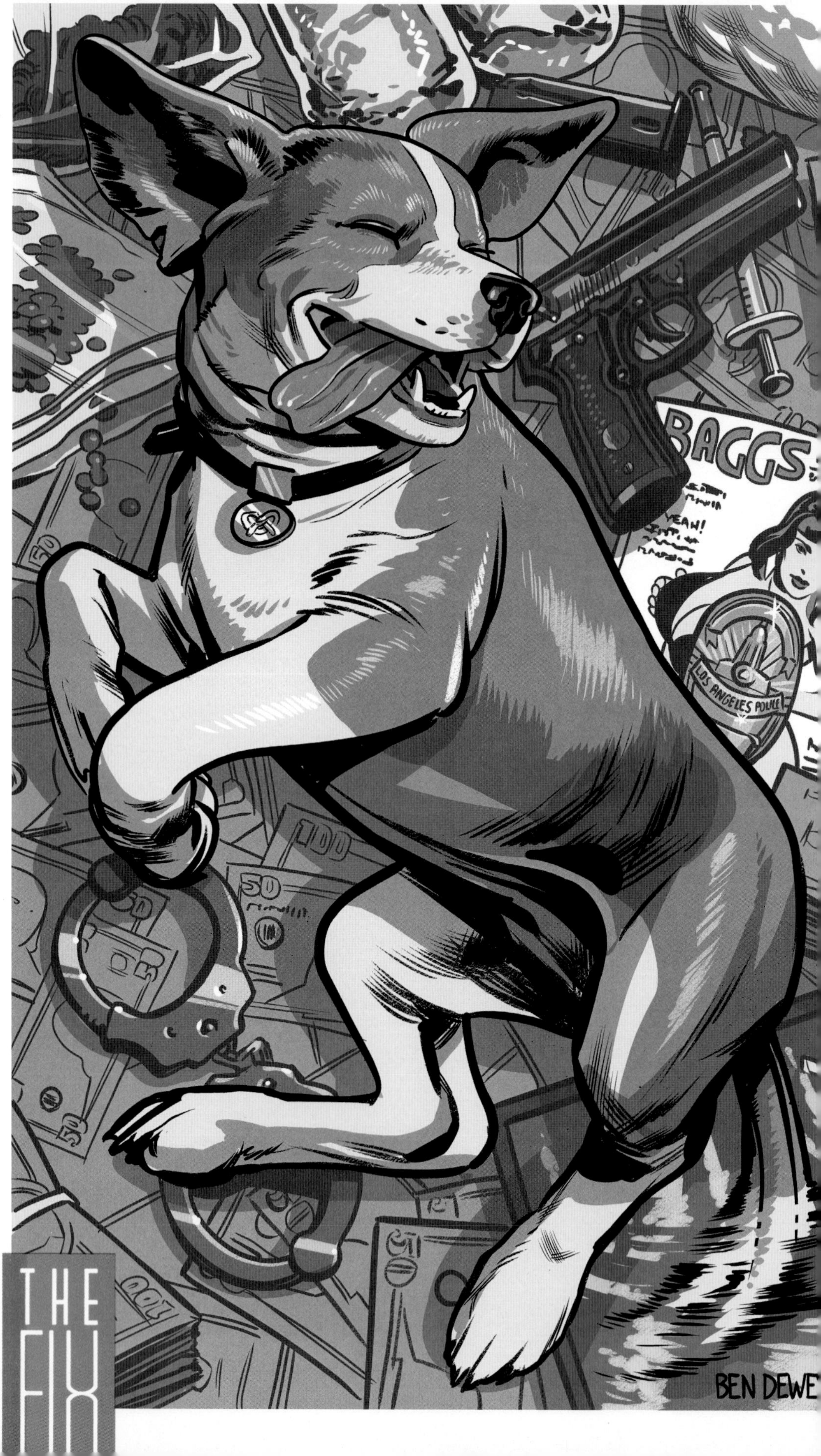
BAGGS
YEAH!
LOS ANGELES POLICE
BEN DEWE
THE
FIX

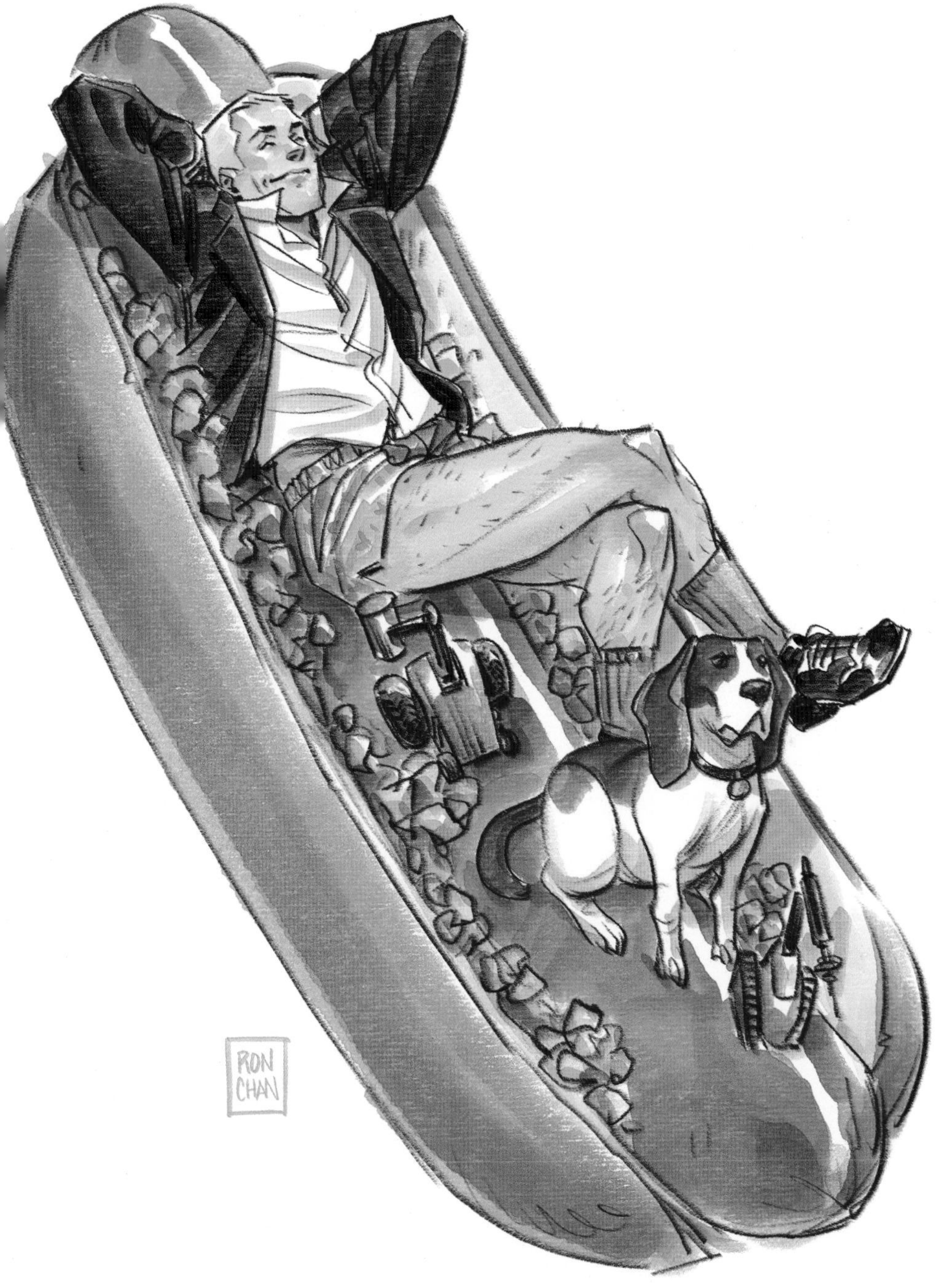
RON
CHAN

THE FIX

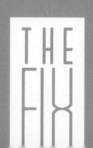